The Genesis Rock

Novels by Edwin Corley

EDWIN CORLEY

The Genesis Rock

DOUBLEDAY & COMPANY, INC.
GARDEN CITY, NEW YORK
1980

All the characters in this book are fictitious and any resemblance to actual persons, living or dead, is purely coincidental.

Library of Congress Cataloging in Publication Data

Corley, Edwin.
    The Genesis rock.

    I. Title.
PZ4.C7995Ge   [PS3553.O648]   813'.5'4
ISBN: 0-385-15018-0
Library of Congress Catalog Card Number 79-7045

This one is for all the lovely Lisas in my life!

Introduction

(On July 26, 1971, after a perfect launch from Cape Kennedy, Apollo 15 sped toward the Moon. Except for a water leak inside Command Module Endeavour, *and an instrument meter with a smashed glass dial inside Lunar Module* Falcon, *the voyage was uneventful. On Friday, July 30, En-deavour* and the Lunar Module separated and after circling the Moon twice, at 104 hours, 42 minutes and 29 seconds into the mission, the LEM set down on a lunar plain. The following true incident was transcribed from official NASA tapes.)*

APOLLO 15: ON THE SURFACE OF THE MOON

Astronauts Dave Scott and Jim Irwin have just dismounted from the mobile "Moon Car," *Rover.* It is August 1, 1971, and they are nearly three miles from their Lunar Module, *Falcon.* Their destination is the Apennine Front, at the base of the gigantic Mount Hadley.

Scott is pointing at a piece of milky-white rock. Although weight has no concept here on the Moon, the rock will weigh about half a pound on Earth.

Excitedly, heard not only by his partner but by Houston Control, Scott says, "Guess what we just found! I think we found what we came for!"

"Crystalline rock," Irwin suggests.

"Yes sir, you better believe it. I think we have found ourselves something close to anorthosite!"

If he is correct, this small rock is at least four billion years old. It has lain, undisturbed, on the lunar surface while, down on Earth, huge mountain ranges have been heaved up from the planet's bowels, then eroded back to dust again. The information contained within this half-pound object may answer many of the questions about the origin of the Universe and its suns and planets which have plagued scientists since thought began.

The discovery is placed in a special collection bag—number 196. Within days, it will have been positively identified. Consisting of feldspar minerals, rich in calcium and aluminum, it is known in textbooks as anorthosite. Because of its great age, existing as it has from the virtual moment of Creation, anorthosite has acquired a convenient nickname.

The Genesis Rock.

The few terrestrial specimens found have always been in the very oldest parts of the continental crusts, suggesting that at one time our Earth must have looked as the Moon does today. Thus, our own Genesis Rock is to be found deep within the Earth, only rarely hurled to the surface by a cataclysmic upheaval such as the one which tore the continents apart to create the Atlantic Ocean.

As alike the Moon rock as to be its brother, it is so rare that few have ever seen one, and even fewer could identify it.

Part One

Science moves but slowly, creeping on from point to point.

—TENNYSON

This would be Jack Springfield's seventh year of living in Central Park. The first winter was hardest—unaccustomed to the sudden snow squalls and violent temperature drops, he had nearly frozen several times before spring. He carried little enough weight as it was: only 143 pounds on his lanky six-three frame. With no excess fat to keep out the cold, and 68 years hanging like lead on his back, it was a near-miracle that the tall fugitive had survived at all.

His lifetime in the Great Smoky Mountains of Tennessee had given him his only edge toward survival. Already an accomplished hunter and forager, during his years of hiding in the Park he had taught himself to be a skilled thief. By the second winter, he knew every acre, every tree, every rock as well as he knew those of his old hunting grounds back in Tennessee.

Jack Springfield thought often of returning to the Smokies. But not for long, and he never acted on the thought. He could not return to Hickory Bluff . . . two blood-deaths and the revenge of the Martin family awaited him there, not to mention the never-forgetting computers of The Law. Those Martin boys, drunk out of their skulls on their own white lightning, had come for him with knives. The twelve-gauge shotgun saved him, dug their graves, and sent him, at 68 years of age, scurrying for a hiding place like some flea-bitten hound caught killing chickens.

He'd thought New York City would be big enough to lose

himself. But he hadn't been off the Trailways bus an hour when two well-dressed men flimflammed him out of his cash money by suckering him into buying a share of a wallet they (and he) had "found" and discovered to be full of $100 traveler's checks. It seemed only fair that Jack and one of the men put up some earnest money while the third man tried to cash the checks. With Jack himself holding the cash, stuffed into a sealed envelope, there didn't seem to be any risk. But the third man never returned, and the other went looking for him and didn't come back either. That was when Jack, his heart sinking, opened the envelope he had been guarding so carefully and found it filled with cut slips of newspaper.

The change in his pockets and eleven dollars he got by hocking his gold belt buckle with the engraved initials of his father, who had bought it at the St. Louis Exposition, kept him going for two days. He slept on benches until the police, tired of rousting him, threatened to take him to the precinct house.

He realized that if an identity check was run on him, the fugitive warrant from Tennessee would probably show up. Somehow he talked his way out of the arrest, promising to leave town and not cause any more trouble.

He had spent the two days, and much of their nights, walking in the Park—somehow it was like home—and so, to collect his thoughts, he went there again.

By morning, he thought he saw a way out. A man could live and get by in this big rectangular place of trees and rocks and buildings and sheds and vehicles. There were birds and squirrels to trap, and plants to eat—not to mention all the leftovers from the folks who had picnics. Cash money, too. He'd already found more than two dollars in loose change under the benches and in the secluded glenns where the young people went to make out.

So Jack Springfield, formerly of Hickory Bluff, Tennessee, became a full-time resident of Central Park, on the island of Manhattan. He stayed out of sight much of the day, sometimes slipping out the East 86th Street exit to spend an afternoon in one of the double-feature movie houses and dine, if he had the extra money, on thick German sausages and beer.

His lodging was often courtesy of the Wollman Memorial Skating Rink behind the children's zoo, or backstage at the Delacorte Outdoor Shakespeare Theatre, where he could usually find a door unlocked after the performance. By the fourth winter, he had discovered what he now regarded as his permanent home: a cavelike arrangement of stones where, somehow, it was always warmer than elsewhere in the Park. Even in winter, the rock floor was pleasantly warm. Gradually, he improved the nook's concealment, until now a person could stand just yards away and not be aware of the entrance into the silent stones.

He had taken to leaving most of his possessions there, and so far none had been disturbed. Perhaps he would spend the whole winter there this year. Since the City had started blasting the new subway, steam escaped occasionally from one corner of the stones, and it was hot enough to heat soup in the small aluminum pot he had found abandoned after a rock concert on the Sheep Meadow.

He was going to have to get another pot soon, though. Even though the steam wasn't all that hot, it seemed to be eating a hole in the aluminum bottom.

What the hell, Jack thought. It hadn't been much of a pot to begin with, anyway.

1

As usual, the Fifth Avenue store windows were leading the holiday season by a good two weeks. November was barely under way, but Santa's workers were already sneaking little touches of green and red into the displays, while the brown and orange leaves of autumn tumbled from the tree branches outside. Still, thought Janet McCoy, as she walked briskly up the west side of Fifth, the Grand Old Lady of New York looked a little dowdy. Of course, it was only 6:15 in the morning, but as an early riser, Janet had seen Fifth even earlier without sensing this dull lack of the luster and glamour that drew shoppers thousands of miles to walk Fifth's magic mile.

Of course, she realized. It's the lights. Or, rather, the lack of them. New York, like most of the nation's major cities, had been forced to accept a "voluntary" power cutback on nonessentials. The effects of the energy shortfall were already becoming apparent when she had left for Iceland ten months before; and now that she had returned, she saw the results with a clear eye—the more so because of her long absence.

Snapped awake at 4:00 A.M. by the east-to-west jet lag, she had been momentarily disoriented in the strange New York hotel room. The summons to return immediately from Reykjavik had barely given her time to throw a few bare necessities into a carry-on suitcase and rush to the airport. She landed at JFK a few minutes after ten, cleared customs, nearly dialed the apartment number, then punched the coin return to get back her money.

It was late, she'd rationalized. Linus would either be asleep after a hard day, or else he would be out entertaining a client.

The third possibility—that he would be at home, but not alone—kept itself obligingly beneath the surface of her conscious mind.

Pausing at Fifth and 38th, nearing the sprawling 42nd Street branch of the Public Library with its stern, guarding lions, she compared the 6:19 of her watch with the 6:20 of a clock in the window of a luxury tobacco shop. She decided that she would stop for coffee at the General Motors Building at 59th Street and call him from there.

There were more people on the Avenue now. Most rushed past her, hurrying to some early job—or returning home from an all-night one. Two young men, waiting for a bus, gave her a long and deliberate up-and-down. At five-four, the bulky Icelandic parka and fur-topped boots made her seem tinier than she was, while leaving it evident to experienced eyes—and the two young men were surely that—that there was plenty of trim, healthy woman under all that nylon and goose down.

Janet gave the taller of the two a wink as she passed, and, red-faced, he began to complain to his companion about the lousy bus schedule. Typical, she thought. Lots of eyeballing, but no action. At 34, she had become cynically aware of how hard it was to find men in an increasing world of boys.

She had been so wrong about Linus McCoy. He came across, loud and clear, as one of the men. Not macho, not posturing, not eternally proving himself. Rather, capable of tenderness, of quiet reflection, of mature understanding and determination. And all of it a deliberately created front.

Janet looked up at one of the library lions and laughed. "Nice Kitty-cat," she said, "Stay just what you seem to be."

A plump woman, rushing south, gave her a strange look,

opened her mouth to ask a question, shut it again, and increased her pace. Janet laughed again.

The sun was beginning to show signs of crawling over the East River. By now it would already have painted shadows across Long Island. And it would be lunchtime in Reykjavik. Her research team would be having their first aquavit at the Borg Hotel.

What did Robinson have on his mind that was so important, to take her away from the Hveragerdi project so suddenly? Oh, her team would function without her—Janet had no illusions of being indispensable. It was just that many of the ideas she had about the project were still unverbalized . . . some existed merely as hunches. With the energy crunch growing more destructive every month, no potential power source could afford to be ignored. She realized that geothermal was low on the priority list, primarily because of the lack of proper conditions in much of the Lower 48, as Alaskans called the mainland U.S.A. Both Alaska and Hawaii had ample heat stored beneath their mountains, however, and if Project Hveragerdi succeeded in liberating only a million barrels of oil a week between those two states, that would still be a million more available for the rest of the country.

Perhaps there had been more private "memos" to Robinson from Perry Bigelow. The 61-year-old geologist made no secret of his displeasure at taking second place to one barely half his age, and a woman at that. Bigelow's prime allegiance was to "the book." Rules were meant to be followed, not questioned or, worse, changed. A solid enough scientist, he had never realized it was this rigidity in him that had kept his career from going further. But even if he had come up with some complaint strong enough to involve Leslie Robinson, the dour Director of the Department of Energy would have given Janet her chewing out on the scrambled telephone circuit. No, it was something else.

Well, she would know soon enough. Her appointment with Robinson was at 9:00 sharp, in the personal suite he kept at the Plaza. Secure with inherited wealth, Leslie Robinson had carved a career out of strip mining in the 50s and 60s, earning a second fortune. Abruptly, he had done an about-face, turning his energy and money toward improving the environment and helping undo the damage his mining had caused. He had served briefly under Carter, but it was not until Howard Foster, the day after being elected, called him back from a South American vacation, that he had formally linked forces with the power of the United States Government. Although he participated in a number of projects—the biggest being the crash rebuilding of huge sections of Manhattan after the abortive, but destructive, Labor Day attack by the Afro American Army of Liberation, which held the city under siege for three days—his principal focus was on the energy shortage. Many of his decisions had been unpopular—but even his most severe critics had to admit that they were designed for the general good, if at the expense of the oil interests, the fat-cat lobbyists, and even General Motors.

His working philosophy was to give his people their heads. And if the results were unsatisfactory, those heads rolled. He had discovered Janet McCoy in Utah, working as a general assistant on the geyser geothermal pilot study. A few hours of going through the files, interviewing other workers, and he had called Janet into a private office.

Knowing the answer beforehand, he asked, "Aren't you related to Senator McCoy of Arizona?"

Janet's smile had always been her principal attraction. If her assets were to be rated on a scale of one to ten, it easily earned a ten. Bodyworks were at least eight; personality around seven; that mysterious attraction known as "it" a solid nine. But tact always came in down around three . . . or lower.

She flashed her ten smile and said, "Only if he has a bastard son. McCoy's my married name. From a snazzy adman back in New York. My Pa's known as 'Red' Willoughby.

Right out of Greyson County, Kentucky. Southwest of Louisville."

"That wouldn't be the Red Willoughby who did the survey up in Alaska for the Valley of the Ten Thousand Smokes?"

"Mr. Robinson, I'm sure you already know that. Why all the games?"

He sighed. "Caught again. I'm trying to be diplomatic, Miss . . . Or is it Ms.?"

"Miss does fine. Unless you're trying to shed some guilt."

Robinson's laugh was full. "None whatsoever. Except perhaps some for not noticing you sooner."

"What's that supposed to mean?"

"It's pretty obvious that you're really doing all the work out here. So why are you being carried as a general assistant?"

"Ask the Department of Energy."

"To all intents and purposes, I *am* the Department of Energy."

"Then shame on you."

She tempered it with another Force Ten smile.

"Would you like to run this project?" he asked. "You've earned it."

She shook her head.

"Why not?"

"Because it's not really going anywhere. It's too conservative. I think we're going to need geothermal energy, and need it bad before the end of the century. At the rate we're moving here, we won't have it in time."

"Where do you suggest we investigate, Miss McCoy?"

"I don't know. Right now, we don't know what to look for, or what to do with it once we find it. But I know where I'd like to spend a year or so looking over someone's shoulder."

"Iceland?"

She gave him a slow nod. "You know, Mr. Robinson, you

do your homework. That's the place—New Zealand would be good, too, but I think Iceland's a few years ahead of them."

"What would you do there?"

"You're serious, aren't you?"

"Deadly so."

She sat down. The trembling that she had been forcing away from her fingers now found an outlet, and for a moment it was as if she were trying to play the Tchaikovsky Piano Concerto on the desk top. Robinson waited, his face impassive.

"First," she said, controlling her voice, "I'd be sure you knew, going in, that I'm not a great big fan of the way they're doing things over there. I think they're just coasting. They're up to their necks in natural geothermal energy, so they've never had any reason to maximize its output. Your Icelander is like the South Pacific native of the nineteenth century, picking breadfruit off the trees and patiently awaiting the arrival of Captain Bligh."

Robinson took out a large briar pipe and ignited some foul mixture within. "I do hope that you wouldn't consider it your obligation to enlighten our Icelandic neighbors."

Janet shook her head. "Not a peep. But I bet I could find areas where they could be doing things better with more output, and adapt it to our own situation."

"Even so," he pointed out, "where would we find geothermal sources of our own? The only two sources we know of, on a commercial level, are here and in California."

"Don't forget Wyoming."

"Yellowstone? The public would hound us to the wall, not to mention the Department of National Parks."

Grimly, she asked, "Not even when daily power outages of six hours become the normal condition?"

"Still," he pointed out, "the chances of capitalizing on anything you learn are slim, at best."

She stared at him. "What's to lose? I know we've got at least nine irons in the fire already. Solar, nuke, crazy stuff like tidal-bore hydroelectric. Maybe none of them will come on line. Maybe it'll take a synergistic mix of several to keep us out of the next ice age. You've seen my file, you know I work cheap. You asked what I wanted—I told you."

Gently, he asked, "And what about your adman husband? What would he say about you trekking off to the wilds of Iceland for a year or two?"

"I've already heard what he has to say," Janet said softly. "It didn't make any difference to Utah. It wouldn't to Iceland."

Robinson looked at his watch. "I'll be back in Washington by seven your time," he said. "Is it all right if I call you around midnight?"

"That's pretty late for you, isn't it? With the time difference?"

He shrugged. "The way I figure it, every hour invested this year will save us a day next year."

"Call away," she said. "I wasn't going anywhere anyhow."

Nor, she thought, crossing 57th Street, with the morning traffic starting to build, am I now. One more block, some black coffee, and we'll see what Linus says about me blowing back into town without warning him.

As it turned out, there wasn't anything said at all. She let the telephone ring twenty times. Nobody picked up. He obviously hadn't been home all night, because if there was one thing treasured by Linus McCoy, it was his morning sleep. He openly boasted about arriving at the corner office provided for him at J. Walter Thompson at "the crack of ten."

Janet put the receiver down. Two more hours to kill. She had a second cup of coffee and a prune danish.

Outside, the traffic was picking up.

Three Fifth Avenue buses, southbound bumper to bumper, roared by.

The countergirl made a rude noise. "You know what they

say about those buses, honey? They're like hookers. They don't like to go downtown alone."

Before Janet could answer, there was a dull *thud,* and the stool on which she sat seemed to shake.

"My God!" she said. "What was that? An earthquake?"

"They're blasting in the Park," said the countergirl. "Uptown somewhere. The new MTA crosstown through the Park."

Remembering when, in the early seventies, Sixth Avenue (or Avenue of the Americas, if you were a purist) had been excavated and covered with heavy planks while a new subway spur was installed, Janet said, "This is going to be a great town, if they ever finish building it."

The new excavation was cutting through the Park from Lexington Avenue and East 96th Street to the same street at Central Park West. It had been budgeted at an original cost of $940 million, and had gone into cost overrun months ago. With each new entry of red ink, the Mayor seemed to add a quart of his own blood. Every time he inhaled a bourbon too many, he let everyone within two blocks know how the city was being rooked by the goddamned Mafia and their Irish cousins from Boston. Meanwhile, the great trench gnawed its way through the once-green meadows immediately north of the huge Receiving Reservoir, which stored water from Westchester and upstate lakes. The tennis courts, near the west side of the Park, had been closed, and seemed likely to fall into the trench if it got any closer to them. Farther north, past the meadows, the residents of Harlem had set up picket groups around their own precious lake, the sprawling Harlem Meer, and threatened dire happenings to any dynamite teams foolhardy enough to venture past West 100th Street and the North Meadow. Although the great fire of the Labor Day Uprising had gutted many of the former tenements which had blighted Cathedral Parkway and points north, the population of the rebuilt area, black and white alike, still felt that the hand of the city was constantly turned against them, and tolerated scant intrusion upon their rights.

Benjamin Keller, Superintendent in charge of the MTA construction project, had already run afoul of the antagonistic Harlemites, and wanted no more part of them. Although many of his trucks came in from Yonkers, they were under strict instruction to stay away from Broadway and Columbus Avenue, using, instead, the Henry Hudson Parkway, although it was illegal, since commercial vehicles were banned from that roadway.

"Send these down to Hizzoner, the Mayor," said Ben Keller, when handed the first thick wad of traffic tickets. He reinforced that command with a telephone call to Gracie Mansion, and the ticket giving ceased.

Keller's argument had been brief: "Do you want them spades getting hold of a whole truck full of dynamite?" he asked the Mayor.

Instructions for a variance in traffic rules were issued from Centre Street that very morning.

Blasting was a more difficult matter. There was no way to enforce the "No radio transmitting" rule with thousands of Citizen's Band radios in the hands of kids and hobbyists, and more thousands of radios installed in taxis. Radio-controlled cabs were scarcest from 6:00 to 8:00 A.M., so that period became blast time.

Even so, Keller caught complaints every day from joggers, dog walkers and environmentalists who accused him of ruining the Park.

So it was not surprising that when, spotting the woman kneeling near a blasted outcropping of gray rock, his fuse blew.

"Hey!" he shouted. "What do you think you're doing? Get away from there!"

The woman—younger than he had thought—looked up. She wore a blue nylon parka and a black fur cap. Her short hair was bright red in the early sunlight. She flashed him a smile that almost cooled down his temper. Then she undid the effect by picking up a small rock.

"Put that down!" he ordered, rushing toward her.

She replaced the stone and stood up, waiting.

"Don't you know we're blasting?" Keller demanded. "Can't you read?" He pointed at one of the signs: "Danger —blast zone. No radio transmissions."

She nodded westward along the deep excavation. "I thought you were working over there. These heaps are at least six months old."

The fact that she was right angered Keller even more. "Lady, this is a hard-hat area. You could get hurt. Do us both a favor and move along."

She brushed dirt from her hands. "Can I see your supervisor?"

This was a red flag to Keller.

"What the hell for?"

The young woman met his eye and this time there was no smile. "I simply want to ask a question about these tailings."

Keller nearly asked her how she knew what to call blast remnants. Instead, he realized that it was almost time for the next blast, and he was falling further and further behind schedule.

"Listen," he said, "*I'm* the super, and I've got work to do."

"How deep did this pile come from?"

"Who wants to know?"

She took out her wallet. Oh, Jeeze, thought Keller. Another EPA inspector.

"I'm with the Department of Energy," she said, flashing an identification card. "This isn't official. I'm just—well, interested in rocks. Some of these"—she indicated the tailings—"are igneous diabase. And I think this one is actually an anorthosite."

"Terrific. So what?"

"So it shouldn't be found near the surface."

Keller heard three blasts of a distant whistle. "Hey, I gotta go," he said. "We're blasting."

"How deep?" she called after him.

He pointed to one corner of the trench. "Right down there," he shouted. "Thirty, maybe forty feet."

"Thanks!" she yelled. He ducked down into the trench and, apparently, did not hear her.

Janet McCoy bent over and, carefully choosing the small milky-white stone, put it in her pocket. Then she looked at her watch. Nearly eight. She decided to stroll down through the Park. There was more than an hour to kill before her meeting at the Plaza.

2

Alexander Cage was late, and the talent coordinator of the *Today* Program was already making up a list of alternates to fill the time. Comedian Kenny Morgan was in town, and his press agent had been trying to place him on *Today*. He'd already been called, and if Cage didn't show within ten minutes, and if one of the other alternate time-fillers weren't used, Kenny would get his big chance.

Or perhaps the early-morning viewers might watch a six-minute interview with the special-effects man who had built the latest wide-screen monster for *The Incredible Centipede*. "It takes three guys riding bikes to make it move," boasted the designer, demonstrating.

Finally, the program's resident critic had an essay condemning the latest Clint Eastwood thriller, and all of his ilk. "Fascist" was used several times as an adjective. So were phrases like "mindless violence" and "destructive role patterns for the young." At one time, this particular critic had favored the terse economy in dialogue and camerawork of Eastwood's films. But that was before the star ignored a request for an interview and, to compound the insult, appeared publicly with Barbara Walters at the latest disco (although Ms. Walters did not get an interview, either).

"Let's rack up the giant cockroach and be ready to go with it," said the program's producer, looking at the sweep-second hand of the big clock above the center screen of his three television sets, which was tuned to NBC and *Today*.

The one on the left offered CBS, and on the right he could watch ABC's *Good Morning, America.* "If we schlepp Kenny all the way over here and don't use him, we'll owe him one. As for the Eastwood piece, with any luck, Marvin'll lose it before we can find time to slot it. This way we can hang loose in case Cage makes it in time for the last segment."

A buzzer sounded. He picked up the telephone, listened, said, "Use the executive elevator." He hung up. "Cancel everything I said. The son of a bitch just came through the revolving door."

"One of these days . . ." said the talent coordinator.

"Right in the old labonza," agreed the producer. It was their shared curse for latecomers.

He dialed the floor director. "When you get a chance to break in, get on the bug and alert Phil that our great big guest finally arrived and we'll slot him in the final segment."

The "bug" was the tiny hearing-aid-like earphone worn by the moderator.

"Final segment," repeated the floor director.

According to the big clock over the NBC television screen, this meant that in exactly 29 minutes the distinguished spokesman for America's oil industry would get a chance to speak his piece for millions of men and women hurriedly gulping a last cup of coffee before rushing to their jobs.

Alexander Cage had not always been a "great big guest" welcome on *Today* and other powerhouse opinion-maker platforms. For the first eighteen years of his public relations career, he had worked in regional—and then national— offices of three of the Seven Sisters—the industry nickname for the world's largest oil companies.

And except for a lucky (lucky for him—not so fortunate for others) break during the Arab oil embargo of 1973, Cage would still be one of the hard-working, high-priced, anonymous flacks behind the glass facades on Park Avenue or downtown Houston.

At the time, Cage was working for the second-largest petroleum importer on the eastern seaboard, and while gasoline lines grew at the pumps and government and industry ran in circles, each frantically trying to blame the mess on the other, Cage happened to be on a photo-reconnaissance flight off Staten Island. Along the coast of New Jersey, he saw, was a vast armada of ships that looked like the Normandy D-day invasion fleet.

"Look at those tankers," he said to the photographer, who regularly worked this area. "There must be fifty of them!"

"Closer to seventy," said the photographer. "And that's just this batch. Down the coast, you've got another couple of hundred. All waiting to unload."

"You mean those things are full of *oil?*"

"Nothing but. Some of those babies have been out there cruising around so long that they're starting to burn their cargo as fuel."

Thinking of the long lines for gasoline and, in some states, the alternate days of sale—based on whether your license plate ended in an odd or even number—Alexander Cage shook his head in disbelief.

"Why don't they unload?" he asked.

"A few of them—the independents—are hoping the price will go even higher. But most of them just can't get a port number. Not enough hookups or docks."

In that moment, the idea that would change his life came to Alexander Cage.

"I want pictures," he said. "As many as we can get."

The photographer glanced at his watch. "How much fuel we got, Hod?"

"Two hours' cruise," said the pilot. "That leaves us plenty to get home."

"Okay," said the photographer. "Let's go take some snapshots."

It was a hard sell to his management, particularly to the Chairman of the Board, old Phil Sanders. But two days later, Cage held a televised news conference, exhibiting the photographs of the tankers, cruising and anchored off New Jersey.

"That's oil which could be heating houses and running cars today," he said, in a quiet, deadly calm voice. "Oil that would eliminate this shortage right now—if we could get it ashore."

Who was keeping it from coming ashore to solve all our problems?

None other than the United States Government which, with its nit-picking regulations and time-consuming paper work had made it impossible to land those millions of barrels of oil the refineries had already bought and paid for.

There were denials, counteraccusations, but when the smoke cleared, the public's attitude toward Big Oil was friendlier, and the Credibility Gap between the Press and the White House had widened.

And Alexander Cage had a new job: Director of the National Petroleum Department of Consumer Affairs. Not just for his own company, but for the entire oil industry. Well, not precisely *all* of it. One of the Seven Sisters and a few independents, disapproving of his tactics, refused to join.

As the years passed, Cage became more powerful—so much so, in fact, that to many he *was* the oil industry. Far from resenting this identification in the public mind, Big Oil was delighted to have someone else to take the heat—and heat there was, unmeasurable BTUs of it, all endured cheerfully by Alexander Cage. His salary was more than half a million a year, his perks (car, apartments in seven cities and four overseas, staff, unlimited travel and expense allowances) would have (and some say, *had*) made the former Shah of Iran green-eyed with jealousy.

So how did it come to pass that he was nearly late for an important interview on *Today?*

The fault lay in a fifteen-dollar Sony digital alarm clock

which belonged to Eve Newhart, his Special Assistant for New York. Cage had such assistants in every city where National Petroleum's Consumer Affairs organization kept offices. Their job was to be his representative when he was elsewhere. In certain cases, such as Eve Newhart's, they sometimes took their job home with them.

There had been a three-hour power outage in Eve's neighborhood the day before, unknown to her because she was already at work. She had shared a late supper with Cage at the Top of the Sixes, and, since it was en route to her Chelsea apartment, spent an hour at Metamorphosis, dancing once and watching the disco's regulars the rest of the time. It was late when they reached West 18th Street, and they'd gone right to bed, skipping even the usual brandy before a flaming Duralog in her reopened fireplace (the firebrick alone had cost some nameless fund buried within the Consumer Affairs accounts nearly a thousand dollars).

Cage had left his suitcase in the private, always locked, office he kept at C.A. He intended to fly to Dallas at noon because he knew that a certain United States senator, spending a postelection holiday at home, would want to speak with him after the *Today* interview. But there was always a fresh suit at Eve's, along with linen, socks, and even a spare pair of shoes.

What there *wasn't* was a spare alarm clock. And the Sony, three hours slow, never even purred.

With the sun prying open his eyelids, Cage glanced at his watch and sat up suddenly.

"Holy shit!" he said loudly. "Eve, wake up. It's nearly seven o'clock. I'm late for the *Today* show."

(Echoes of horror must have radiated down the RCA building's very girders. By edict of the late Frank McGee, its host until his death, *Today* is a Program, not a mere show, a tradition continued through the years.)

While he dressed rapidly, Eve called NBC and assured the *Today* talent coordinator that Alexander Cage was speeding to the studio and not to worry.

Whereupon the talent coordinator began to worry at full speed, because she had been sold this same bill of goods by more than one tardy guest.

But now . . . well, the bastard *was* actually in the building. Still, one of these days . . .

3

When *Today* was conceived, its format was intended to give the viewer snippets of news and information, often repeated, so that during its two-hour air-time the harried viewer with only a half hour or so to tune in would get the essence of the day's important activities. As a result, much of its reportage was duplication of that transmitted in earlier segments. An especially important "live" interview in the first hour might turn up as a news item in the second.

By being late, since he had been slated for the last segment of the first half hour, Alexander Cage lost that bonus second exposure. But, delighted that their top guest for the day had showed up after all, the moderator plugged the appearance so enthusiastically that Cage drew nearly 30 percent more viewers than he would have ordinarily.

One, captured without the hype, because she had been strolling through Central Park carefully examining the rock outcroppings, was Janet McCoy, who returned to the coffee shop just as Cage was being introduced.

Another, called to the set by his wife, Harriet, was Jack Ward of North Fork, Texas. It was only 7:40 in North Fork, which—on Central Time—received the last hour of *Today* live, and then a replay of the first hour on videotape. Jack Ward had been to Houston, where he and Harriet spent some three hours too many at The Ranch, a sprawling beer and dance joint which occupied two and a half indoor acres just east of the city. The beer hangover—and no beer can leave a more lasting imprint of its presence than Pearl—was a dull throb behind his eyes.

But Harriet's voice calling, "Hey, Jack, that no-good sumbitch is coming up on TV!" roused him out of the sack. That "no-good sum-bitch" needed no identification. He could be none other than Alexander Cage.

Jack Ward, thick of waist, jet-black hair thinning, struggled into the shower, where two minutes of ice-cold spray shocked his body—if not his mind—into wakefulness. He wrapped himself in a towel and lurched out into the living room. The big Advent seven-foot television screen was filled with a tight close-up of a can of dog food, and a familiar voice was extolling the merits of "meat a dog can really eat."

"Now, Jack," warned Harriet, "don't you go throwing anything at that Advent screen. You know you can't hardly wipe spots off it."

"Hush, woman," said Jack Ward. As the dog wolfed down the Alpo, he added, "I thought you was coming back to bed after you got them kids off to school."

"I meant to," she said. "But then they said *he* was going to come on, so I woke you up."

"What's he selling today?" grumbled Jack.

"You oughtn't let it bother you so much."

"He's a goddamned liar," said Jack. "He's got so many twists, you could use him for a corkscrew."

"He helps the oil business."

"That's his story. People ain't all that dumb. Sooner or later they're going to catch up with him like I did, and that'll be all she wrote—the pencil's busted. Except all the good oil folks'll take the mud right along with Old Cage-arino."

"Well, when they had that accident in the Provo Field, he kept it out of the papers."

"Sure he did. By making it all out to be the fault of the workers. Harrie, I blew that mother out, remember? I saw those poor bastards, fried to a crisp. They was like little burnt gunnysacks, with their arms and legs scorched down to flippers. Cage came out real strong about better training and supervision, but I didn't hear any mention of second-hand equipment and wore-out gear. They had the insurance settlements all signed by them poor families and those charcoal-broiled men in the ground inside of two days, and hardly a word in the papers or a peep on TV."

He got up and lurched into the kitchen, returning with a cold can of Coors.

"What's more—" he began.

"Shhh," said his wife. "He's talking."

Jack Ward struggled to pick up the gist of what the trim, sleek man on the huge television screen was saying. At 63, Alexander Cage was dignified without being stuffy; authoritative without being overbearing; dryly humorous without being a buffoon.

". . . more than enough oil for the next several centuries," he was saying. "If we'll only accept the responsibility for paying its true price."

"What exactly is 'true price'?" asked the moderator.

"We must accept the fact that the days of cheap energy are gone forever," said Cage. "It's no credit to our government or its regulations that for decades we've been riding on the backs of the OPEC nations, literally stealing their natural resources to increase our own standard of living. The very basis of our system of government is free enterprise. But when it comes to the necessities of life, the power barons of Washington decree, 'No, there won't be free enterprise in this area. *We'll* tell the public what's good for them, and make it stick by controlling prices, output and distribution.' And they do, meanwhile wasting billions of dollars searching, they say, for alternative energy sources."

"Isn't it a good idea not to put all our eggs in one basket?" asked the moderator.

"Is it a good idea to set up a secret project in, of all places, Iceland, wasting taxpayer money, to study how the Icelanders heat their homes with steam from hot springs?"

"It seems sensible to know what's worked elsewhere."

"Only if we have access to the same resources here. But, except for a few isolated geysers in the Far West—where hydroelectric power is already taking up the slack—we don't have any hot springs to draw upon. Even if we did, did you ever try to run an automobile on the output from a geyser?"

"Well," said the moderator, "there were steam cars—"

"Which burned charcoal or some other fuel to create the steam. No, oil is still our answer. But we must face the fact that we can no longer literally steal it. We're going to have to pay the going rate, like everybody else."

"Even if gasoline goes to a dollar and a half a gallon at the pump?"

"What's so sacred about that price? In Europe, years before the 1973 embargo, they were paying that—and more—for gasoline. Why are we so special? The government has to make it possible for domestic oil production to earn a profit, and only then will we be free of our present bondage to the OPEC nations.

"But, no. The politicians would rather appropriate millions for some college girl to spend on geothermal nonsense that will never so much as boil an egg in this country. Do you know who they put in charge of this mammoth Icelandic project? A young woman named Janet McCoy, who was formerly a mere assistant on some proper, modestly funded research we were doing here in our own country, in Utah. A month later, she was handed the keys to the treasury and put in charge of studying what any schoolboy—or girl—ought to know: that if you put hot water into pipes and run those pipes through a house, then the pipes will heat the house. What her study doesn't—and won't—tell us is where are we going to find all that hot water?"

The moderator chuckled. "Well, if I don't say 'station break' right now, we'll find it pouring down our necks. This morning's guest has been Mr. Alexander Cage, Director of the National Petroleum Department of Consumer Affairs. And now, a station break."

In North Fork, Texas, the station cut to a commercial plugging the North Fork Toyota dealer's Leftover Sale. Jack Ward, his arms and legs scarred from burns received while earning the reputation of being the best man to cap burning oil wells since Red Adair, scratched a recently acquired scab on his wrist and growled, "If that turkey would put only half of his mouth and money behind drilling safety, there'd be one hell of a lot less wells to blow out—and fewer men hurt."

"And even fewer jobs for you," his wife pointed out. "Then how would you pay for your next jet plane?"

"Shoot, honey," said Ward, "a man can't fly more than one at a time anyway."

4

Leslie Robinson used the remote control to click off the 23-inch RCA. The *Today* moderator faded in mid-smile.

His guest, a slim man of perhaps forty, totally bald, and sporting a Guardsman's moustache, put down his coffee cup and said, "Ouch."

"How bad an 'ouch,' Waldo?" asked Robinson.

"Ouch as in, that's one more log fueling the fire your girl is going to have to walk through," said Waldo Wynn, Director of NASA. "There's been enough opposition to women in the space program already. Those three washouts last year didn't help any. The MCPs can point and say, 'Two got pregnant and one went batty.'"

"MCP?"

"Male Chauvinist Pig," said Wynn.

Robinson shuddered. "Are they still using terms like that?"

"Where have you been? In a fallout shelter? Leave it to the ladies to come up with a real butt-scorcher when they decide to call names."

Smiling, Robinson said, "That sounds vaguely MCPish to me."

"Sure, I'm a closet card-carrying antifeminist. Seriously, Les, maybe we ought to hold off for a while. You know as well as I, that loudmouth's going to make all the newspapers, and drag your girl right along with him."

"Janet McCoy is an extremely skilled, totally qualified and very determined young *woman*."

"And a late one, too," said Wynn, glancing at his watch.

"I thought you called her the original Miss Punctuality." He chuckled. "Rather MCPish, too, wouldn't you say?"

Feigning a groan, Robinson said, "I'll be glad when everything settles down, so we can have a sense of humor again. I feel like the principal at a kindergarten. If Johnny gets an extra cookie, Jane has to have one, too. Whether or not she wants it. Everybody's a minority but me. Sometimes I wish I were female, black, and gay. Then—"

Waldo Wynn never learned what would have followed "then," because at that moment the doorbell rang.

"Pardon me, boy," he drawled, "is that the Chattanooga Choo-Choo?"

Robinson opened the door. Janet McCoy, flushed from hurrying, said, "Sorry I'm late. I was watching someone on *Today*, and lost track of time."

"Six minutes late," Robinson said sternly. "I think that's some new kind of record."

As he led her in, knowing he was only joking, Janet still could not stop herself from continuing to explain. "It was Alexander Cage, with Speech Number Three. Pay we must, and all. But this time—"

Gently, Robinson said, "We know, Jan. We watched, too." He had led her over to the window, where Wynn stood. "Janet McCoy, may I present an admirer of yours, Waldo Wynn." He helped her slip out of the blue parka. "Mr. Wynn is—"

"I know, I know," she said, holding out her hand to the ferocious-looking man. "Big cheese of the space stuff." She popped a hand over her mouth. "Whoops! I was thinking Moon, and that jumped to green cheese and . . . I meant to say, 'big wheel.'"

"Cheese fits better," said Wynn. "Since your boss doesn't seem likely to, may I call down and order breakfast for you? I understand you flew in from Iceland last night."

"Thanks, I had something," she said. Now, without her bulky parka, Waldo Wynn could not help admiring her figure. Slim, yet full-breasted, her body curved in to a narrow waist, flared to hips that filled her tan slacks just tightly enough before descending to long, well-proportioned legs. Her face, bare of makeup, glowed from the cold wind she had faced all morning. Her hair, in a neatly trimmed page-boy, was a rich golden red without the harshness of copper that was too often a tattletale of touchups.

She could hardly have missed noticing his examination.

Janet cocked her head and let half a smile leak out. "Do I pass?"

With a double meaning she would not yet understand, Wynn said, "In every way."

Robinson, who had been pouring coffee for everyone, said, "I'm sorry we had to yank you away from the Project on such short notice, Janet. But even though the phone lines are scrambled, I didn't want this to reach you that way. Somehow the telephone distorts things. I find myself saying too much, or not enough, and it never seems to come out precisely the way I planned."

"I know what you mean," she said, accepting the coffee. "Thanks. This makes my third cup, though. One more and I go into orbit without a capsule."

Wynn stared at her. "Why did you say that?"

Puzzled, she looked back. "What? Orbit? I don't know. Too much caffeine gives me a worse jag than champagne." She turned to Robinson, and the light touch left her voice. "Hey, just what the hell is going on here? Did you know what Cage was going to say today? Is that why I caught the Red-Eye Express?"

"No, not at all," he soothed. "Sit down, Janet. We're talking about two separate things at the same time. Let me try to put things back on the track. First, I wanted to speak to you personally about a matter pertaining to your career. I didn't want to use the phone because—"

"There's no body language, no eye contact. I know. That's when I said the wrong word, like 'orbit.'"

"Furthermore, I wanted you to meet Dr. Wynn—"

"Oh, shit," said NASA's Director. "Janet, if he's calling Ph.D.s 'Doctor,' you and I are both in trouble."

"Let me spread the butter my way," said Robinson. It was evident to Janet that he and Wynn were close friends, used to friendly back-and-forth bickering.

"Spread it fast," said Wynn. "I want to get that eleven o'clock shuttle to Washington."

"All right," said Robinson. "To keep from being embarrassed by a public turndown, if Waldo and I read you wrong, what we brought you here to ask is, would you like to be assigned to the space program as a geoscientist, with the Moon as your personal project?"

Janet McCoy gulped. There was no other way to describe the sound she made. She had often read of people gulping, and now she herself had done it, too.

"How's that?" said Robinson, leaning closer.

Janet gave a weak laugh. "I said, 'gulp.'"

"I take it, then," said Waldo Wynn, "that our offer interests you."

"Interests?" The laugh was wild this time. "Of course it does. If it's real. Not just some figurehead kind of thing to keep minority pressure off you."

Wynn went on. "I further take it that being the first woman on the Moon is half of the inducement."

"More than that," she said. "But scratch the 'woman' part. I just want to go."

"Well," said Wynn, "that's too bad, because the Moon shot is only a front. We have no intention of actually sending you there."

"Oh," said Janet. "Well, I know it's no mean accomplishment, being invited to join the program in any capacity, but if I'm going to have a ground job, I think the one I'm doing now is more important than . . ."

Her voice wound down. She sensed that Wynn had not finished his say.

He gave her a broad wink that made him look like Attila the Hun.

"Your actual, secret destination," he went on, "would be Mars."

Jack Springfield was so accustomed to the explosions from the subway construction that, like those living near a railroad track, he was not disturbed by the noise, but rather by its absence.

"Fire in the hole!" they called it, when a blast was getting ready to ignite. He had slipped over to the work site many times—his tool chest was richer now by a hammer, two stone chisels, and a screwdriver. And there were always rags and bits of wood—things a body could use to fix up his place. Jack Springfield had no animosity toward the MTA subway workers at all. He thought of them as good neighbors.

Because it was cold, and because he had a squirrel to cook, Jack had allowed himself the luxury of a small fire this morning. There was always plenty of wood to be gathered—the danger was in someone spotting the smoke. But he had stockpiled dead, dry wood, which burned virtually smokeless, and he kept the fire tiny.

His pot was propped on three stones which contained the embers. He fed them carefully, allowing only the smallest flame. Once he had the squirrel tender, he could continue stewing it over the steam that rose from the almost invisible fissure in the rocks.

Jack had snares throughout the park, although he kept them well away from paths where playing children might come upon them. And he never set them until dark, revisiting them before dawn to collect the occasional catch, and to disable them during the day so they would not capture animals which might struggle and attract attention. He had found this fat gray near The Ramble, just north of The Lake where the boaters gathered in summer and the ice skaters in winter. Cut by deep gorges, The Ramble was one of his favorite hunting grounds. He had only to be careful to stay away from the paths and trails. Once, in a Springlike March, he had caught a large white rabbit—probably an escapee from some Easter party. He dined well on it for nearly a week.

Poking a fork into the squirrel, which he had quartered and put into the water along with some wild garlic roots he had picked along the edge of the bridle path, he decided that the meat was nearly tender enough to place over the steam to simmer.

The earth trembled, and a second later, he heard the rumble of an explosion from the north. Judging the sun's angle, he thought, *They're late today. Usually they don't touch them off after eight o'clock. It's plumb past nine by now.*

Patiently, he let the fire burn down. No sense in wasting good heat. Then, using a piece of flannel shirt as a potholder, he lifted the pot and took it over to his steam fissure.

The steam was gone.

He vaguely remembered that it had first appeared when the blasting began, months ago. He had never questioned its origin. Once, in a discarded newspaper, he had read that Con Edison, the city's utility company, sold steam to commercial buildings for heat, conveying it underground in huge pipes. The old man had merely assumed it was his good luck that one of those pipes had begun to leak under his hiding place.

Now it looked as if that last explosion which, come to think of it, had been bigger than usual, had rearranged the pipes again and cut off his steam supply.

Jack Springfield had not lived 75 years to let a minor setback like this disturb his tranquillity. He would make do. Maybe the steam would come up somewhere else. Or at least, if the pipes were close enough to them, the rocks might remain warm, leaving the cave inhabitable for most— or maybe all—of the winter.

He carefully pushed some twigs into the little fire. It looked as if Mr. Squirrel was going to get cooked the old-fashioned way this morning.

5

This Central Park, which Ben Keller was violating with his high explosives, and which was a jogger's paradise, and which harbored old men on the lam from the highly efficient police of Hickory Bluff, Tennessee, and which represented the Last Frontier for millions of New Yorkers, had originally been a swamp and a garbage dump for the sprawling infant city of New york.

The elite of the city had decided that, like all the respected cities of Europe, New York should have parks and playing fields.

The original plan had been to create many small ones, scattered around the city, but the city plan drawn up in 1811, with a grilled pattern of streets, limited this creativity, forcing the planners to take advantage of the only relatively unbuilt area: a wilderness located in the precise center of the city. Drawing up a plan, titled "Greensward," they entered it on the last day of the competitive period, April 1, 1858.

"They," for the record, were Frederick Law Olmsted, perhaps the first true environmentalist of the emerging nation, and Calvert Vaux, an English architect.

Their restrictions were great. The new park's requirements were strict: there had to be enough room for a hall suitable for music or exhibitions. No less than three playgrounds, of fixed sizes, were required. Furthermore, there had to be a mammoth parade ground, an ice-skating lake, at least one formal fountain, gardens galore, and—more important than any aesthetics—no less than four primary routes to carry traffic east and west. Budget? No more than $1.5 million.

Today, that sum would barely meet sandblasting of the statues located within the park. Even in 1858, it was Poverty Row, but barely possible.

It has often been questioned whether Olmsted and Vaux came up with the best design. But no one questions that they sold their idea better than anyone else. They sent artists into the field who drew "before" and "after" versions of the available landscape. Where, in the "before" section, a flock of sheep might have grazed on a tawdry hill, the "after" sketch showed a cloud-dazzled hillside with dashing waterfalls and trees which, while appearing to be in the wild, spread their green limbs in an exquisite pattern that delighted the eye.

Both men were ahead of their time. The Park represented profitable employment for a few years. But they saw further than that. They knew, without speaking of it to each other, that if they did not preserve this precious relic of the wild, it would soon be overwhelmed by concrete and buildings, forever erasing the few remnants of the natural past. Gone would be the gray outcroppings of natural stone; the birds would flee to less occupied space; the natural waters would be blocked, polluted, or both; the constantly increasing parade of horse-drawn carts and carriages would rip up the precious grass and contaminate it with endless piles of dung.

Their Grand Design was so creatively massive that it convinced the judges of the competition. The result was that Olmsted was awarded the post of architect in chief, which amounted to dictatorial powers. Vaux labored at his drawing board.

Within a few months, three thousand men were at work transforming the garbage dumps and squatters' camps into the master plan conceived by Olmsted and Vaux. The blasting which occurred daily dwarfed what came more than a century later when the MTA began digging its huge trench across the waistline of the Park.

Progress was halted by the Civil War, and Olmsted, who was irritated by the corruption of Tammany Hall, joined the war effort. There he found the forces of bureaucracy unwilling to accept his assessment of the real reasons for the battle lost at Bull Run. Driven out of the military service by his very dedication to it, accused of "most insanitary habits of life. He works like a dog all day and sits up nearly all night . . . works with steady, feverish intensity till four in the morning . . ." Olmsted returned to his first love: Central Park, still unfinished, but gay with children playing, strolling gentlemen and ladies, and the tranquillity of carriages clip-clopping.

But Olmsted was obliged to move on, due to the corruption of Boss Tweed's Administration, which sought to sell off concession spots in the Park, which had originally been planned to be free of such commercialism. At any rate, a board took over all Park activities, giving the Administration authority to profit from the Park in any way that it might engineer a deal.

Some of these projects included a statue of Boss Tweed in the costume of a Roman emperor, to be mounted among the statues of the poets. Another was a raceway for trotters. Most of these ill-conceived ventures came to naught when Tweed was arrested, and by 1872, Olmsted was back in charge—but only for a while, for the established Tweed cronies declared that Central Park could "become a nuisance and a curse to the city." Twenty years after he had first studied the swamps and rock outcroppings that he had envisioned as America's finest park, Frederick Law Olmsted resigned, vowing that he was forever quits with that siren dream, Central Park.

Inevitably, Vaux took over. But not even he could stop the inevitable slide toward shambles, begun by Boss Tweed's removal of the thousands of trees so carefully cho-

sen and planted in the early years of the Park. By 1885 th
Park had reverted almost completely to its shantytown in
carnation. The slope was ever downhill, until finally, i
1899, the automobile was admitted to the Park roads.

In one sense, the internal combustion engine destroye
the dream that was Central Park. In another, it saved it. Th
first fantasies of a pure park were gone. But now that mor
of the public saw it, albeit through the windshield of
Stanley Steamer, more of what was left was saved. Ye
paths and green swards of land and streams were covere
with concrete to provide passageway for the insolent char
iots. But other hills and rocks and meadows survived, de
spite the distortion that the new way of life had forced o
what had been, once, a dream of majesty, beauty, and recre
ation for all.

It wasn't what it might have been. But Central Park sti
became one of the most used, most enjoyed, most admire
parks in the world.

6

"The Moon made my knees go shaky," Janet confessed. "But Mars? I may have to lie down."

Waldo Wynn chuckled. "It's a biggie, I'll agree. And I'd be lying if I told you there's any kind of guarantee. We're recruiting nine people for a three-man . . . three-*person* . . . assignment. At the end of the first year, two will be phased off into other assignments, if they want them—or be discharged from the program. Six of those remaining will be trained for both Lunar and Mars expeditions. The seventh will be a backup in case one of the six drops out. Near the end of Year Two, the teams will split, with one definitely scheduled for Mars, the other for the Moon."

Robinson said, "You see, that's when we'll be in just the right opposition with Mars to allow a successful round-trip mission. If we went any sooner, and conditions there didn't remain consistent with the Mariner profiles we've received, it could be dangerous for the crew. The less time they spend on the surface, the better—at least on this first trip."

"I think I could handle another cup of coffee after all," Janet said. "If you don't mind, though, there's one really big question you haven't answered."

"What's that?" asked Wynn.

"As the little girl who got hit by a falling piano always says, 'Why *me?*'"

The two men smiled. Wynn started to speak, but Robinson got there first.

"No one is more qualified than you, Jan," he said. "No man, no woman. You've grown up with volcanoes. When you were twelve, you helped your father predict the second eruption of Pacaya, down in Guatemala. You've had more pumice under your fingernails than polish on them. You received the highest graduating marks ever given by Dr. Fred Bullard's geology class at the University of Texas."

"Aha," she said. "But you know, also, that I never got my Ph.D., and that, to a career in Academia, is comparable to shooting oneself in the forehead with a .357 Magnum."

Robinson shrugged. "You were offered two and turned them down."

"Honorary nothings," she said contemptuously. "Front-office public relations types trying to get some free publicity space just before the big annual fund-raising drive."

"I agree," said Robinson. "Turning down those degrees did you far more good than accepting them would have. But knock off the modesty bit, Janet. We don't have time for it this morning."

"The Eastern shuttle waits for no man," Waldo Wynn hinted.

"Okay," she said. "Granted, I'm damned good at what I do. And furthermore, there's nothing so special about women being in the space program anymore. The mission itself can work, because we'd make it work. So the next big question is, just what has to be accomplished?"

Waldo said, "We want to know if the volcanic activity that we know exists on Mars would support a geothermal energy system. If so, it's possible we could plant a colony there. Conventional fuel just couldn't be transported, and as you know, we're really being cautious about nuclear power. We're checking the Moon out, too, but the chances there are nearly zero."

"All right, I think it's terrific. How many other women are there in the program?"

"On your level? None."

Janet frowned. "What about Katherine Redford?"

Wynn said, "She made the final short list. But not the cut." He took a folded sheet of paper from his pocket, handed it to her. "Here. I thought you might want to know who your coworkers would be."

Janet examined the list of nine names carefully. They were in alphabetical order. All were men except for herself.

She pursed her lips. "Okay, I can't quarrel with your choices. Present company excepted, you went after the best. But if you were seriously considering Katy—"

"We honestly were."

"Then I bet I can tell you whose slot she nearly got."

"No bet," said the NASA Director.

"Chicken!" said Leslie Robinson. "I'll buy in. If Janet loses, she buys us lunch the first time we're all in Houston." He glared at Wynn. "Put up, old buddy."

"Put up what?" asked Janet.

"Or we owe you dinner at the swankiest place you can name," said Robinson.

"Oh, hell," said Wynn, "I'm in, but we're being hustled."

"Lars Morgan," said Janet. "He's good, but he's got a rep for forgetting the team and taking off on his own."

Waldo Wynn gave a bearlike growl. "You and your big mouth," he told Robinson. To Janet: "You're right. It was nearly a toss-up. Lars got picked because he's also a skilled photographer, as you are. But your Mrs. Redford gets the first slot if any of the original nine falls out during Year One. After that, there wouldn't be enough training time."

"Why not now? She could learn to use a camera. I'd teach her."

Wynn shook his head. "There's no affirmative-action program in outer space, Janet."

She shrugged. "It's a good list. I'm proud to be on it. And I'll bury the modesty bit. I *deserve* to be on it. Okay, fellows, what do you want from me?"

"Do you need time to think it over?"

She shook her head. "No, because I guess I've been thinking about something like this ever since I learned to read. But what I *do* want is plenty of time to get Iceland in shape. I know the official line down here on good old Earth is that geothermal doesn't look too promising, but I think the Department of Energy is being overly conservative."

"Meaning me," said Robinson. "I hope you're right, Jan. Nothing would please me more than to be proven wrong. With this energy crunch, we can use all the help we can get."

Wynn said, "We want to make our selections public as soon as possible. Everyone else on the list has already agreed to come on board. Now that you have too, we think that President Foster might include the Mars project in to-day's news conference. It'll probably be the only cheerful thing he has to report."

Janet smiled. "You guys were cutting it pretty close. What if I'd stalled? Or said no, flat out?"

"Then your friend Katherine Redford would have been one very happy lady," said Wynn.

They were still chuckling when the distant explosion shook the windows.

7

Still smarting from his encounter with the curious, red-haired young woman, Ben Keller arrived at the face of the trench to find hopeless disorder and confusion. The whistle, which had summoned him, was not the signal for "fire in the hole" after all, but an emergency call from one of the crew handlers.

"What the hell's going on here?" demanded Keller.

A pneumatic drill had tumbled over, crushing lines from the big Ingersoll-Rand air compressor which powered the drill and most of the other tools. One air line, completely severed, was whipping about like a dying snake.

"Cut off that goddamned air!" Keller shouted. He called the crew handler over. "I turn my back for two minutes, and the whole damned place falls down!"

Tony D'Amato, the handler, spread his hands. "We were drilling out one last hole, Ben. Al had his charges ready to place. Then the drill hit something extra hard in there, and the torque started spinning the platform. Before we could cut off the drill, the wheels went right out from under her."

"Why the hell wasn't the platform braced against torque?" Ben asked, and then turned away without waiting for the answer he already knew. The wheeled platform which supported the long drill, and which was raised and lowered like an elevator, had not been braced because that took extra time; a commodity of which Ben Keller was running dangerously short. He had taken a calculated risk and had lost. He would do it again under the same conditions, he knew. There was no blame for Tony. Drills almost never jammed so suddenly that they toppled.

It would take at least an hour to clear the mess away and set the charges. Then he would have to take more risks. A foreman who did not was not doing his job. So he would now risk blasting after 8:00 A.M. It was not too high a hazard. The transverse road was well marked with "No radio transmission" signs, and even with the current crop of Hispanic drivers who could not speak or read English, let alone find an address in Greenwich Village's twisting streets, the low output from the modern mobile radios represented no real danger. The original prohibition against radios dated from the thirties when brute force instead of sophisticated electronics was the only way to push a signal through the jungle of stone and metal buildings. The transistorized mobile units today put out less than twenty watts, compared with a thousand back in the primitive days of vacuum tubes.

And perhaps there was another way he could pick up some lost time. He called out, "Hey, Tony, get Al and let's have a cuppa joe while they clean this crap up."

Their breaths steaming in the chill air, the three men cupped the white polystyrene cups in their hands to warm numbed fingers.

"I miss the old cardboard cups," Ben said, trying to ease the tension. "They kind of melted into the coffee and gave it *body*. This plastic stuff is like drinking out of the old lady's hot water bottle."

"Coffee's not as good anymore, either," said Al Taylor, the explosives man. "They water it down next to nothing."

"Look," Ben said. "About the drill—I ain't blaming nobody but myself. Okay, we lost an hour this morning because we didn't brace it. But we've been saving maybe half an hour every day for the past month by *not* bracing it. So we're still way ahead of the game."

"Just so nobody got hurt," said Tony D'Amato. He had worked in construction all his life, like his father and brothers before him. Two had died, and all had eventually been injured on the job. Tony did not like shortcuts. Too often they went sour and somebody wound up in the hospital.

"Al," Ben said, "I figure at least an hour before we're going to have that mess cleared. How many more holes do you need to plant charges and take down the rock bridge at the same time we blast the face?"

The "rock bridge" was a span of harder stone which had resisted their earlier demolition efforts, and which was being held back for a separate attack.

"Six, maybe seven if we space them along the fracture point," said Al. "But—"

"Tony, get your guys up there with hand drills. Get Al to show you where he needs the touchholes. We'll hit the face and the bridge all at once and pick up that time we lost."

"Ben," Al said hesitantly, "that's going to call for a good twenty percent over our authorized blast load."

"But the charges are in different areas," argued Keller. "We'll pull the men way back, all the way around the bend. Block traffic in both directions. The overhang'll keep aerial debris down to normal. Where's the complaint?"

"I don't see any real problems," admitted the demolitions man. "But you know the rules . . ."

"Screw the rules!" Ben snapped. "We're behind time now and losing more every minute. If you say it ain't safe, that's it. I'll go along with you. But not for lousy rules."

Al considered. "It's safe enough," he said. "As long as we do a good job of clearing the area. But—"

"No buts. Al, you and Tony get moving. I'll take over on the cleanup."

Shortly after 9:00 A.M., the fallen equipment and its scattered pieces of broken metal and shorn hoses had been dragged away from the granite rock face that awaited demolition.

Al and Tony, working at top speed, had drilled new holes

to topple the rock bridge. Al's team had planted high explosives in all the holes, and the wires snaked back to a common connective point behind a protecting knoll.

Men were stopping traffic with red flags. They took their orders from distantly blown whistles. The prohibition against radio transmission applied even to the walkie-talkies carried by the work crews. Some wire-connected telephones were used, but only between the foreman and Al Taylor.

"How we doing, buddy?" asked Keller.

"I'm on my way back now. But like I said, we're twenty percent over specs."

"Let me worry about that."

In a moment, Al came around the knoll. He looked around and, satisfied, gave four piercing blasts on his whistle. Answering whistle calls came back.

"Let her blow," Keller said.

"Fire in the hole!" Al bellowed over a bullhorn. All around the work site, whistles blew again. Then there was silence.

"Stand by," Al said. He twisted a mechanism on his detonator.

"Ready to blast," he said.

"Let 'er go," Ben said.

"Open your mouth!" Al said automatically. With his mouth open, a man was less likely to have his eardrums burst by the shock wave of an explosion.

He pressed the handle of the detonator.

A hundred yards away, the earth, and the granite rock, and the trembling trees above the layer of sod, gave a lurching quiver and settled, in a cloud of swirling dust, into the bottom of the trench.

Where the workmen huddled, the explosion's impact was more powerful than usual, and as they dug their fingers into the dirt, an artificial earthquake shook their bodies.

The rolling thunder of the blast sped away from them. A cloud of dust rose into the morning sky.

"Holy shit!" Ben said. "That was big enough for me." He grabbed up the bullhorn. "Is everybody okay?"

A chorus of yeahs came back.

Ben found that he was trembling. Maybe he'd nearly cut it too close this time.

But what the hell. Nobody was hurt, and he was back on schedule.

8

Chief Charles Nelson Neal, head of the 22nd Police Precinct on the 85th Street transverse, across the Reservoir from Ben Keller's trench (which the Park police had jokingly renamed "the Panama Canal") felt the old stone building shudder. Dust settled from the ancient ceilings.

Neal got up and went out into the duty room. The men there were cursing and picking up papers and small items which had fallen from the edges of their desks.

"What's happening up at the Canal, Chief?" asked the desk sergeant. "That one felt like it went clear through to China."

To another sergeant, a buxom woman in her mid-thirties, Neal said, "Better give the contractor's field office a call. Make sure there hasn't been an accident."

"You got it," said Sergeant Linda Zekauskas. She consulted a typed list of special numbers and dialed.

When the Park had echoed the city's prosperity in the 1870s, and the new attraction drew crowds from the wealthy of nearby Fifth Avenue, naturally they had to be protected from ruffians and pickpockets. The newly organized Central Park Police did this job and did it well.

A generation of planning, planting, and care had left the Park grounds in full bloom for most of the year. The designers planned well, with trees and plants blossoming at staggered times.

Poet Walt Whitman described the Park in 1879: "Private

barouches, cabs and coupes, some fine horseflesh—lapdogs, footmen, fashions, foreigners, cockades on hats, crests on panels—the full oceanic tide of New York's wealth and 'gentility.' It was an impressive, rich, interminable circus on a grand scale, full of action and color in the beauty of the day, under the clear sun and moderate breeze."

The Central Park policeman of the period wore a dark uniform with light stripes around the cuffs and the bowler-like round hat made famous by England's "bobbies." The mounted patrol, which still existed at the moment Sergeant Zekauskas was placing her call, wore uniforms more suited for riding. The wage in 1879 for eight hours was $2.40 a day, with each man on duty seven days a week. Today's paycheck was considerably larger. And backing up today's horsemen were police on motor scooters equipped with two-way radios. Despite a reputation gained in the sixties as a mugger's lair, the Park had aways been well guarded and now, with highly efficient, low-wattage lighting dispersed along its paths and drives, was well illuminated at night except for those wooded areas where young lovers—and, unfortunately, the occasional mugger—liked to stroll. At one time, using infrared scanners and sound detectors developed during the Vietnam war, the Park Police had announced that every foot of the Park was under protective surveillance —either visual or audible. The hue and cry that went up surprised Chief Neal. It seemed that, to the citizens of New York, there was such a thing as *too much* protection. The expensive equipment was removed, and the lovers and muggers plied their usual occupations again, undisturbed.

Sergeant Zekauskas made her report: "I talked with Keller himself, Chief. No problem. He said they were blasting through some heavier rocks—that's all."

Chief Neal gave a nod. Still, when he took his usual late-morning tour around the Park, he might just drop by the big trench and see for himself. Something was tickling at the back of his mind, and he had learned long ago not to ignore that signal.

When Central Park was officially conceived in 1857, the Park Commissioners made no mention of statuary and monuments. The craze did not strike the country until after the Civil War. But by 1873 it became necessary to form a Committee on Statues. Some twenty pieces of sculpture had already been offered.

Olmsted and Vaux had envisioned a park "purified by abundant foliage . . . means of tranquilizing and invigorating exercise, kept free from the irritating embarrassments of the city streets . . . free from the incessant emphasis of artificial objects."

Nevertheless, the statues had launched their invasion, and nothing—not even stringent rules which included being judged as works of art by the Presidents of the American Academy of Design, the American Museum of Art, and the American Institute of Architects—could keep them out.

Over the next century, quite a few impostors sneaked inside the Park's walls and were positioned without regard to their destructive effect on the landscape. Amazingly, some fine works also found homes in the Park.

The Bethesda Fountain, carved by Emma Stebbins, was one such, and dominates The Terrace overlooking The Lake. But Daniel Webster, on the West Drive at 72nd Street, did not fare so well. The 14-foot, crudely executed monument perches on a 24-foot granite base, with Webster's "Liberty and union, now and forever, one and inseparable" carved on it for all time. This might have pleased Mr. Webster, but proved to be an "attractive nuisance" for roving bands of street artists with their aerosol cans of spray paint.

More successful exhibitions of the sculptor's art were William Shakespeare, on the Mall—the formal tree-lined avenue stretching from just north of the 65th Street Transverse to the Concert Ground above Bethesda Fountain. The playwright was in good company—Beethoven, Robert Burns, and an exciting naturalistic work by Christian Fratin, *Eagles and Prey*, which depicts two eagles dining on an unfortunate young mountain goat.

The three potential statue-donators, who had been strolling around the Park this morning since seven, passed the only abstract sculpture there, Jean Arp's *Threshold Configuration*, a little south of the Metropolitan Museum of Art. Ten feet tall, cast in harsh stainless steel, it looked to them like some strange slug crawling on its belly.

"Ugh!" said Arlene Blake. "Who sneaked that atrocity in?"

The older of her two male companions, Professor Jess Hawley, chuckled. At 67, he was erect and moved his thin body with the grace of a dancer. Not for nothing did he jog around the Reservoir every morning at exactly 5:00 A.M. Once, two years ago, an ambitious would-be thief pursued him. The Professor never left the path for safety on nearby Central Park West. Instead, he left his assailant fainting on the ground, wheezing like a beached whale. Now retired from his post at New York University, Hawley filled his days with reading and in helping his old friend, Mrs. Blake, fight what seemed to be an endless battle with the Parks Department, the New York City Arts Commission, and some dozens of pressure groups who simply did not want to see another statue in Central Park, no matter what. Somewhere in her early sixties (a gentleman to the last, Professor Hawley refused to consult *Who's Who* for exact dates), Arlene Blake had been trying for five years to get permission to donate a twice-life-sized sculpture of Harry S Truman. So far, her every approach had been stonewalled, filed and forgotten, buck-passed to some other department or committee, or received with great enthusiasm from an administrator who was never heard from again.

The pudgy, puffing young man (well, relatively so; he was still on the sunny side of 40) laboring along the path with them was Marlon Whyte, the sculptor of President Truman, whom he had portrayed striding along on one of his vigorous early-morning walks. Whyte had gained considerable fame among the city's collectors with his intensely realistic portrait busts. All he needed to gain national exposure

—even international—was to have a major work displayed somewhere where TV cameras roamed.

And Whyte was in a hurry. He was constantly pleading with Mrs. Blake to offer the statue to Washington, D.C.

Her answer was always the same: a hearty laugh and, in her deep, almost baritone voice, the admonition: "Forget it, baby. They were so goddamned relieved to get Harry out of town, you don't think they're going to stick a statue of him up in Lafayette Park, do you?"

Whyte would have settled for a corner of the Capitol Building mall. After all, he pointed out, the President had often taken his brisk walks there.

Mrs. Blake would have none of it. She had commissioned the sculpture, she had been advancing regular sums to the sculptor, the Truman was hers, and she wanted him nearby.

Clients, thought Marlon Whyte. You can't get along with them, but you sure as hell can't get along *without* them.

If only somebody would get on the stick, before his secret leaked out. He could get very healthy financially in a year, break out of these $3,000 portraits . . . but only if the true method of his ultrarealism remained unknown.

If his clients knew that the "photos for research" Whyte always took were actually laser holographs, which—in the privacy of his Long Island studio—were used to carve his masterpieces, mechanically, aided by computer instructions, . . . well!

Those two ancient stringbeans had gotten ahead of him again. Puffing, Marlon Whyte hurried to catch up.

The three were paused on the north shore of Belvedere Lake, north of the 79th Street Transverse.

Professor Hawley had just indicated a site, near the footpath. "Harry'd look good right there," he said.

Mrs. Blake had begun to nod agreement.

Then the earth trembled beneath them. The sound came an instant later, preceded by a rush of chilled air that caught up the fallen leaves and scattered them.

"Those subway people!" she declared. "They're destroying this park!"

Hawley did not answer. He was staring at the middle of the small lake.

Huge bubbles were bursting to the surface. The ripples they generated lapped against the shore.

Then the bubbles stopped.

Mrs. Blake sniffed. "Do you smell something odd?" she asked.

The Professor tested the air. "No."

"That pipe has ruined your sense of smell," she grumbled. "It's as if someone were striking matches." She turned to Marlon Whyte for confirmation, but he had his mind elsewhere. Mrs. Blake had noticed that of him more and more in recent months. Maybe the poor boy needed to go off somewhere and have some fun. He was so dedicated to the Truman statue that it was beginning to affect his concentration.

Another bubble belched through The Lake. This time even Hawley smelled it.

"Sulfur," he said.

9

Leslie Robinson's Plaza Hotel room faced north. He, Waldo, and Janet went to the window and looked down over Central Park. Far to the North, where the haze bent the sky down toward the leafless trees, a black cloud of smoke rose hundreds of feet into the air.

"They're blasting the new subway line," Robinson said.

Janet, who had heard more than one dynamite blast in her day, said, "I think they went a little heavy on the TNT this time."

"Progress!" growled Waldo Wynn. "It'll kill us all in the end."

Janet laughed. "I like you," she said. "Go ahead, tell the President he can shout my name from the Oval Office. I don't care if I *am* your token female. It's too good a chance to pass up."

"Good," said the NASA Director. "I'll make my shuttle flight after all."

"I'll brief Janet on the Mars intentions," said Robinson.

Janet spread her hands. "What's to brief? Obviously you guys are thinking of a long-range station there. You need energy, and you don't think you can get enough—or the right kind, from nuclear power alone. So if we can fuel our generators—and turn over the oxygen producers, and heat the joint with geothermal, we're in the colonization business. If not . . . well, back to the old drawing board."

"That's about it," said Wynn.

"Did it ever occur to you, Gunga Din," she asked, "that there's another planet in the Solar System that needs more or less the same prescription?"

"Where's that?"

"Here," she said, gesturing out the window. "This planet. Earth."

When the NASA Director had gone, Robinson reached out both hands to the young woman and clasped her to him.

"I'm glad for you," he said. "You'll do a hell of a job."

"I think I can," she admitted. "Otherwise I'd never give up on Iceland. Les, we're on the very edge of some real breakthroughs there. I hate to bug out just when things are getting hot, even if I've got until January."

"Somebody'll have to take over," he said. "Who do you suggest?"

"Promise me you won't gasp and fall down."

He raised a hand. "I promise."

"Perry Bigelow."

"I may just fall down after all," Robinson said. "Surely you're aware of how disloyal he's been to you? He's snowed me under with memos accusing you of everything but selling out to the Russians."

"I know. But he's still a really good volcano man. He just needs supervision, and I think he'll take it from any one of the other project assistants already out there. In the form of 'suggestions,' of course. He just couldn't accept being bossed by a woman—especially an upstart like me."

"Are you sure?"

"Les, my primary concern is for the Project. I'm as sure as anyone can be. He can do it. And he will, just to prove how wrong you were originally to put me in there over him."

"Okay," he said. "If that's the route you want to go, I may even leak a few white lies to him. How we were glad to lose you to NASA. If we're going to let his ego pull the load, we might as well give it all the fuel we can."

"I would have been disappointed if you'd suggested anything else. That's the old CIA man I knew and loved."

He repeated patiently, for the fiftieth time, "I was never associated with the Company."

"And cows don't moo at milking time."

Changing the subject, Robinson said, "This is going to come as a slight shock to Linus."

"I know."

"The Mars part is a real submarine. You can't let it get within a mile of the surface. You can talk Moon, but—"

"Trust me," she said. "Neither of us is famed for sharing family secrets. Thank God. We've both got some doozies."

He said hesitantly, "Linus tries."

"I know he does. So do I. Bug out, boss man. The McCoy clan doesn't fink on each other."

"I've learned that," he said. "I'm sorry, Jan. The breaks seem to hide from you."

"It's what I asked for. I cut my own cards," she said. "And I deal them from the top. Don't feel sorry for me, Les Robinson. I'm doing exactly what I want, and if I get a splinter under my tiny little fingernail, I can pry it out myself. I'm the one who put it there."

He said, "I've got to get down to a meeting with the U.N. Ambassador. Use the place as long as you want. Take a nap. You look beat."

"Maybe a phone call," she said.

"Be my guest. I'm glad you decided to hook up with Waldo. We go back a lot of years, and if I don't miss my guess, he's already got his eye on you. Not to worry. He's good people."

She caressed his cheek for a brief moment. "So are you, Mr. Robinson. Too bad you remind me so much of my Daddy."

Only half-joking, he said, "I'll take Electra if I can't do any better on the open market."

She tickled his ribs, and he withdrew, chuckling.

"I just bet you would," said Janet McCoy.

Jack Springfield's hideway was between the Shakespeare Garden and Belvedere Castle, looking down over Belvedere Lake. It was fully ten minutes after the explosion that he came out of his burrow. By then the turbulence that had disturbed the Lake was gone, but he smelled the sulfur instantly. The steam which had, until moments before, wafted from the rocks in his cave had a touch of the same distinctive odor.

North, the black dust puffed into the air by the blast was still settling down on the MTA trench. Back in Tennessee, Jack had used explosives frequently.

"That was a big 'un," he mumbled.

By now, he had learned how to blend into the normal crowds which visited the Park. His clothes were clean, and while ruggedly outdoorsy, with flannel shirts and heavy wool pants, did not stand out from many of the would-be woodsmen who practiced in the Park. He carried a surplus Army musette bag over one shoulder. Within it were enough supplies, money, and spare clothing to keep him going for several days if he could not, for some reason, get back to his cave.

Across the Lake, he saw three people—a woman and two men—staring into the water. He remembered seeing them on other days in other parts of the Park. His safety depended on such memory.

He made it a point to stay well out of their sight, in case they had noticed him previously.

He detoured North, between the Delacorte Theatre and the Great Lawn. As he walked rapidly, almost trotting, the odor of sulfur seemed to follow him.

Something was very wrong.

Maybe the big blast from the subway trench had busted those Con Edison pipes right in two.

Jack Springfield's whole nature told him him to stay out of it, not to get involved.

But if things kept going downhill and they sent in a bunch of people, just pawing around without knowing what they were looking for, they could easily stumble on his snares and his hidden caches of food and materials—and especially his hiding place.

He headed north, past Winterdale Arch, Summit Rock, the Children's Playground and, on Central Park West, found a telephone booth.

Although he restricted his contact with the authorities to practically nil, Jack knew how to get their attention.

He did not make the mistake of calling the Parks Department. Instead, he dialed the New York Daily News, asked for the City Editor, and told him, "Hey, mister, they set off a big explosion up here in Central Park, and it busted all them Con Edison steam lines. The whole place smells like sulfur. And there was steam coming up through the rocks." This was no lie. There had been steam in the rocks . . . before the explosion. Now it was gone.

The editor pressed him for details. He gave those that he knew for sure: the larger-than-usual explosion, set off later than usual, and the pervading smell.

Eventually, after trying unsuccessfully several times to get Jack's name, the editor thanked him and hung up.

A call to Con Edison got the editor put on hold, which he did not like very much. He hung up again and dialed a friend at City Hall.

"You'll hear from somebody in ten minutes," promised the friend.

Actually, it took eleven. The caller was one of the vice-presidents in charge of steam sales.

"It can't be us," he asserted. "We don't even have any steam lines running through the Park."

The editor said ominously, "This sounds like a pretty dangerous situation, sir. Can you absolutely guarantee me that there aren't any of your pipes down there?"

He could tell the vice-president was sweating. Over the years, Con Ed often rode free and easy with the public trust. How could anyone guarantee anything?

The vice-president decided, "We shouldn't have anything there. But back forty, fifty years ago . . . well, look, I'll send in a man to check."

"With one of my reporters?"

"Most irregular . . . wait and see . . ." and all that jazz. Plus eventual capitulation.

"My guy'll be waiting for you at the Miner's Gate," said the City Editor.

Each gate to the Park had been named for a group of workers. In later years, other names had been added: the Woodman's Gate, the Girl's Gate, and even the Stranger's Gate. The Miner's Gate was at Fifth Avenue and East 79th Street.

By the time this arrangement had been completed, Jack Springfield had abandoned the pay telephone on Central Park West and had reentered the Park through the Mariner's Gate at West 85th Street.

Jack was not pleased by the morning's events. Big changes meant big risks, and at his age, even as spry and limber as he was, he did not enjoy big risks anymore.

10

Linus McCoy had gone slightly gray around the temples in the ten months since Janet had seen him. It was the first thing she noticed when his key clicked in the Gramercy Park apartment and the door opened.

As usual, he wore no topcoat. The pale blue Brooks suit was one of the six "uniforms" he kept for the office. Once, when he had been promoted to account executive on the $4 million Ease Soap account, one of his copywriters had joked, "Now maybe Linus can afford two suits."

The next morning, the other five blue suits of his business wardrobe were hanging in Linus's office. He left them there all day, never referred to them, and never heard another joke about his wardrobe.

Two years older than Janet, he seemed even older. Perhaps it was his quiet, serious attitude; he listened carefully, replied concisely, seldom joked, and yet seemed to be enjoying whatever his companions were. Linus was as at home in a Soho jazz bar as at the New York Philharmonic—and would be properly dressed for either. His casual attire tended toward bulky sweaters and tweedy jackets. Formal wear leaned toward ruffled sleeves and heavy silver jewelry made to order for him by a craftsman in Taxco, Mexico. He liked to dress and looked well when he did.

It was in Taxco that he and Janet had met. He was returning to the capital from Acapulco; Janet from a field expedition. He stopped at the Linda Loma Motel for lunch, parking his Mercedes Mark X9 in the shade near the pool. Janet had just arrived in a dust-covered Land Rover. They both reached the bar at the same time and he gestured for her to order first.

"*Un cerveza, por favor,*" she told the bartender, who then looked at Linus.

Linus shrugged. "He thinks we're together. *Un margarita, mi amigo.*" He smiled at Janet. "Join me?"

"Not until I wash down some of this dust. You could grow forty bushels of corn in my throat."

She was brushing dust off her khaki shirt, so well worn that it looked like suede. Then, realizing some of it was settling on his sport jacket, she lifted both hands, fluttered her fingers nervously, and said, "Sorry. There are those who think I shouldn't be allowed indoors."

Gesturing at the patio around them, Linus said, "You aren't. And I've seen dust before."

Introductions came just before the drinks, and they made a casual toast to that champion of Mexican roads, the inter-city bus driver who, owning the entire road, drives on "any side he wants to!" Then came the obligatory "What do you do?" and "Where are you from?" and "Let's have lunch together."

The food was simple, but delicious. Tiny bits of fried chicken, an avocado dip, beans and tortillas. They both ignored the lettuce.

Linus nodded at it and said, "Faster than a speeding bullet."

Janet laughed. "I hear you talking. Of course, in Acapulco, you get the safe stuff flown in from the States, don't you?"

He tilted his head. "It pains me to tell you this, but are you aware that a goodly portion of the fresh lettuce eaten in the United States is shipped in from Mexico?"

"And there I was blaming it on my father's heavy hand with the olive oil!"

"Is he a geologist, too?"

"Was. He died last year."

"Oh. I'm sorry."

"Don't be. He'd gotten too old to do the things he loved
He seemed to live only for my returning from a field trip
My report to him had to be more complete than the one
made to my bosses."

"Who are?"

"Right now, I'm on a grant from the University of Texas
My alma mater." She pushed the lettuce around on he
plate. "How do you know stuff like that story about the let
tuce?"

"I'm in advertising. One of my accounts is the Mexica
Tourist Board. That's what I was doing in Acapulco—attend
ing meetings and planning next season's campaign."

"Acapulco!" she said, making it an unpleasant word.

"I know," he said. "But to most tourists, Acapulco i
Mexico. That's why I always drive down—I can see more o
the real country."

"Well, I don't want to bruise your pioneer spirit," sh
said, "but if you do all your driving in that chrome and
fiberglas torpedo out there, you haven't seen one tenth o
the true Mexico. Even in the Land Rover, there are places
haven't been able to reach without hiking for two or thre
days." She tapped her beer bottle, and the bartende
brought another Carta Blanca. Linus shook his head to
refill of the margarita.

"Yes," he said. "I can see you hoofing it up the side o
some new volcano, stopping only to take Polaroids fo
Daddy's Report."

The bartender was pouring Janet's beer. She waited unti
he left, then leaned forward and, her eyes meeting Linus'
unblinkingly, said, "Listen, buster, you don't know me we
enough to make a shitty crack like that."

She got up, peeled off a handful of pesos, and threw then
on the table. "You'd better stick around for half an hour
The road down to the main highway is narrow, with a thou

sand-foot dropoff. You wouldn't want to dent your nice new toy."

He knew the road well, and knew she would take delight in making him eat dust all the way. So he ordered coffee and waited. He resisted the offer of a complementary brandy, smiling at the steadiness of his hand as he held the coffee cup. Who says you can't take just one and quit? He'd been strictly on the wagon for the whole week in Acapulco, with not even one thirst-quenching beer to break the monotony of fruit juice and coconut milk.

He paid *la cuenta*—the bill—putting aside the twenty-odd pesos the girl had thrown down. Maybe he would encounter her in Mexico City and return it. In their preliminary conversation, she had mentioned meeting friends there.

As it happened, he caught up with her within a few miles, broken down on the exit for Cuernavaca. From the way the Land Rover leaned to the right, it looked as if a mainspring had given way. He pulled up behind her and got out.

"Need help?" he asked.

"The Safety Patrol'll be along pretty soon," she said, referring to the government repair trucks which patrolled the Mexico City–Acapulco road to aid tourists.

He had knelt to look under the Land Rover. Not only was the mainspring fractured, but the shocks were leaking oil.

"You need a tow," he said. "By the time the patrol shows up and radios for help, it could be dark."

She had parked the Rover, with its cameras and delicate equipment, in a dozen jungle clearings, and never lost so much as a scrap of rope. But she knew, here on the artery of "civilization," that abandoning the vehicle was an invitation to having it stripped and looted.

"If it's not too much trouble," she said hesitantly, remembering her hostility to him earlier, "maybe you could detour into Cuernavaca and send a tow truck? I've got traveler's checks and—"

"Better idea," he said. "You take my nice new toy and make the arrangements. You're certainly going to have to stay overnight. Meanwhile, I'll guard your trusty steed and make sure nobody gets light fingers."

Janet hesitated. But what he suggested made sense.

"Okay," she said. "And thanks. I'll drive carefully."

"Carefully but fast," Linus McCoy said. "I don't want to be out on these roads after dark any more than you do. Every cow and goat in the country takes his evening stroll right down the center line."

He briefed her on the gearshift of the sports car, warned her that the brakes would stand the Mercedes on its nose, and waved as she shifted up from first to second, speeding down the exit ramp.

The sky was a cobalt blue. At this altitude, the breeze was brisk, almost cold. He walked around the Land Rover, making sure everything was fastened down and secure, and then crawled under the steering wheel to wait. Half an hour for her to get into town, another half to start the slow wheels of rescue moving, the return trip . . . two hours at least. With a contented sigh, he found a rolled-up sleeping bag and positioned it between the two seats so he could stretch out.

Naturally, no sooner was he comfortable when he heard a truck engine and looked up to see one of the green-and-white Safety Patrol vans pulling onto the shoulder.

The driver spoke English well, relieving Linus of his limited Spanish. He shook his head sadly over the plight of the Land Rover. Meanwhile, his assistant had jacked up the right rear wheel and was examining the damage. He rummaged in the van and came back with a block of wood.

"This will make it more safe to tow," said the driver, whose name was Manuel. His assistant beckoned for them to help. As they lifted, he jammed the wood under the broken spring. When the jack was lowered, the Land Rover remained almost level.

Linus had explained that help had been sent for. Manuel nodded, but with the wisdom of one who has seen much, warned, "If for some reason, señor, help does not reach you by four of the afternoon, you must drive carefully toward

Cuernavaca. You will find a Pemex station eleven kilometers from here. It is safe to park there during the night. This place is not good."

"Bandidos?" Linus joked.

Manuel did not find it humorous. "Sometimes," he said. "Most often, the Coca-Colas. The teen-agers. They move quickly. The engine would be out of this machine in ten minutes."

Linus decided not to ask what might happen to the driver. He reached into his pocket. "*Muchas gracias*," he said, taking out some pesos.

Manuel waved both hands, "No, señor. *La mordida* is forbidden. It has been our pleasure to assist you."

Not wanting to let them go without some gesture of thanks, Linus said, "Is it forbidden to share a drink—*un tequila*—with an *amigo?*"

The driver hesitated. It had been a long day. And it was not actually forbidden . . .

"Thank you," he said.

Shit, thought Linus, realizing that his car—with the unopened bottle of tequila he was taking back as a gift—was somewhere miles away.

"*Un momento*," he said. He opened the rear door of the Land Rover and rummaged through several cardboard boxes stacked there. He was ready to give up and disappoint the Mexicans when he found a bottle of rum, nearly full. There were no glasses or cups, though.

He handed the bottle to Manuel who nodded his thanks and took a healthy swig. "*Muy bueno*," the driver said, passing the rum to his assistant, who lowered its level another inch before returning the bottle to Linus.

He had started to put the cap back on when he realized that both men were looking at him. It would be an insult not to drink from the same bottle they had shared.

Just a little one, Linus told himself. Without wiping the bottle's neck, he took what was intended to be a mere taste.

But the rich rum kept gurgling until he had downed at least two ounces of the liquor.

Manuel laughed and gave him a friendly punch on the shoulder. "Some *hombre, mi amigo,*" he said, taking the bottle again and punishing it once more. Another shot for the assistant, a second chug-a-lug for Linus, and with hearty laughs and cries of "*Adios,*" the green-and-white Safety Patrol truck was on its way, leaving the American weaving under the bright sun, holding a half-empty bottle of rum in his hand.

By the time Janet returned with the tow truck, the bottle was empty and Linus was snoring, sprawled across the two front seats and the sleeping bag. She tried to wake him, then realized that even if she succeeded, he would be in no condition to drive. She told the tow-truck driver that she would follow him in the Mercedes, and down the mountain they went, a battered Mexican truck towing a lopsided Land Rover, followed by a young, red-haired woman driving an American advertising man's nifty new toy.

Now she looked up at him, in the door of the New York City apartment they had not shared together for almost a year, and said, "Hello, Linus. You're looking well."

Slowly, with hardly a click of the lock, he closed the door behind him and, without taking his eyes from her own, moved toward her.

11

Jack Springfield had been telling the truth without knowing it. While his own tiny plume of steam had vanished after the big explosion in the MTA trench, several other fissures now leaked white mist into the chill November air. Two of these were in the trench itself, and now Ben Keller was anxiously studying the terrain maps which had been drawn up long before the first shovel of earth had been turned.

According to the maps, there were absolutely no underground cables, steam lines, water conduits, or sewage pipes anywhere near the positions of the escaping steam. So far, the soil and rock he had excavated had matched the map exactly. Topsoil, much of it brought in more than a century ago as fill for this originally swampy section of the Park, was mixed with clay and sand. Much of it had since been carried away by rain and melting snow. Some remained, however, covering the weathered fragments of bedrock which makes up the bulk of the Park's soil.

Three different rock formations form New York City's foundation. Just north of the Park lies the soft Inwood marble, so easily eroded that the East and Harlem Rivers carved their beds out of it. Farther north, with most of it in the Bronx and Westchester County, is the oldest formation, Fordham gneiss, which underlies the others.

South of Harlem, and thus the principal bedrock of Central Park, is Manhattan schist. It is sturdy, hard to erode, and easily supports the heavy loads of the city's natural and man-made edifices.

Grooved, usually on the north side, by the ponderous weight of the Wisconsin Glacier, which covered them under a thousand feet of ice some forty thousand years ago, the outcroppings of Manhattan schist were the principal barrier to Ben Keller's trench. Part of the excavation, planned there because of the easier digging, ran through an area of regolith—a blanket of rock bits remaining from glacial debris.

Ben Keller was no geologist, so even if he'd examined it, he would have seen nothing unusual about the bit of rock the red-haired young woman had found earlier that morning. But his map indicated that there was only a thick layer of ancient stone beneath his trench, with nothing natural or man-made that could possibly be leaking steam.

Maybe heat from the blast itself had heated trapped water to the boiling point, and it was now bubbling in deep underground crevices. That seemed logical to Keller, so he put the oddity from his mind and turned back to clearing the blast debris in an attempt to get back on schedule.

12

The *Daily News* photographer attracted no attention, with his Nikon F strung casually around his neck, and a Rollei Mini 35, only half the size of the Nikon, tucked in his jacket pocket as a backup camera. The tourists beginning to throng Fifth Avenue, many of them Japanese, often carried two or more cameras and a gadget bag as well, filled with extra lenses, film, and other thief-attracting valuables.

The Con Edison inspector was a large man, weighing at least three hundred pounds. Like a young Jackie Gleason, he was nimble on his feet and, unconsciously, because of his resemblance to the comedian, had adopted some of his mannerisms. He arrived in a yellow Dodge with the company's name lettered on the door.

"Hank Lawson," he said, slipping easily from the Dodge's right seat. The photographer shook hands with him and said, "Tom Chastain."

"Your editor said he had some information about broken steam lines in the Park. That's funny, because according to our records, we don't have any lines there at all."

"Beats me," said Chastain. He had already clicked off two shots of Lawson while the fat man was getting out of the car. You never knew; a human interest shot of Lawson dwarfing the vehicle might make the paper while a waft of smoke coming out of the ground would give your editor the ho-hums. "All I know is that I was supposed to meet you here and follow you around taking some pictures."

His casual, making-it-sound-easy approach concealed that he had one Pulitzer prize and had been nominated twice more.

"Wait for us," Lawson told the driver. Although this was a No-Parking zone, the official "emergency" powers given Con Edison would protect the Dodge from a ticket.

"What are we doing way down here?" asked the photographer. "I thought they were doing all the blasting further uptown."

"We've got to check out one of the lakes," said the Con Ed man. "Then we'll go up to the subway site." He nodded at the waiting car. "By Company wheels. I don't like to walk."

"I don't blame you," said Chastain.

They took the path alongside the Metropolitan Museum of Art's parking lot, climbed past the weathered Obelisk.

Chastain had done his Central Park homework, having published a photo essay on it in the revived *Look* magazine. He nodded toward the tall tower of stone, popularly known as "Cleopatra's Needle."

"You guys keep polluting the air, and that thing's going to fall down," he grumbled. "A hundred years here has aged it more than three thousand in Egypt."

"Egypt doesn't have two million cars pouring hydrocarbons into the atmosphere," said Lawson, sidestepping the jibe. The pace set by the photographer was beginning to wind him. Sweat trickled down his cheeks. Oddly, he felt no conscious resentment. He was accustomed to being tested.

They came over the hill and looked down at Belvedere Lake. Beyond it was Shakespeare's Garden, where all of the flowers mentioned by the Bard are planted. Towering over the flower beds was a Stratford oak, transplanted from Stratford-on-Avon. Now, with most of the leaves gone from the trees, and the shrubs and flowers dormant for the oncoming winter, the landscape was bleak and harsh.

"Looks all right to me from here," said Lawson. Three people—two men and a woman—were climbing slowly up the path. The photographer found a nice composition in his viewfinder and preserved it on film with a click of the shutter.

"What did you expect? That somebody'd taken the stopper out and let all the water drain away?"

The two groups were only a few yards apart.

"Hey," said the photographer. "I know her. That's Arlene Blake."

"Who?" said the Con Ed man, who had never been closer to the inside of Gracie Mansion than through the face of his television set.

"She was married to Mayor Blake. Remember him? Got drowned on vacation five, six years back."

Lawson remembered the Mayor's name, vaguely. Such people moved in another world from his own, hemmed in by power substations and the ever-present grime and muck of the work holes in the streets ("Dig we must . . . for a growing New York.").

Chastain nodded as they drew abreast of the two men and the elderly woman. "Good morning, Mrs. Blake."

She tilted her head as she replied, "Good morning."

The photographer laughed. "Tom Chastain, ma'am. *Daily News*. You wouldn't remember my face, but I took some shots at your daughter's wedding that you liked, and you wrote the paper to ask for prints. I made them myself. I don't like those automated prints going out with my name on them."

"Oh yes, I certainly remember that incident. Thank you very much, Mr. Chastain." She introduced her companions, and the photographer presented Hank Lawson.

"Consolidated Edison?" said Professor Hawley. "Have you come to investigate the lake?"

Lawson, quickly, asked, "Were you there? Did you see anything?"

Marlon Whyte, always uncomfortable when he was left out of a conversation, said, "Bubbles."

"Who?" said Lawson, who had once dated a nightclub showgirl who called herself "Bubbles."

"Not who, what," said the sculptor. "They came up right in the middle of the lake."

"Most unusual," said Professor Hawley. "Not at all like the gas release one sees in the spring, when a lake is turning over." He was referring to the temperature inversion, most noticed by fishermen, when warm water, trapped all winter at a lake's bottom, frees itself and rises to the surface.

"You mean lakes bubble sometimes all by themselves?" asked Lawson, sensing a way to get Con Ed off the hook.

"It's quite common. But I've never seen one behave as this one did."

"Well, I know one thing," said Lawson, "We don't have any gas pipes down there, or anything else."

"Mention the sulfur," said Mrs. Blake.

"Oh, that," said the Professor. "Yes, there was a most definite odor of sulfur."

"Like someone striking matches," said Marlon Whyte, who had a retentive, if sometimes selective, memory.

Lawson sniffed. "I don't smell anything," he said.

"It dissipated quite rapidly," the Professor said.

The three had strolled around the Shakespeare garden for a while, discussing what they had seen, and decided to return to Fifth Avenue by way of the lake to see if the bubbling had recurred. But all seemed back to normal.

"You didn't call the newspaper, did you?" asked Lawson.

"Us?" said Mrs. Blake. "Good heavens, no. Why would we do that?"

"Somebody did," said the Con Ed man. "Well, thanks for the information. I'll pass it along."

"You will?" said Mrs. Blake. "To whom?"

Lawson shrugged. "My boss. We make reports on everything. Then they get put in the computer."

"Which does what?"

Lawson made a wry face. "Who knows?"

13

She had not even planned to go to the apartment. Of course, she wanted to see Linus, talk with him, but her suitcase was still at the hotel. So when she reached him at J. Walter Thompson, told him she had flown into town unexpectedly and was probably going back to Iceland in a day or so, she was surprised when he said, "Hon, why don't you shoot over to the apartment? I've got an eleven o'clock meeting, but I can kill it and be right down."

"I called you this morning," she said.

"Client business. Lancaster, Pennsylvania."

"Where?"

"The Armstrong Cork account. Listen, let me cancel that meeting. I'll see you by noon. 'Bye."

He was gone, leaving the drone of the dial tone.

Well, there were some books she wanted, and she needed a few odd items of clothing. She could fill an extra suitcase while she waited.

Then he had come through the door, and before she had a chance to say any of the things she had planned so carefully, the suitcase had somehow tumbled to the floor, and Linus had mounted her and even as she gave little cries of, "No, no . . ." she guided him into her and, in some distant corner of her mind felt amazement that she was so ready. He penetrated easily, and deep, and still it was not enough. She threw her legs around him and, matching her movements with his thrusting, felt a deep tingling warmth spreading upward, an internal earthquake with her sex as its epicenter.

It had not been that way in Mexico. There he'd done absolutely nothing. The repairmen helped her get the unconscious man to the hotel, where a clerk who spoke little English nodded his sympathy, made a drinking motion with his hand and chuckled, "*mucho tequila*." Janet registered him, and two young Mexican bellboys half-walked, half-carried him to the elevator.

"Don't forget his suitcase," she said. She had taken it out of the sports car's trunk.

"*Por nada*," said the clerk.

Janet went outside, where the tow truck was waiting. They towed the Land Rover to a nearby garage, discussed the truck's illness and the cure—and, most carefully of all, the bill. When all had been satisfactorily concluded, Janet sternly warned the garage owner that the equipment in the Land Rover was all listed with the police and should be kept under lock and key all night. She had agreed to pay for night work to fabricate a new spring, and the Land Rover was promised for nine in the morning. With luck, that meant she might have it after lunch. That would give her plenty of time to reach Mexico City before dark.

She had already sent her luggage up to the room, but since it was early, she had rummaged through the boxes and found a battered copy of *Volcanoes* by Peter Francis. She liked the casual, yet accurately informative tone of his prose. Speaking, as she often did, to lay audiences whose only conception—bred by movies and television—of a volcano which was a cone-shaped mountain that hurled bright red lava into the air, with or without the optional sacrifice of screaming virgins, she often found it useful to crib from Mr. Francis.

The small restaurant on the ground floor of the hotel was open. She asked the clerk if dinner was being served.

"*Si, señora*," he said. Then, giving an exaggerated yawn,

he gave her the room key, explaining in a mixture of Spanish and broken English that he would be closing the desk soon, but that the restaurant would be open until midnight.

Janet smiled her thanks. By midnight, she intended to be long asleep. Out in the mountains, it was up with the birds and under the mosquito netting before the pests began their evening rounds. After an expedition, she always had a hard time readjusting to normal North American meal and sleeping schedules, let alone those of the Mexican cities where dinner was often begun as late as eleven.

She found the waiter more fluent in English and, without too much difficulty, ordered a tall rum with lime and bottled water. Janet had traveled enough in Latin America to be slightly cynical about *aqua pura*—many of the bottles, she suspected, were filled at the nearest faucet—and the ice was undoubtedly made with tap water. Still, one took as few risks as possible.

She knew long-time residents of Mexico City who stoutly denied there was any water problem in Mexico at all. When asked about their big jugs of purified water, it was explained that they "tasted better" in coffee, or scotch, or that they were present only to reassure visitors.

Janet had suffered the effects of the dysentery known variously as "Montezuma's Revenge," the "Mexican Two-Step" or *turista,* too often and too severely to find the subject amusing. And, as a constant traveler, she knew that, even when foreign water was not polluted, the mere change in its physical ingredients—higher or lower in mineral content, or pH—acidity or alkalinity—was often enough to cause distress. That was one reason why she stuck to beer, or bottled soft drinks, when she was unsure of her surroundings. Here in Cuernavaca, a tourist center, the water and ice at the hotel should be safe.

Her highball came and she squeezed the quarter of a lime into it. The fresh taste of the clear rum and the tartness of the fruit was her favorite combination. She would have to remember to buy more tomorrow. Mr. Linus McCoy had made one very dead Indian out of her traveling bottle.

A moderate drinker herself, Janet was no stranger to the problems of those who either could not stop, or could not handle, their drinking. Of course, perhaps she was being too hard on her new traveling companion. He had been moderate at lunch. And it was obvious that someone had stopped to help with the Land Rover. That block of wood had not inserted itself under the broken springs. Then they had probably celebrated.

Have a heart, babe, she told herself. Be generous to the poor guy. He and his eighteen-thousand-dollar car in a country where farmers live on two hundred dollars a year.

Not fair, she thought. Sour grapes, maybe?

She sipped her drink and browsed through the Pelican edition of *Volcanoes*.

The author advanced the notion that if volcanoes had identities or personalities, like the gods primitive tribes thought them to be, they would fall very close to the Christian God—pure, screaming schizoid. Serene, sheltering, generous to crops during their dormant periods, they turned violently destructive without apparent cause, dealing out indiscriminate death by fire, choking ash, falling stones, or poisonous gases. And certainly such volcanoes abounded in the history of the world—real and mythological.

But, as Janet had learned through study, from her father, George "Red" Willoughby—acknowledged as one of the world's best volcano-chasers—and from her own extensive experience which had placed her, while still in her early thirties, in the small group of geologists who were genuinely expert in the field of volcanic study, there were many other kinds of volcanoes. In fact, there were so many varieties that it was sometimes simpler to explain what a volcano is not rather than what it is. A volcano is not a coral atoll . . . although some coral atolls are attached to underwater volcanoes, extinct and otherwise. Nor is a volcano animal or vegetable, although it can be as treacherously violent as any mountain lion and as placid as any baked potato.

Her original ambition had been to specialize in learning to predict eruptions, because advance warning would have saved hundreds of thousands of lives over the years. Instead, while she still worked on that aspect, Janet found that more and more of her time was spent in attempting to find ways to harness the natural forces of volcanoes to bring assistance to a world starved for energy.

Volcanoes, in their many guises and varieties, already aided Mankind in many ways. Perhaps their most important contribution was the soil: so fertile that nations use former volcanic ash to feed millions who would otherwise starve. This is particularly true in tropical areas, such as Indonesia, where heavy monsoon rains soon wash nutrients out of ordinary soil. The steady addition of volcanic ash and pumice keeps the slopes tillable.

A thousand years before Christ, a black, glasslike lava flow known as obsidian was as important to civilization as steel is today. Shaped into tools harder and sharper than any other substance available, obsidian also found use as mirrors when flat slabs were highly polished. But, like everything which falls prey to Man, even obsidian was corrupted, and by the early 1500s, when Cortez conquered Mexico City, then known as Tenochtitlan, the Spaniard found the black lava formed into sacrificial knives which carved living hearts from the victims of Aztec priests. Today, in the form of jewelry, living hearts are touched by obsidian in a different way.

Gold, too, draws strength from volcanoes. While the yellow metal, on which virtually all the trade of history has been based, occurs virtually everywhere, even in the oceans, its presence is so diluted that only where it has been concentrated can mining the ore become profitable. One such concentration, caused by an ancient volcano, was Colorado's famed Cripple Creek, where, eons after being formed, the volcanic pile had weathered down several hundred feet from its original peak, leaving the rich veins of ore close enough to the surface to be worked relatively easily.

And so it went . . . huge finds of silver, copper, iron—and, especially, sulfur—were made in and around long-dead volcanoes, to enrich the world as if in payment for the destruction brought by their creation.

Janet finished her dinner and had a glass of wine with some cheese. The cheese, white—apparently made from goat's milk—was delicious. The wine, however, was a mistake. To protect its own industry, Mexico places an extremely high tariff on imported wines, which rarely travel well anyway in the extreme heat. Janet always hoped to be proven wrong, but each time she ordered a local wine, it was as she feared: bitter, aged with chemicals, made drinkable only by the knowledge that it cost one tenth the price of the most inexpensive French *vin ordinaire*.

She realized, stifling a yawn, that she had spent hours sitting there, reading, and thinking. How many rums had she drunk? Three? Not that it mattered. She didn't even have a slight buzz from them.

Paying the waiter, who leaped to draw back her chair (he, too, had been stifling yawns; Janet was the only diner in the room, and lack of work had made him drowsy), she said goodnight and went out into the lobby.

The outer doors were closed, quite obviously locked—or at least barred by a heavy wooden beam. And the desk was closed. She looked at the key number. Eight.

The corridor floor was of brown tile, and her feet, even in rubber-soled climbing boots, seemed to make an enormous amount of noise.

She found the room at the end of the hall. Its door was at least eight feet tall, and covered with carvings of flowers and birds. It looked as if they had given her the best room in the house.

When she turned the key in the lock and it clicked and the heavy door swung open, she revised that opinion. This wasn't merely the best room in the old-fashioned hotel, built when style and graceful living were prized.

It was the bridal suite.

And there, snoring in the canopied bed, where the servants had deposited him, assuming he belonged to the *señora* with the flaming hair, was Linus McCoy, a beatific smile on his face.

Janet laughed.

Linus, stroking in and out of her with that rolling motion that let him prolong his own pleasure almost indefinitely, while exciting her to repeated climaxes, said, "That's not a coming laugh. That's a something's funny laugh."

"I was just thinking about that first night, down in Mexico. What a washout you were."

"So you say. I take the Fifth."

"You sure as hell did. A whole fifth of rum."

"Don't remind me. All I remember, next morning, is asking you why you didn't buy a better grade of booze. My head kept falling off."

"No, my dear," she said, cupping her hands around his flanks and feeling the alternating clenching and unclenching of his muscles as he kept up the rhythmic stroke. "You asked much, much more."

He slipped his tongue into her ear. "Go ahead," he whispered.

"It's not fair," she murmured. "I come and come and you only can once."

"Liar. Sometimes twice, and remember that New Year's, when we got stoned on Charlie's grass? Three big ones, baby. Without once taking it out. Be fair. We may have our problems, but that isn't one of them."

"No . . ." she said, her voice thick. "Don't stop."

She said more, much more, but in her passion, the words ran together, or were not words at all, but a cacophony of sound keeping pace with the surges of pleasure that rippled through her body.

Then she arched, feeling his spasm begin. She felt the cords in her neck tense into iron cables as she stared, unseeing, toward the ceiling and made the half-laughing, half-screaming sound that accompanied only her most violent orgasms. Everything blended into a whirling mixture of almost unbearable sensations and wordless cries and the wet slapping of flesh on flesh.

Then, as if falling from a great height, silence.

Linus withdrew. Janet, shimmering with perspiration, fell back on the pillow.

He covered her with the blanket, tossing the drenched sheet onto the floor.

"You take a nap," he said. "I'd better hit the shower. I have to at least put in an appearance at the office later."

She mumbled something that he did not understand and dozed off.

14

Hank Lawson, the Con Edison man, posed stiffly before the twin plumes of steam deep in the MTA ditch, while Tom Chastain took three quick shots.

"I don't think this is my job," said Lawson. "I'm supposed to investigate this stuff, not take pictures with it."

"Humor me," said the *Daily News* photographer.

"Humor *me*," said Ben Keller. "What the hell is this all about?"

"Someone reported your blasting had broken some of our steam lines," said Lawson.

"Maybe it did," agreed Keller. "But none of the maps showed them there."

"Your maps are right," said Lawson. "They aren't there. We don't have a steam line within a quarter mile of this site. We go up and down the main streets. We bypass the Park, because by the time we were laying lines, the Park was off limits. I don't know where this stuff is coming from, but Con Ed is not to blame."

"I figured so," said Keller. "Maybe the blast heated up some underground water and now it's just bleeding off."

"Probably," said Lawson. To Chastain: "Are you finished?"

"Just about," said the photographer. "Listen, get over there a little closer to that one by the bulldozer. I've got to take something back, even if it's only you saying, 'They don't belong to us.'"

The quote appealed to Hank Lawson. He carefully ma neuvered his bulky frame to a point just inches upwind from the banner of steam that bubbled from the rock fissure.

"How's this?" he asked.

"Fine," said Chastain, clicking off his first shot. He had just pressed the shutter release for the second when the rocks themselves seemed to explode and, with a scream louder than that of the dying man, the steam enveloped Hank Lawson and, instantly, boiled him inside his skin. The photographer kept shooting reflexively, and it was an irony of the dancing wind that during the twelve seconds it took him to burn to death, Hank Lawson's face was completely unmasked by the bubbling mist, so Chastain's camera caught every emotion and reaction—from the first simple ac ceptance of instructions to curiosity about a sudden sound to a bewildered combination of shock and fright to the first twinge of pain to agony—absolute and mindless—to the glaz ing of dead eyes and the snorting cavern of a mouth trying to scream when all breath is gone to the lowered curtain of death as, its body suddenly limp beneath it, the face fell downward, out of the clear patch of air and into the scald ing steam.

"Fire in the hole!" shouted Ben Keller, reverting to the only emergency phrase that his numbed brain could recall. "Run for it!"

They did. The workers. Keller. And, his camera bouncing against his chest only a little slower than the pounding of his heart, the photographer from the New York *Daily News*.

To those north of the Great Lawn, the steam was almost invisible. But behind it, distorted by its presence in the air, the light from the sun was bent until it formed, with one end seeming to touch down in the Children's Playground and the other brushing the top of the Metropolitan Museum of Art, a perfect, shimmering arc.

Couples, strolling around the North Meadow, pointed and said, "Isn't that beautiful? A sun-shower rainbow!"

Part Two

Maui, the Polynesian hero, stole fire in the netherworld and brought it to the surface. From that moment, all people have had fire—sometimes, to their despair.

15

The trouble with radios, as convenient as they may be compared to finding a land line, wire-bound, to send messages over, is that anybody else with a similar radio can overhear everything that is said.

Tom Chastain found the Con Edison car waiting outside the Woodman's Gate, at Fifth Avenue and 97th Street. He leaped into the front seat and demanded of the driver, "You got a two-way?"

"Sure, but—"

"Let me use it."

"Where's Hank?"

Without answering, the photographer grabbed the microphone and, pressing its Push-to-Talk button, said, "Calling Newsdesk. This is Chastain. Come in."

The *News* had three scanner monitors, their circuits searching all available frequencies for traffic. If it locked into an unproductive message, the scanner—with the mere touch of a button—could be urged to enlarge its search.

It was Scanner #2 which intercepted the photographer's call. A rewrite man hit the switch and said, "Newsdesk. Come in, Shutterbug."

"Take this down."

"Taping." These days, no rewrite man relied on mere memory or fast fingers on the typewriter keys. He taped— and wrote—at the same time, later using the tape to reinforce his original message reception.

"I've got pictures and I'm on the way in. Copy starts. 'At approximately eleven-forty this morning, in the deep trench being carved across Central Park by the MTA, a burst of steam from deep within the earth blasted through the surface and enveloped Consolidated Edison investigator Hank Lawson.' Check that Hank. It's probably Henry. More copy: 'Reports of steam coming from the granite rocks of the Park had been phoned into this newspaper, which instigated the investigation. According to Con Ed records, no underground steam lines or equipment have ever been placed in the area which might cause such an effect. Mr. Lawson, caught in an explosion of the unexplained steam, died instantly. Endit.' But more to come. You'd better put some guys out on the street. Meanwhile, I'll get these shots down to the lab."

"Got you, Tom. You all right?"

"Just scared. I'll get over it. But don't sit on this. If I figure right, it's big enough that there ought to be feedback from the Mayor on down."

"Got you, Shutterbug. Come on home. Newsdesk out."

"Out."

The driver had been staring at Chastain. Now he found his voice. "Hank? Dead?"

"As a mackerel. Listen, run me down to the *News*, will you?"

The driver flared, "Like hell! Get out. I've got to do something about—"

"Bud, there's nothing you or me or anybody can do. Wise up. You heard what I told the desk. We've got to get that Park shut up tight, or more people are going to get hurt."

The driver did not answer, but he put the Dodge in gear and headed downtown.

Radios being what they are, the scanners at two of the city's television stations also picked up Tom Chastain's report. One ignored it. The nearest person was a writer whose only interest was in writing the Great American Novel exposing the crass commercialism of television, which paid him $415.78 a week to subsidize his subversive moon-lighting, most of which was done on company time. But the other station had two senior newsmen in the radio room before Chastain's transmissions had ceased.

"Is it worth a flash?" asked the noon anchor man.

"Not until we check it out," the news editor said. "This could be some kind of hype. Who's nearest the scene?"

"Harry and a crew are setting up to shoot some stuff at the Guggenheim," said a third man, consulting a clipboard. "The new bit with the rolling carpet, so the folks don't have to walk. They could send a go-fer over, find out what's going on."

"No," said the editor. "Scratch the Guggenheim. Send the whole crew over to the trench. If it's real, they'll need every minute they can get. If it's a phony, all we've lost is the people mover, and we can get that later. Big apologies to the museum staff, of course."

"On the way," said the radio man. He took up a microphone and called, "Cronkite, come in." This always brought a laugh from the uninitiated, because Walter Cronkite, until his retirement, had always been on another network, and still did his occasional guest shots there. But the evening anchor man of *this* network admired Cronkite greatly. Besides it often confused—at first, at least—other media eavesdroppers listening in on the same frequency.

"Do they have a microwave dish?" asked the news editor.

"I think so. We'll messenger one up if they don't."

"Cronkite here," said a harsh voice from the radio.

Tersely, the radio operator said, "You guys got a dish with you?"

"Ten-four," said the man on the other end of the transmission.

"Okay. Here's Sid. We got a hot one. Maybe."

Sid, the editor, explained the situation. "You guys get your butts out of there right now. Leave somebody expendable behind to smooth down the ruffled feathers. As soon as you're at the scene, give me a buzz, with enough for a flash if it's warranted. Get the dish set up and start transmitting live, no matter what or how rough. We'll put it on a delay here, and if it comes in too chopped up we'll cut to anchor and let him ad-lib. Got it?"

"Ten-four," said the voice.

The editor clicked off the radio. "I wish the hell Harry had never gotten into CB radio," he complained.

The first negatives which Tom Chastain held up for inspection showed the Con Ed inspector getting out of the Dodge. They were followed by the shot of Belvedere Lake with Mrs. Blake and the two men coming up the path.

He handed the strip to his assistant. "Print the second car shot. Recorder on?"

"Rolling," said the assistant.

"Caption, Hank Lawson—remember to check if it's Henry —on his way to tragic death. Well-liked Lawson was X years old, leaves Whoosies as survivors. Get the correct age and names."

"Gee," said the technician, "I wish I'd written that."

"Shut up," said Chastain. "Move your ass. I've got another strip almost ready."

This was the money strip. If the editors had any sense, they would run it as a six- or seven-frame sequence—starting with the first curious look down toward the steam from the fat man through the agony of his death and concluding with his form, huddled on the ground, blanketed with caressing vapors.

"Here's the car shot," said the assistant. Chastain glanced at it. Under the safe light it looked flat, but he was sure that it would make a good halftone. The *News* used a sixty-five screen: each square inch of picture was broken down into sixty-five patches of light, dark, or in between, which when seen from reading distance blended together to give an impression of continuous tone. He only hoped the steam would read as white, without darkening Lawson's face so much that expression was lost.

Although he almost never manipulated negatives when time was short, he told the assistant, "If you have to, dodge out the guy's face. I want to hold all the detail we can."

The assistant, who had by now seen the second strip of negatives, said, "Yecch." Like so many darkroom technicians, his senses had been so carefully trained that his mind could reverse the negative and he could actually "see" the picture as it would be when it became a positive print.

"One man's 'Yecch' is another man's Pulitzer," growled Tom Chastain. But his heart wasn't in the insult. In the short time they had walked together, he had come to like the fat man. Still, if he hadn't taken the photos, someone else would have.

"This is Cronkite," said a voice over the television station's radio.

"Go, Cronkite."

"Affirmative on that flash. Steam escaping from MTA excavation has killed one man, slightly burned four others. No names yet, but ambulance and police units have already responded. We are shooting tape and will begin transmission bursts as soon as the microdish is in place."

"Roger," said the radio man. "Keep sending and we'll record everything that comes in. Good work."

"Ten-four," said the voice.

The radio man groaned.

16

The nagging drone of soap-opera voices helped Janet to doze. She vaguely remembered Linus saying something about that evening, but it was too much trouble to think about that now.

"*Are you seriously trying to tell me you're carrying Jeff Burlingame's child?*"

What on earth had she done? Sex had never been a problem between her and Linus, but with things the way they were, she certainly had not come here with the slightest intention of going to bed with him—let alone almost hurling herself between the sheets only minutes after he opened the door. And it wasn't from being horny, either. There had been plenty of opportunities in Iceland, and she had nearly taken some of them. Her libido was quite normal and content, thank you.

"*Well, you may have his child, but you will never get him. Marcia Burlingame will go to her grave before granting him a divorce . . . especially if it's to marry you!*"

She sat up quickly.

My God! The things I said! The things I did! We were like animals. I submitted to everything he wanted and begged for more.

Janet rushed into the bathroom. The mirror was still steamy from Linus's shower.

Dimly: "*Surely you realize that an abortion is the only way out . . .*"

Christ, who writes those stupid things anyway? She turned the shower on full blast, tested it with a finger, and turned the single knob toward "Cooler". The bottom of the stall was made of some nonslip material, and it was rough against her feet as she stepped in and slid the glass doors shut.

The water and the thick soap suds washed away the perspiration and tingled against her thighs when she directed the pulsing spray there.

What the hell good does it do to be your own woman when all that stands between you and domination is the closing of a bedroom door?

Janet's experiences with masturbation had been limited by a sense of shame that plagued her for weeks after she tried what a roommate had suggested and found that it *was* possible to bring herself to a climax. She felt absolutely no desire to repeat the experience, although it had been months since she had had normal sex with a boy who was a friend, but not a *boyfriend*, back in Kentucky during the holidays. She thought about it a good deal, and listened while her friends boasted of their conquests, real and imagined, but felt no compulsion to seek out sex merely for its own pleasure.

She knew that she wasn't frigid; on the few occasions where the boy—or man—was experienced enough, she had felt the full range of passion and its reward. It was just that she didn't feel the need for it all the time, or even notice its lack.

Oh, she had been intimate with relative strangers—men she met at a party or even picked up in a resort bar on one of those long Fort Lauderdale weekends. Mechanically, the experiences had been satisfying enough. Emotionally, they left her empty and a bit ashamed.

Another friend, this one an already-divorced 24-year-old female chemist, advised her, "Don't sweat it, Jan. You haven't found the right man yet."

"Why does everything have to revolve around that?"

Janet demanded. "Why must all happiness and contentment revolve around a woman having a *man?* I thought that was what we were trying to get away from."

Now, ten years later, showering, Janet felt a smile creep up and spread her lips. How young and stupid could one be?

Her friend had merely said, "I know you're into Lib and all that, but that's only one part of the world. God, I remember the first time I met Ray. I swear, Jan, the first time he looked at me, I could actually *feel* my legs parting."

Because she somehow did not want to accept this point of view, and because her accusation (she told herself) was true, Janet said, "But now you're divorced from him."

"And I'll stay that way. But that doesn't mean I don't miss the good part."

Almost bitterly, Janet said, "You mean the part between his legs?"

Her friend was not offended. "That, and his hands, and his lips, and especially his tongue." She squinted at Janet to see if she had shocked the younger girl. She had. "Oh, I know. That probably sounds dirty to you right now. But one day it won't."

Angrily, but trying to hide it, Janet said, "If everything he had was that terrific, I don't see why you walked out on him."

"Because," the friend said sadly, "when you add up everything at the end of the week, there's more to life than fucking."

Janet turned off the shower and found a dry towel on the shelf over the medicine cabinet. She pushed the bathroom door open so she could hear the sound from the TV set. Let's see how Jeff Burlingame's mistress is getting along.

Instead, she heard a male announcer: ". . . We expect to have live minicam coverage from the accident's location momentarily. To repeat, a Consolidated Edison inspector was killed this morning when scalding steam errupted from an excavation site in Central Park, where the MTA is constructing a cross-park spur connecting the IRT Lexington Avenue and Broadway lines . . ."

Damp-dried, and knowing she chafed easily between the legs, particularly after sex, Janet opened the medicine cabinet, looking for talcum. The Johnson's Baby Powder she normally used was not there—she vaguely remembered packing it when she had left for Iceland. But there was a round box with a French name and the label, "talcum." It made no impression on her, except that it would do since there was no Johnson's. It was only when she opened the lid and saw, carefully nestled in the pink talcum, the large rubber ring, that Janet drew back and, without realizing she had spoken aloud, said, "That shithead son of a bitch!"

She had tried a diaphragm once, years ago, and found its last-minute insertion to be too cold-bloodedly interruptive of the mood. But she still remembered what one looked like.

Before she realized exactly what she was doing, she had flushed the diaphragm down the toilet and scattered the pink talcum all over the bathroom. She stomped out into the bedroom, dabbing at herself with the towel.

She supposed that there were clean panties and bras still in her dresser, the one nearest the window. But the anger that blotted out everything but the memory of that obscene rubber ring refused her permission to look anywhere else in the apartment. She rummaged through her suitcase, found some slightly tattered cotton briefs. She'd forgotten to bring an extra bra, though. It would have delighted her to go braless, wearing the clean blue blouse with her nipples drawing men's eyes while her own, meeting their glance, would be glacially cold. Go ahead. Look, but you can't have it!

But it was cold outside and getting colder. She would wear the one she had.

She was fully dressed, had found the note Linus left, with his left-handed italic printing: *see u at six at DOWNBEAT, Lex & 42. Drinks, then steaks at CATTLEMAN. Luv. me.*

She made a grumbling noise and threw the note, crumpled, at the window. It bounced back and hit the television set, and drew her eye to the picture there.

That was the excavation site she'd visited this morning.

She sat on the edge of the bed and listened carefully.

". . . had been blasting, as usual. But this morning passersby noticed steam rising from the ground and telephoned newsmen, who contacted Consolidated Edison. The utility company, which states that it has no facilities beneath the Park surface that might cause steam to appear, nevertheless sent an inspector to examine the site."

The camera lingered on a canvas-covered object lying next to a plume of white steam emerging from the shattered rocks of the big trench.

"Moments later, there was what seemed to be an explosion underground, and the inspector, whose name is being withheld pending notification of next of kin, was trapped by a blast of steam and killed."

As intent as she was to the television reportage, Janet felt a twinge of anger. Yes, it would be bad for the victim's family to learn of the accident over TV. But now the wives and relatives of every single Con Ed inspector were hanging by their fingernails, praying that it wasn't *their* man under that canopy of drenched canvas.

Her blue parka was stretched over the back of a chair in the living room. She went over and, from its pocket, took the small chunk of rock she'd found that morning in the MTA trench.

"Oh, my God!" she whispered, examining it closely.

Her anger with Linus forgotten, her own self-revulsion erased, her pride in being asked to join the Space Program completely ignored, she picked up the telephone numbly and dialed a familiar number.

A formal voice answered, "Department of Energy."

"Mr. Robinson, please."

"I am sorry, but Mr. Robinson ts in confer—"

Janet cut her off. "This is Janet McCoy, and I'm declaring a Priority One emergency call. Interrupt him."

There was a pause, some inaudible whispering, then the operator said, "I will connect you with Mr. Robinson."

In a moment, she heard his voice: "Janet, what's wrong? Don't tell me you've changed your mind—"

"Les, please listen. I'm on my way over right now. But take my word for what I'm going to say, and start acting on it immediately."

"On what?"

"Have you seen the news?"

"Janet, I've been in meetings for the past hour and a half."

"Okay, listen close. I don't know who all has to be contacted—Civil Defense, the Mayor, the Red Cross—but they'll listen to you a hell of a lot faster than they will to me. Are you recording this?"

She heard a click. "I am now."

"Good. Leslie, get your TV sets and radios on. I'm watching Channel Four, and they're still broadcasting it. Don't wait for me to get there. I've got the proof, but go ahead without it. Every minute counts."

"Counts for what?"

"For evacuating the city," she said.

"Janet, what on earth—"

"Leslie, damn it, listen!" she almost sobbed. "I don't think anybody knows it right now except me, but if my facts are right—and I think they are—we've got a volcano getting ready to erupt under Central Park!"

"That's impossible."

"Les, believe me. This morning I found a Genesis Rock lying right on the surface. Get things moving—I'm on my way!"

Jack Springfield sensed—rather than saw—the accident. He had gone back into the Park after making his telephone call. At first, he wandered around the familiar paths and trails. With his carefully honed instincts, he realized something was decidedly wrong. The rhythm and normal sounds of the Park had changed. And now that he was actively looking for change, he noticed the most major one.

The birds were gone. Many had migrated earlier, but more stayed, particularly the gray pigeons, who were there all winter, mooching for scraps and breadcrumbs. Now none remained.

And the air itself seemed different. Sort of charged, the way it is just before a big thunderstorm.

It had a different smell, too. He had always noticed a touch of sulfur in the steam from the fissure in his cave. But now the acrid odor seemed to permeate everywhere.

He approached the subway excavation through the South Meadow, near the tennis courts. Usually, the trench was the source of considerable noise—the shouts and jokes of the workmen, the low rumble of machinery, the occasional RAT-TAT-TAT of a jackhammer.

All was silence now.

Then, before he could see down into the excavation, he felt the air pressure change suddenly. He threw himself to the ground, and did not see the plume of steam shoot up above the lip of the trench. He heard yelling, and a watery, hissing noise.

That was enough for Jack Springfield. He took to his heels. Today looked like the perfect time to take in a movie. A double feature, if he could find one.

Too many funny things were happening. Let the joggers and the tourists have the Park until things calmed down.

17

Probably the best-known apartment building in New York City is located at 1 West 72nd Street, on the corner of that street and Central Park West.

It took four years to build for its owner, Singer Sewing Machine heir Edward S. Clark. The ultimate in luxury for its time, it still retains much of its prestige—thanks to the celebrities who own its sprawling eight- and ten-room apartments with their high ceilings. Stars of the stage and screen, such as Lauren Bacall, John Lennon of the Beatles, actors Robert Ryan and James Whitmore are only a few of the luminaries who have lived there.

During its construction period, the building had two nicknames: "Clark's Folly," because of his apparent stupidity to invest so much money so far north in the wilderness, and "The Dakota" because he might just as well have located his apartment house in "the Dakota Indian Territory."

"The Dakota" survived, much to the relief of subsequent managers of the building. Such a romantic name is far easier to sell than something called "Clark's Folly."

The Dakota had a Germanic feel to its architecture, with turrets, bay windows, dormers and above all, a grandness of size. Even today it dwarfs most of its neighbors. In 1884 it had no neighbors, except shabby farms and wooden shacks.

Naturally, although all of the apartments are spacious and well built, with thick, soundproof walls, service elevators for each kitchen, and intense privacy (to enter the Dakota, one must be cleared through what looks like a walled courtyard in old Munich, complete with sentries), the most favored ones are those which overlook Central Park.

Daytimes, in spring, the blossoms are a crazy quilt spread out below. Summer brings a green curtain of trees and lawn. Fall presents the bursting colors of falling leaves. And even winter has its appeal, with the Park resembling a stark black-and-white woodcut of some desolate darkling plain.

But it is at night when the Park is its loveliest, year round, when seen from above. Thousands of lights dance through the evening mists, each forming its own little yellow circle against the dark carpet below. Automobile headlights thread their way between the rock outcroppings, tiny electric beams that should, by rights, be in the main window of the city's great toy shop, F. A. O. Schwarz.

If it had not been for the view from her Central Park West window, where—like a sleek blond cat—actress Joan Weldon liked to curl, watching a world that never sensed, let alone saw, her scrutiny, Alexander Cage would have caught his plane to Dallas, and perhaps the history of New York City might have been written differently.

Cage had gone to Joan's apartment directly from the *Today* interview. He had promised to stop by for a quick cup of coffee.

They had met two weeks earlier in London, where she was finishing scenes for the latest Agatha Christie thriller, *Murder in Buckingham Palace*. To be sure, Miss Christie had never written such a book, but the producers weren't bothered by that minor detail. A screenwriter had hashed together two of her earlier novels, which had—unfortunately for Miss Christie's heirs—been sold outright many years ago, and now, resurrected from a pile of "properties" were carried on the books as "assets" when a formerly major Hollywood studio had been sold, its back lot to be converted into high-rise apartments and its corporate structure to concentrate on "releasing" films rather than making them, while diversification was achieved by taking over a chain of hotels.

She said, "You would have made an excellent actor, Alex."

Kissing her—a "hello" kiss, not the lovemaking ones they would share one day soon—he asked, "What makes you say that? All I did was answer questions."

"Plus projecting honor, integrity, candid truth—when you and I both know that you didn't believe a word you were saying."

This sobered him. "You're wrong, Joan. Yes, I present the views of the oil industry. Some of the issues may be open to controversy. But—"

"Never kid a kidder, Alex. I've had two weeks to study you. I've read your book. I've listened to your speeches. We've talked around the subject, but even avoiding a question, you answer it."

Flattered, he said, "I thought I was the only one in the world who knew I'd published that book. I think the publisher sold around nine copies."

"They sold more than twelve thousand in hardback, and the paper edition is required reading in at least a dozen universities. Not bad, since it amounted to a manifesto for virtually turning the country over to the Oil Barons. You nearly had me believing what you said. And that makes you a very dangerous man, Mr. Alexander Cage. Luckily you don't really believe it yourself, or somebody'd have to assassinate you to save the country."

He studied her. He had never allowed himself—not ever—to question the positions he presented on behalf of the oil industry. He could not afford to, he realized subconsciously. Because with the first serious doubt about the honesty of his commitment, his usefulness would cease. Yes, he would exaggerate, he would jawbone, he would even withhold part of the big picture. That was fair, according to his private code.

But to deliberately lie?

He pressed a finger over Joan Weldon's lips.

"And I think you are a very dangerous woman, Miss Joan Weldon."

Realizing that she had the power to destroy him, she chose not to use it.

Instead, she gave him a chaste kiss on the cheek. "Let's hope you never find out," she said.

Now, as she sat in her window perch, looking down at the Park, which seemed more barren each day, she heard Alex call, "Joan, do you want some coffee?"

"No," she said. "Turn on the TV, will you? Channel Four. A girl who did a bit in the Christie thing has a running part on one of the soaps. She wasn't very good in the film, but the director didn't give her much of a chance. I'd like to see if she's any better doing things her own way."

She heard a click, as he asked, "Don't soap operas have directors, too?"

"Barely. They're so busy plotting camera positions, it's up to the talent to find their own interpretation and deliver it on cue."

She slipped down from the padded window seat and went into the kitchen. The little black-and-white set had been installed for the primary pleasure of the live-in cook/maid/companion . . . who had carefully been given to-day off. It was not that Joan worried about Lydia's knowing—or even seeing—a male visitor. It was embarrassment to Alex that she wanted to avoid. If their friendship became an affair, if he came to New York frequently, if . . . well, there were so many ifs she could handle when they arose.

"That's her," she said, pointing to a young woman who was seated in what was obviously a doctor's office.

"*. . . but how can I tell him? He's always been so proud of my figure. And now, you're going to . . . to . . .*"

The young man playing the "doctor" practically oozed compassion: "*It's not the end of the world, Laurie. And it doesn't have to be the end of your attractiveness to your husband. Believe me, I know.*"

"Oh, sure, you know! And how would a MAN know? What would you say if someone told you that they had to cut off your . . ."

"My, my," said Alexander Cage, who only rarely saw daytime television. "I hope all the kiddies are in school."

"You might as well kill it," said Joan. "I've seen enough. She's one of the unlucky ones, with just enough talent to get by and keep her hoping."

"Maybe she'll get that so-called big break," said Cage.

"That would be the cruelest thing in the world that could happen to her," said Joan. "Once she's had her own spotlight, and loses it, she'd have to be a remarkable person to survive. Think of how many who have gone right down the chute—drugs, booze, mental wards . . ."

"Perhaps she'll marry rich."

"If she does, I pity the poor son of a bitch," she said. "I told you, turn it off. I've got calls to make. And you have a plane to catch."

Knowing he had said something that had touched too close to whatever fears and insecurities she carried inside, Cage reached for the "off" button. Before he touched it, the picture cut abruptly to a newsroom set and an announcer said, "We interrupt our regularly scheduled program for this Channel Four news flash. An unexplained eruption of scalding steam killed one man and injured several others this morning at the MTA subway excavation in Central Park. . . ."

"Joan," said Cage, "if you don't mind, I'd like to listen to this."

She made an "I don't care what you do" gesture with her hand and went back to her window seat.

The klaxon of an emergency "whooper" siren drew her attention to the street below.

An ambulance was speeding up Central Park West.

18

"You mean you haven't done a goddamned *thing?*"

Janet McCoy's shouted question was so piercing that everyone in the suite of Department of Energy offices on the 48th floor of the Pan Am Building heard it.

Leslie Robinson's patient reply was inaudible outside his private office.

"I've done plenty," he said. "All I could until I knew more than you told me on the phone."

"I told you we have an incipient volcano right in the middle of nine million people," she replied coldly. "I think it's already starting to erupt."

"I have lines open to Civil Defense and the Mayor," said Robinson. "I'm trying to get through to Waldo on the shuttle flight."

"What good can he do for us thirty thousand feet over Maryland?"

"Volcanoes are out of my field," he said. "I'm an administrator, not a scientist. But Waldo will know every competent geologist with volcanic experience close enough to do us any good."

Janet sat down. Plumped down was perhaps more correct. Her legs were trembling, and she realized that she had been superimposing her own fear and indecision over the Director. He had acted swiftly and, in view of the wildness of her warning, with prudent effectiveness.

"I'm sorry," she said. "It's been a day."

He slid open a bottom drawer of his desk, offered a bottle of Old Granddad. "Some frostbite medicine?"

She shook her head. "I'm okay. Here's what happened. You know that big hole they're digging across Central Park for the subway?"

He nodded.

"Well, they had an accident a little while ago. They were blasting, and some steam came up through the rocks. Con Edison sent an inspector out, although they say there aren't any steam lines or anything else under that part of the Park. The inspector got in the way of what sounds to me like a geyser effect and was boiled like a lobster."

"Couldn't there have been some groundwater in a crevice, that the explosion superheated?"

"I sure hope so. But this makes me think otherwise."

She took the small rock from the parka's pocket and pushed it across the desk.

"What is it?"

"A Genesis Rock. Maybe four billion years old."

"Where did this come from?"

"The subway excavation. The foreman told me they found it less than thirty feet down. It should have been more like thirty thousand."

He shrugged. "I'm still lost."

"You know how a volcano is formed?"

"A mountain blows up and spouts lava."

"Sometimes. Not always. But, with no exceptions, a volcano is a hole—call it a chimney or a vent that pokes up from the interior of the planet, where the heat may be as high as a thousand degrees centigrade. At that heat, rock—minerals —in fact, *anything*—melts into a thick liquid we call magma. When the pressures get great enough, or if there is a gas explosion, this magma is forced to the surface. If it breaks through, we have what you call a volcano. But sometimes it cools before reaching the surface, and hardens into what are known as dikes. Dikes are actually streams of magma which go down deep into the earth like roots of stone. Genesis

Rocks are usually found at their base. When I saw this one this morning, I took a walk down through the Park."

Robinson hefted the weight of the rock in his hand. "I gather you found something else."

"I found that the Park is literally riddled with dikes. If you just glance at them, they look like veins—usually vertical —in the rock formations. Remember, when these dikes were formed, they were hundreds of yards, possibly miles, beneath the surface. The constant weathering of millions of years have worn the country rock down to where it is now— and the dikes have become visible."

"But active? All this took place, as you say, millions of years ago. There are no volcanoes on the East Coast, or any signs of there having been any."

"There weren't any human beings on the Moon for millions of years either, and now your buddy Waldo wants me to go there."

"Speaking of which—" he said, pressing an intercom button. "Mary, any luck getting through to Mr. Wynn?"

"We've just spoken with the Eastern pilot, sir. He's having Mr. Wynn brought up to the flight deck."

"Buzz me when he's on."

Janet said, "What I'm saying is, one, there's this rock on the surface when it ought to be thousands of feet down; two, no matter how thick the bedrock is, it could be riddled with dikes or sills—"

"Sills?"

"Like dikes, except they cut across the country rock in a horizontal direction."

"Complete my education. What's country rock?"

"Any local rock. In our case, I happen to know it's a very hard species called Manhattan schist. I know, because I saw them, that the country rock here contains dikes. I'd guess, down deep . . . maybe two hundred, maybe a thousand feet . . . that there are sills, too. In fact, now that I remember my basic training a hundred years ago down in Texas, the Palisades rock face across the river *is* a sill." She furrowed her brow. "Sure it is!" As if reading from a computer screen inside her head, she said, slowly, "The most famous sill in the world, the Palisades sill, was formed when the supercontinent of Pangaea tore apart and began the continental drift that separated Europe and Africa from North and South America."

Robinson sighed. "Millions of years ago, no doubt."

"They've carbon dated specimens at around 240 million."

"Yet in all that time, we've never had a volcano. Why are we suddenly so blessed?"

"The reason we haven't had a volcano is because, according to our current thinking, certain areas where the continents were torn apart have subsurface weaknesses which allow the magma to rise to the surface more easily than in other, less stressed parts of the world. But remember: those stresses are always changing. An area safe today might be tomorrow's danger zone."

A buzzer sounded. Robinson pressed the intercom. "Yes?"

"Mr. Wynn is on Two."

"Thank you." He punched a key. "Waldo?"

"What's up?" came the NASA Director's voice. "You've got a cockpit filled with very frightened birdmen here."

"Nothing to do with the flight. Listen, we need to know how to get a couple of the best geothermal experts available into my office in the next hour."

"You've got one of the best there is around there somewhere. What's wrong with Janet?"

"She's already here. And she's raised a problem that I think needs some backup thinking by a couple of other big-brains."

"Okay, the first thing you do is call the Geothermal Institute on Park Avenue. Ask them where to find Mort Weisman and David Black."

"Are these guys on your Mars list?"

"No, but they're top-grade. Failing that—they may be out of town—ask, right out in front, for the best available people under the time and location circumstances."

"Will do."

"And check their names with Janet. She'll know the hot ones."

"Thanks. Call me when you get to your office."

"I presume this has nothing to do with our conversation this morning?"

"No," said Leslie Robinson. "That's still Go."

"Good," said Waldo Wynn. "Call you later."

Robinson hung up the phone. "Mort Weisman and David Black."

"The best you could hope for," said Janet. "Use my name."

Tersely, Robinson gave instructions for the two scientists to be tracked down, at the "urgent request of Miss Janet McCoy."

The steam in the MTA trench had dwindled down to a bare mist seeping from the rocks. But all work had ceased. Awaiting orders from higher up, Ben Keller was not about to risk further lives.

Had the heavier-than-usual blast liberated some destructive underground force? Was he responsible for the Con Ed man's death? Keller tried to force those questions from his mind, without success. Normally, he returned to his home in Kew Gardens with at least half a dozen boastful stories to relate to his wife, Agnes, while she prepared supper.

He had no idea what he was going to tell her tonight.

Linus McCoy tried to keep his voice calm. "I know, baby, but she blew into town last night without warning. She'll be here a day or two—that's all."

Paula Armstrong, not of the Lancaster, Pennsylvania Armstrong Cork Company, but of the Armstrong hostess at the reopened *Le Valois* restaurant, was not particularly delighted by the message Linus was relaying.

Her voice was sharp: "You told me you were through

with her. Now all of a sudden she's back in the apartment. What happens if she starts going through the closets?"

Linus, who had been worried about that very thing, reassured her: "She's in town for one day, for some kind of meeting with the Department of Energy. And she's got a hotel room."

Paula had not left too many of her things at the apartment. Even if Janet went looking for a coat or sweater, the chances were good she'd never notice the strange clothing. Janet had never been very interested in clothes, and more than once had worn a dress for months before looking at it in bewilderment and asking, "When did I buy this rag?"

"It was a gift from your humble servant, Linus McCoy," he would reply.

In truth, she had probably bought it herself off a 14th Street discount rack.

"No, not tonight," he told Paula. "She's been in Iceland for ten months, baby. I've got to at least take her out to dinner."

Dinner was all right. But Paula told him, in no uncertain terms, what would happen to a certain portion of his anatomy if he used it to perform any husbandly duties.

Arlene Blake, in her Fifth Avenue apartment, saw the news flash and immediately dialed Professor Jess Hawley.

He had seen it, too.

"We'd better communicate what we know to someone who can take action," said Hawley.

"I'm on speaking terms with the Mayor," she said. "I helped his wife get settled, and he owes me."

"See him in person," suggested the Professor. "No phone calls. Meanwhile, I'm going to bike down to the Museum of Natural History. Believe it or not, there's some muscle in those back rooms behind the dinosaur bones."

Chief Charles Nelson Neal hit his fist on the desk sergeant's battered podium. "I should have checked it out," he grumbled. "I had a bad feeling about it."

"Terrific!" said the Dispatcher, Sergeant Linda Zekauskas. "The way your luck runs, you'd have arrived just in time to get boiled yourself."

Neal had already ordered a protective cordon of police around the accident site to keep sightseers away. He had the 97th Street Transverse closed to all traffic. His urgent report to the Police Commissioner had already been sent by Telex. For one not given to foreseeing the future, he had reacted promptly and properly to the emergency.

So why did he feel so guilty, as if he had fumbled the ball on the defensive team's one-yard line?

Having made a dozen superb prints of Hank Lawson's death for the late-afternoon edition, Tom Chastain washed his hands carefully to remove all hypo odor, thanked his assistant, strolled out the door of the *News* building, had a cold mug of half and half, left his change on the bar as an indication that he would be back shortly, went into the ammonia-smelling men's room, locked the door, and knelt to puke his guts up into the rust-stained toilet bowl.

The efficient secretaries of the Energy Department were able to track down both Mort Weisman and David Blake, both of whom promised to be at the Pan Am Building by 5:00 P.M. Janet McCoy spoke briefly with both of them and, without revealing what she suspected, persuaded them to bring along everything they had, of personal research, or in books or articles, about the substrata of the Manhattan area.

At the same time, Leslie Robinson made the same request of the New York Geothermal Institute. Once again, a mention of Janet's name brought instant cooperation.

Between all the business calls, Janet managed a personal one to J. Walter Thompson. She was trapped at the office and would be unable to meet Mr. McCoy, as she had promised.

Linus's secretary, who was anything but deaf-and-dumb, gave a satisfied smile as she wrote down the message and left it on his desk. It was about time somebody caught up with that joker.

The first time she was positive that Linus had cheated on her, Janet had left the apartment in a cold rage and, using her credit cards, flew to Kentucky where she reopened her father's house and spent nearly a week staring out at the Rough River and, in a daze, preparing meals, bathing, and trying to think.

She had disappointed Linus, she knew, by insisting on continuing her field work. But she had canceled more expeditions than she undertook.

"You're my goddamned wife!" he shouted at her, when he came home unexpectedly at noon and found her studying maps of the island of St. Vincent, where new volcanic activity was brewing. "You're supposed to be here with me, not camped up somewhere on a crummy mountain!"

"It's my *work*," she protested. "And it's just a survey. A week—ten days, at most. Why don't you take some vacation and come with me? It's a beautiful island."

"Just like your damned *beautiful* Valley of the Smokes up in Alaska? I've still got welts from those lousy mosquitoes. Thanks, lady, but you stick to the kitchen, and I'll tend to the *work*."

"That was never agreed on," she flared.

"Since when does it have to be agreed on? You know what a wife is supposed to be. Every time I need you—or want you, which is the same thing—you're way the hell off in South America getting your jollies by staring down some crummy lava pit."

She folded the maps and went into the bathroom. When she came out, he was gone, and he did not come home until after midnight. He was drunk and smelled of a musky perfume, but she tried to ignore it as she undressed him and rolled him into bed.

There, nude, it was impossible to ignore the fresh nail welts on his back.

So she sat, dazed, in Kentucky, refusing to answer the phone. It was only when he came down and, hugging her, actually wept, that she was persuaded to return to New York.

But from that awful week until she left for Iceland, feeling almost criminal as she noticed the unmistakable signs of other women on him or his clothing, hating herself when she called and found him out of the office, when he'd told her he would be in meetings all day, Janet felt herself drifting slowly away from the man she had promised to "love, honor and obey . . ."

Obedience had never existed. Honor was gone now, too. Love?

Janet found herself wondering what it really was, and if it still bound them together.

Alexander Cage had canceled his Dallas flight. He reached Eve Newhart, asked her to call the office and get everybody who could dial a phone to start calling the oil industry's top demolitions experts and ordering them to report to him in New York within the day.

Eve asked, "Since when is there oil in Manhattan?"

Cage answered, "Power comes in different colors, Eve. Start dialing."

19

The construction site had been cordoned off. Two almost-invisible plumes of steam wafted up into the chill air of the November afternoon. Distantly, the never-ending sound of city traffic went unheard by the investigators, who carefully examined the fissures in the gray rocks. They were so used to the background noise that it was unconsciously blocked out of their minds.

Once, when brought directly to a trading post north of Fairbanks, an Alaskan Eskimo family had fled in terror a hundred yards from its front porch.

When asked to describe what had frightened them, they said that a terrible noise had tried to get inside their heads to eat their brains. It sounded, they said, like a dull "*Mmmmmmmmmmm*" coming from the very bowels of the earth.

Eventually, it was discovered that the trading post had just been connected to a main power line from the south and it was the hum of the sixty-cycle alternating current that the Eskimos heard. Since they had never been near electricity before, their minds were open to the constant sound it makes, near the bottom of our threshold of hearing.

Similarly, many native groups around the world have had to be taught to "see" photographs. Until their eyes, coordinated with their brains, were able to fuse two-dimensional objects into an image acceptable to them, a photo was simply something flat with smudge marks on it.

So it was today with the new team from Con Edison, with the MTA crews, with the media—TV, radio, newspaper and a horde of free-lance photographers. They looked at the steam and saw only the results of an overambitious blast. They looked at the fissured rocks and saw only stone. They had a dozen theories, the most prevalent one being, "Whatever it is, it's going away."

Nobody in Central Park had yet learned how to look at a baby volcano.

Mort Weisman, who lived in Manhattan, was at the Pan Am Building early. A stocky man with a flourishing red beard, he fumbled with a thick briefcase as he shook Janet's hand. "I've heard about nothing but Project Hveragerdi ever since you went to Iceland," he said. "I even almost wrote you to volunteer. But"—and here he almost glared at Leslie Robinson—"I've made it an absolute rule never to work on government projects."

"A rule I wish I'd been taught at my mother's knee," agreed Robinson. "I'm going to have a very weak drink. Is it against your principles to join me?"

"We Jews are very temperate people," said Weisman. "Every chance we get. Scotch?"

"Coffee," Janet said firmly.

Robinson, who had heard rumors about Linus McCoy, rejected a first thought of pointing out that this was his office and his hospitality.

"You're right," he said. Besides, if she happened to be right about the threat to the city and if word got out that they'd all been drinking . . . "Excuse me. I'm going to make sure we have a skeleton staff. One can be our coffee maven."

"Keep a couple of messengers," said Janet. "We're going to need them. Let's use the couch," she said to Weisman, as Robinson left. "What did you bring?"

"Nothing you couldn't get a dozen other places," said the geologist.

"Except that you've got it *here*," Janet pointed out.

He unrolled an odd-looking map. "This is based on bore holes made over the years. They go down through the country rock, into the igneous layer."

"And?"

"That's it. Solid casts all the way. Nothing fluid."

"No signs of magma?"

"Only in its hardened form. Two hundred, two hundred and fifty million years old."

"How about Central Park, specifically? Layer by layer."

He checked identification numbers on the chart, fumbled through several smaller ones until he found what he wanted.

"Here we are," he said. "Want to tell me what we're looking for?"

"Not yet. I don't want to color your independent opinion."

"Okay. But first, do you believe in the Pangaea theory?"

"Only if it's part of the orogeny concept."

An orogeny is when layers of rock, which may have been horizontal, are pushed and twisted, like a crumpled sheet of paper. Some parts become hills and mountains. Others become gorges and valleys. The orogeny theory of the New York area is that, some 450 million years ago, a cataclysmic crushing together of landmasses crumpled New York's rock formations just like that imaginary sheet of paper.

"But," said Weisman, "without the original orogeny, the next one, a hundred million years later, wouldn't have left us with our present landscape."

He now referred to the theory that some 350 million years ago, Europe, Africa and North America had fused together into a single gigantic continent which today's geologists call Pangaea. The result of their collision was another earth-rending orogeny, throwing up more mountains and actually folding the layers of Manhattan schist—particularly in the area which is now Central Park.

"That's the only way we can account for the tilt of the formations in the Park—near the Lake . . . here"—he indicated a section of the chart—"they dip nearly seventy degrees. Now, according to our bore holes, the loose regolith consists of soil, then sedimentary cover. Some of it is glacial drift, only fifteen or twenty thousand years old. The drift and the regolith may be a few inches thick, or as much as fifty feet. But—sooner or later—our drills hit country rock."

"And that continues down to the limits of your drilling?"

He nodded. "Janet, I think I know what you're thinking, but nothing I've seen or read gives me any reason to believe there could possibly be volcanic activity under Central Park, the city, or this whole section of the Eastern seaboard. We've made too many test bores. If there were activity down there, we would have found some trace of it."

"How recent are these bores?"

"The ones in Central Park?" He studied tiny symbols on the chart. "The deep ones, thirty years and older. Shallow ones for the MTA excavation go back a couple of years. Relying on the earlier deep exploration, they went down only far enough to be sure there was no cavitation or other foundation problems."

She handed him the rock she had found that morning and told him where she'd gotten it.

"Janet, it could have been forced to the surface in a dozen ways. It's probably just part of a dike that didn't weather as fast as the surrounding outcroppings. That thing you're holding might be only a hundred million years old."

She sighed, put it on the desk. "Which is approximately the age I feel right now."

Mort Weisman made a "me, too!" gesture.

She stared at the bit of gray rock. "God, Mort, I hope you're right. But what if you aren't? What if this *is* a Genesis Rock? Can we take that chance? That steam had to come from somewhere, you know."

"I do, and I don't think we should let up for a minute. I honestly believe there's some, as yet unthought of, explanation for it. But, with Mr. Robinson's permission, I'm going to use his phone."

"He's probably out lassoing reluctant overtime slaveys. Be my guest."

"Thank you. First, I intend to call my family, tell them to put their collective asses into our bank-owned Pinto, and haul those asses up to Middletown to spend a few days with the doting grandparents. I'll claim I'm involved in a day-and-night project, and that this is a good time to get brownie points against the visit for the holidays that we aren't going to make because . . . well, I don't know because what, but I'll wing it."

She touched his arm. "Mort, I'm sorry. I've alarmed you in spite of these—" indicating the charts. "Then what?"

"Then," he said, "you and me and Dave Black, if he ever gets here, are going to tear these surveys apart until we're willing to bet nine million lives that the books and tests are right, and our dear little Janet McCoy is wrong."

"Boy," she said, handing him the telephone, "do I ever hope that you can!"

Linus McCoy's phone jangled.

He picked up the receiver.

Paula Armstrong said, "Congratulations, Ralph Kramden."

He had just received Janet's message canceling their drink date, and was irritable. "What the hell's that supposed to mean?"

"Don't you ever watch reruns of 'The Honeymooners'? Jackie Gleason is Ralph, and he's always threatening Alice: 'Pow! One of these days, right to the Moon!'"

"Har har, de har har," he growled, going along with the gag. Le Valois served only luncheon and early evening cocktails. If he couldn't patch things up with Janet, he might just hook up with Paula. If he went out alone, crawling the singles bars and discos, he knew he'd never be able to control the booze, and there was an important client meeting coming up in the morning. "But I still don't know what good old Ralph's got to do with me."

"You haven't heard?"

"About Jackie Gleason? Or the Moon?"

"About your oh-so-famous wife, friend. Don't you executive types have radios or TV sets? My God, it's your business!"

"It's my business to *make* advertising for TV, not to *watch* the stupid stuff," he said.

"Well, make an exception. The President had a press conference a little while ago. Try Channel Seven—their news is going on right now."

"Thanks," he said. "You at the place?"

"I work here, don't I?"

"I'll call you back."

"Could be. Or it might just be that I won't be important enough for you to talk with anymore."

She hung up without waiting for a reply.

There was a small Toshiba color set perched on the wide window bay. He turned it on, switched to Channel Seven.

The anchor man was just finishing a description of the accident in Central Park. Linus had not heard of it yet, and wondered why the death of one man in a city of nine million had drawn such attention. Before he could speculate further, the announcer continued: "President Howard Foster held a scheduled news conference this afternoon, and spoke of the economy and the worsening situation in Asia. Then he made a surprise announcement that had feminist organizations cheering in the streets. Here, on videotape from Washington, the President of the United States."

The picture cut to the Oval Office. Foster, still pale and thin from a bout with the flu, sat behind the old John F. Kennedy desk.

"Normally," he said, "the folks down in Houston make announcements about new NASA projects and personnel. But, since I have a personal interest in this one, I suggested to Director Waldo Wynn that he let me be the spokesman. He replied, 'Sir, if I'm in the Capitol, it's my responsibility to speak for NASA.'" Foster paused for effect. "So I sent him to New York."

The reporters chuckled, except for Mrs. Bernice Knight, who was already sketching out, in her mind, the inevitable three-part question she would ask the President, no matter what he had just said.

"If Mr. Wynn is watching me on TV in New York, may I take this opportunity to thank him for giving me a pleasure which comes but rarely."

He took up a sheet of paper. "NASA has just released the names of nine scientists, all specialists in geothermal energy, who will begin a two-year training program for an extended study of the volcanic activity on our Moon." He had obviously expected a reaction here, waited for it, and when none came, continued: "In these days of energy shortages, it behooves us to search every avenue which might help us relieve the problem. Already, teams of scientists are exploring ways to use our own natural supply of such virtually cost-free power. Now, we know it's a long shot, but perhaps waiting for us on the Moon may be a shortcut, a hint, a way of stepping into the future without all the trial and error between now and then. Thanks to our splendid scientific community, NASA found no shortage of candidates for this important work. Yet only nine could be chosen, and I thank the separation of executive offices and field commands that the almost overwhelming decision was capably made by NASA's director, Dr. Waldo Wynn.

"Our representatives on the Moon two years from now are, in alphabetical order—all save one—Dr. Ralph Allen, presently Director of geothermal studies at the University of New Mexico; Dr. Samuel . . ."

Foster continued reading names until he had listed eight, all of whom were men.

He paused. "The congratulations of our nation, and of course, my own, have been richly earned by these men. As for the final member of the team, I have held her name for last—not because she is any way more qualified, or more special, than the others except in one respect: I know this young woman, or at least *did* when she was but a little girl, and I cannot resist showing a little familial pride."

He put down the sheet of paper. "The ninth member of

the Lunar team is Janet Willoughby McCoy. I met her many years ago when, as the junior Senator from my state, I accompanied her father, Dr. George Willoughby to the Hawaiian Islands and observed the volcanic activity there. Our chief cook, bottle washer, candid camera-person, and at all times, entertainer *par excellence* was a young ten-year-old vixen named Janet Willoughby. Since then, I have watched, from a distance, this amazing young person emerge as a scientist and explorer equaled by none. I feel sure that of the eight men on the Lunar list, not one begrudges Ms. McCoy her assignment alongside themselves. I had no foreknowledge of this honor in store for her, so I hope my loyal opposition on the other side of the aisle will excuse me of any possible conflict of interest."

His voice changed. The wrap-up was coming. And Mrs. Bernice Knight was furious. She had been prepared to berate the Administration for having eliminated women from the Lunar program, and now Foster had drawn her fangs. Frantically, she scribbled another of her multi-layered questions.

Foster concluded: "More than one spinoff of the space program has benefited us here on the planet Earth. Our sophisticated weather satellites alone have saved many thousands of lives by tracking storms which might otherwise have surprised and killed coastal populations worldwide. Now we face a new challenge, and in the forefront of our legions march nine of the best, the most courageous: eight men and a woman. Their first steps, taken today, are the beginning of a journey of half a million miles—leading, perhaps, to the greater prosperity of all Mankind. And that includes Womankind, too, Janet. Good luck to you all."

Then, briskly: "Questions?"

From the corner of his eye, he saw that old shrew still struggling with her pad. Was this the lucky day he might catch her with her bloomers at half-mast?

"Ms. Knight?"

Alas, no. Winging it, she began, "Mr. President, my question has three parts, if you don't mind. First . . ."

He sighed and listened carefully. There was no respite today. Unknown to anyone but the closest members of his staff, he had a tiny earplug beneath his hair, transmitting, by bone conduction, facts and suggested answers from a team of fast-thinking experts in another room. As Mrs. (although to call her so was at any man's peril) Knight rambled on, a brisk voice summarized what she had said and predicted where she was headed. Therefore, before her amplified voice had stopped echoing from the high ceiling, he had begun a response which met her question head-on and with candor.

The remainder of the Press Corps waited patiently. Mrs. Knight, like the playing of the National Anthem at a baseball game, was a tradition which had to be observed before the real business got under way.

In New York City, staring at a Toshiba portable TV set with disbelief, Linus McCoy reached for his telephone with numb fingers.

"Sally," he said, "see if you can track down my wife. Try the local branch of the Energy Department first. Then NASA here in town."

His secretary had already been called by a friend on another floor who had heard the original "live" broadcast of the press conference. She could not restrain herself, caught up in the excitement, from saying, "Congratulations, Mr. McCoy."

"Why?" he snapped. "What did I do?"

David Black had a briefcase just as fat as Mort Weisman's. He resembled Dean Martin, right down to the tousled hair. But his voice was pure Georgia cornpone.

"Hate to be so late," he said. "I had to come down from Columbia, so I stopped off and had a look at that MTA trench. Miss McCoy, I know what you're thinking, and I'm scared stiff that you may be right. I think we got us a volcano brewing right here in Fun City."

Janet smiled. "Dr. Weisman here disagrees."

"Hey," said Weisman. "If this can't be Mort and Dave and Janet, I'm taking my glove and going home."

Janet held out her hand. "Hi, Dave."

David Black took it, observed it carefully as if it might be something good to eat, then gave it a hearty shake.

He dumped the contents of his briefcase on Leslie Robinson's desk and said, "I don't doubt that Mort here has given you proof conclusive that there's no way in the world there could be a sill or pools of magma anywhere beneath this city . . . at least, any closer than a depth of hundreds of miles, which is true of the entire world." He nodded at the charts spread out on the sofa. "Those bore charts bear that out, and I agree with them."

"Before you go any further," said Weisman, "even though I believe Janet's on a false trail, I think enough of her instincts to have already called my family and told them to get the hell upstate until further notice."

"Good thinking," said Dave Black. "I didn't wait to get here. I sprung twenty cents on a pay phone. The Black clan is on its way to Westport, which is perpetually upwind from this helluva town."

Weisman asked Dave, "What did you see in the Park?"

"Two distinct breakouts from a deeper fumarole," said Black. "It could be down a hundred meters, or a thousand, but it's venting its way up, and taking into account the geyser effect this morning, the pressure must ebb and flow."

"If it's pure geyser, we may not be too badly off," Janet said. "After all, Old Faithful's been spritzing for centuries without doing any real damage."

Dave gave her a sickly grin. "Come on, if you believe that, you still wait up for the tooth fairy. Either we've got a real bastard down there, getting ready to do his own thing, or we've got something fairly innocent but as yet unexplained. Frankly, I'd feel better continuing this meeting up in Westport, so you know where I stand."

"Do you have anything to show?"

"Yes," said Black. He smoothed out an aerial photograph, taken, obviously, from several hundred miles up. "This is infrared. Must be twelve, thirteen years old. The warmer areas show up light. Notice the coastal area? And the waters offshore? Dark. No excess heat worth noticing."

"Season?" asked Janet.

"Winter. Now, take a look at this one."

"Shit," said Weisman. "That has to be summer."

Black pointed at dates imprinted in the lower right-hand corner. "Sorry. Early January." His finger traced a light, almost invisible streak which began a few miles off Staten Island and, gradually increasing its seaward angle, curved up into the North Atlantic. "Taken last year. We didn't take too much notice of it. An inversion layer of warmer water . . . maybe the Gulf Stream swinging off course a little. I almost threw it out. But it got filed and forgotten. Then I heard about the steam bath in the Park, and pretty soon I got a call from the Department of Energy, mentioning the name of Janet McCoy who, as we all know, is supposed to be in Iceland studying—of all things—geothermal energy. The old bean put two and two together and got—"

"—water on the brain," finished Mort Weisman. "There could be any number of causes for an increase in ocean temperature over a period of ten, twelve years. You mentioned a couple yourself."

"Shhh," said Janet. She compared the two infrared photographs. "What you're suggesting, Dave, is that there isn't any volcanic activity directly under the landmass. That it's . . ."

He finished: "That it's out thataway somewhere. Maybe along the plate fracture that feeds Iceland. And, like the water that gets in your roof at one corner of the house and runs along the beams until it leaks on the floor somewhere else, we've acquired a flow of magma—maybe it's creeping along a sill that's opened up recently—which is trying to surface right under the city."

She sat down heavily. "That isn't exactly what I wanted to hear."

"Coffee!" said a cheerful voice. Leslie Robinson had returned. "The phones are ringing off the hooks out there, Jan. The President just made his NASA announcement, so I went out for the stuff myself." He looked around at the disarray which had consumed his normally neat office. "What hit this place? A hurricane?"

"No," said Janet McCoy, without humor. "Just a volcano."

20

"You're always welcome, Mrs. Blake," said the Mayor's wife. Arlene had telephoned to see if she might visit to speak with His Honor, Perry Knox. "Perry isn't here, but his office called a few minutes ago, and he's on his way."

"Suppose I come over in a few minutes?"

"Please do. I've been wanting to show you what I've done with the study. We'll have tea."

"With a little brandy," said Arlene Blake.

Annie Knox giggled as she hung up. That Arlene! So much fun, and so full of jokes.

But Arlene Blake had not meant it as a joke. Her hands were trembling as she waited for the doorman to hail a taxi. She had just received a call from Jess Hawley.

Without preamble, he said, "Things aren't good, Arlene. The geology boys over here are jittery, to say the least. There's the bare possibility that we may have witnessed a minor volcanic eruption. The word is that the Department of Energy's called in some volcano experts."

"I'm on my way to see Perry Knox," she said. "Do the museum people think there's any real danger?"

"They frankly don't know. According to all that's holy, there's no way in the world a volcano could turn up around here."

Seriously, she said, "Perhaps what we're dealing with isn't all that's holy. Thank you, Jess. Are you going home?"

"Yes. I'll wait for your call. And maybe I'll do a little packing."

"Maybe we all will," she agreed.

"That's it?" said Leslie Robinson. "Janet's hunch, and some infrared photos which, for all we know, might be part of the Gulf Stream?"

"In addition to a dead man and two unexplained steam leaks out of solid bedrock," said Mort Weisman. "I agree, we're operating in the area of bare possibilities. I'm not convinced. But I'd rather push this thing and look like an idiot than be safe and sensible and, when it turns out I was wrong, have a couple of million deaths on my conscience." He turned toward Black. "Dave?"

"I agree with Mort, Mr. Robinson. Except that I tend to lean more toward the possibility of there actually being a volcano rather than not."

"And I know where you stand," Robinson said to Janet. "Well. This is a fine kettle of fish. What do we do now?"

"Lay our case before the Mayor and the proper authorities," she said. "Recommend immediate evacuation."

"With resultant panic, accidents, inevitable destruction, and looting? What if we're wrong?"

"What if we're right?" she replied.

The buzzer on his desk sounded. He pressed a button. "Yes?"

"The Mayor is on One. And Mr. McCoy is on Two. Also, every newspaper and TV station in town is trying to reach either you or Miss McCoy."

"I'll talk to the Mayor," he said. "Janet, why don't you take your husband's call outside?"

"He can wait," she said.

He shot her a glance.

"Oh, what the hell," she said. "He'll just keep calling."

She left. Robinson clicked the proper button and said, "Mr. Mayor? This is Les Robinson."

Knox's voice boomed strongly enough that the two geologists could hear it clearly.

"I understand that you've got some kind of emergency related to that Central Park accident," the Mayor said.

"Yes, sir. I think it's important enough that we should get together immediately."

There was a pause. "I'm committed to a dinner," said Knox. "Can we do it on the phone?"

"I'd rather not," said Robinson. "Believe me, sir, I wouldn't intrude on your time if I didn't believe this matter was vital to the city. And time is critical."

The Mayor made a "hmmmm"ing sound. "Tell you what," he said. "Come on up, and we'll get at least a few private minutes. That is, if you don't mind the trip."

"We'll be there immediately," said Robinson.

The Mayor laughed. "It's obvious you aren't familiar with the way the streets run around here. Nobody gets to Gracie Mansion *immediately*."

"I was upset at first about being canceled," Linus told Janet. "But then I saw the President on TV. Why didn't you tell me this morning?"

"I couldn't until the official announcement had been made."

"I'm proud as hell of you," he declared. She let the silence grow. "Let's go out as soon as you can get away," he said. "We'll really celebrate."

"I don't think so," she said. "First, it's likely I'm going to be tied up until all hours. Second, I wasn't snooping, but I found some strange talcum in the medicine chest." He didn't answer. Anger flared in her. "Damn it, Linus, I've got my pride. It's bad enough, you playing around outside. But letting your *friend* store her contraceptives in my own bathroom is too damned much!"

He stammered, tried to pretend innocent bewilderment. "Oh, shut up," she told him, cupping the telephone mouthpiece. Too late, probably. The whole office must have heard her outburst.

"All right," he said. "You've got the right to be mad. But let's see each other and talk."

"Not now. I've told you, I'm tied up. Later." She paused. "If there *is* a later."

"And what's that supposed to—" he began, but she had hung up.

"*Who?*" bellowed Jack Ward.

His wife repeated, "Mr. Alexander Cage, on long distance from New York City."

"Tell him to take that there Empire State Building and shove it up his—"

She had her hand over the mouthpiece. "I think you ought to talk with him, baby. He says it's professional, and I hear money in his voice."

Jack slid off the sofa, his bare feet plumping down with a slap against the tile floor.

"That makes it different," he said.

Into the phone, he shouted, "This here's Jack Ward." He had never gotten used to the idea of talking over a wire. Opening a window and yelling was more his style, and with the amount of voice he employed when using a telephone, that style was nearly as effective as Ma Bell's amplifiers.

"Alexander Cage, Jack."

"You don't know me well enough to call me 'Jack,'" Ward said.

"You don't know *me* well enough to call me some of the things you have in the past," said Cage. "So let's leave it as Jack and Alex. I've got a job for you. Good money, and you're boss."

"Who pays the bills?"

"National Petroleum, which is to say, me."

"So long, Mr. Cage."

Jack Ward hung up. His wife gave him a sharp look.

"Don't worry," he soothed. "He'll be right back. That old boy's hurting. You're right, old lady. He's drooling money like a rattler dripping venom. The only trick is, how to grab it without gettin' myself snakebit."

The telephone rang. Instead of making Cage wait, Jack picked up on the first ring. "Howdy, Mr. Alex. Nice to hear from you again so soon."

"You crotchety bastard," said Cage. "Don't you hang up on me again."

Jack did. Promptly.

"Now you've done it," said his wife. "He'll take his business over to the Jeffers crew."

"No he won't," said Jack. "I'll give Cage this: he's a man knows what he wants and won't settle for nothing less."

"I think you're shoving a mite hard."

"That was just to remind him of something he told me."

"What's that, hon?"

"You just listen."

They waited ten minutes this time before the telephone rang again.

Once more, Jack picked it up on the first ring. Before he could say a word, Cage's voice shrilled, "What the hell are you trying to prove?"

"Just that I'm my own man when it comes to dealings between you and me, Mr. Alex."

There was a ragged sigh that trembled wires all the way from New York City.

"You've proved it," said Cage. "Now can we talk business?"

"It's your nickel," said Jack.

"It's my five dollars, the way phone rates are," blustered Cage.

"That bad?" soothed Ward. "Tell you what, if this deal you got for me is as good as you say it is, I'll get me one of them toll-free 800 numbers so's you and me can talk all day for free."

Cage sputtered. "I want you to come to New York," he said finally. "Tonight. There's a midnight plane out of Houston that'll get you here for breakfast. Five thousand consultation fee, and I'll pay expenses."

"Consultation about what?"

"It's in your line of work. That's all I want to say on the phone."

"What if I look at your job and decide I can't do it?"

"You still get the five."

"What if I could do it, but don't want to?"

Cage's voice was grim. "You've got a rotten mouth, Jack, but the word is, deep down, you're a decent person. If you *can* do this job, you'll want to."

"Thanks for the kind words," said Jack Ward. "Maybe I might even reconsider some I've used about you."

"I'll wire your ticket to Houston," said Cage.

Dryly, Jack Ward said, "Don't bother. I'll take it out of the wife's petty cash."

Ben Keller, hovering around the Con Edison and MTA experts like a mother hen, thought he heard something.

"Get back!" he shouted. "Here it comes again!"

In a mad scramble, experts, photographers, policemen and onlookers who had somehow penetrated the police cordon, ran for safety.

One of the plumes of steam danced higher, shimmering in the television lights.

The tiny fissure in the rock made a belching noise, and a gob of water shot less than six feet into the air. It splashed into the reflector of a CBS quartz light, and the bulb exploded.

The sound elicited a gasp from the crowd, which fled back even further.

After a moment of silence, the fissure said, *"Glip,"* and the steam vanished completely.

One ambitious reporter had already transmitted "Mystery

Geyser Erupts Again." By the time he radioed a correction, the first flash had already been broadcast.

The city, its collective ear tuned to the electronic town crier, felt a gentle tug of panic at its heart.

21

"You never come to visit," complained the Mayor. "All you do is badger the poor Commissioner of Parks with your Harry S Truman statue. Don't you know that Irv Sonn is a Republican? Offer him one of Nixon walking Checkers, you'll have your permission in ten days."

Arlene Blake smiled. "It's good to see you, Perry. I've meant to drop by, but . . . well, I'm sorry. And I'm afraid this isn't a social visit, either."

The Mayor glanced at his watch. Annie had found a reason to leave the study which, as she had hinted to Arlene, had been done over since her own residency in the Mayor's mansion. "I've got a damned dinner for a visiting fireman, the Mayor of Seattle. But there's always time for you. More tea?"

"Annie promised me a brandy," she answered. "Better pour one for yourself—I think you're going to need it."

"Don't tell me you're thinking of running against me next election," he said, pouring two small brandies.

She accepted hers, lifted it to toast: "To the old days."

He repeated, "The old days," and they sipped.

"Perry," she said, choosing her words carefully, "I have reason to believe that this city and everyone in it faces immediate serious danger."

"How did you know we were planning to default again?" he joked.

She raised a hand. "Be serious, Perry. You know Professor Jess Hawley?"

He nodded.

"He and I were walking in Central Park this morning. Of course you know about the accident?"

"Yes. We're investigating." He sipped some more brandy. "In fact, some people from the Department of Energy are on their way up to discuss it with me in the next few minutes."

He barely refrained from looking at his watch. Arlene Blake gave a little laugh. "I get the hint, Perry. I'll be brief. Jess has talked with some of his egghead friends at the Museum of Natural History, and they agree that it's barely possible that what happened this morning was the eruption of a minor volcano."

The Mayor frowned. She noticed. "You don't seem surprised, Perry."

"Between you and those people arriving from the Energy Department, I'm suddenly getting bad vibes about tonight's dinner guest. Something tells me the Mayor of Seattle is going to spend the evening discussing needlepoint with my wife."

Annie, who had just come into the study, said, "If it's good enough for Rosey Grier, it's good enough for the Mayor of Seattle. Dear, four people from the Department of Energy just arrived. They told Hawkins that you're expecting them."

"I am," said the Mayor. "Arlene, why don't you stay? I respect your opinion. You can slip me the high sign if those Washington city slickers try to slide one past me."

"You're on," said Arlene Blake.

Ben Keller actually put his ear to the fissure. There was no draft—hot or cold—coming from it.

"Don't hear a damned thing," he said.

Flashbulbs were recording this moment of foolish heroism for the morning editions. TV minicams were already transmitting it, via microwave dish, to their stations where video-tape machines recorded thirty pictures a second along with their accompanying sound.

Not to be upstaged, an MTA executive pointed. "The other one's dying down, too."

Ben Keller got up from his knees and, pointedly ignoring the cameras, strolled toward the small trailer that served as a field office for the contractor. En route, he was set upon by several TV cameramen and their reporters who shoved microphones at him and, in a jumbled overlay of strident voices, began shouting questions.

Keller raised his arms. "Hold on!" he yelled. "One at a time." He pointed at one reporter, the way the President does in his news conferences. "You."

"You're in charge of this excavation, right?" asked the reporter.

"In charge of the work that goes on. Somebody else actually owns the hole. The city, I guess."

"Do you think the danger's over?"

"Looks like it. My guess is we heated up some underground water, that's what come shooting out like Old Faithful. Now that it's cooling off, I think we'll be able to go back to work. The city needs this subway, you know."

"How do you plan to protect your work crew?" asked another reporter.

"I figure we'll wait until morning, then drill out those rocks, relieve any pressure that might still be down there. We'll operate the drill by remote control, so if she blows again, there won't be nobody in the way."

"But what if the water hasn't cooled after all?"

Keller gave a short laugh. "You just saw me put my ear down to that hole, didn't you?" He pointed above the lobe. "You don't see no boiled eggs in there, do you? You can take my word, boys. Whatever it was, it's all fizzled out."

Gracie Mansion sits right on the north end of its own park: Carl Schurz Park, which runs along the East River from 84th to 89th Streets. Surrounded by expensive apartment buildings, the park overlooks the river from a high promontory caused by the four lanes of the FDR Drive tunneling under it.

The Mayor had been right when he told Leslie Robinson that nobody got to Gracie Mansion in a hurry. The one-way streets, with the heavy traffic around three hospitals and Hunter College, once one of the world's largest for women, combined to make driving stop-and-go.

The Mansion itself was constructed in 1799 for an affluent merchant named Archibald Gracie. In 1917 it became the official residence of New York City's Mayor. Unlike the White House, Gracie Mansion is not open to public tours.

Even the Mayor has to be careful where he puts his feet, for most of the period furniture is on loan from antique collectors and museums. When leaving office, Mayor Fiorello LaGuardia had to pony up $950 for a sofa he had systematically destroyed over the years by bouncing up and down on it in the heat of anger or enthusiasm while dictating speeches and correspondence.

"Sorry we're late, Mr. Mayor," said Robinson. "You were right about the traffic."

With the introductions over, the four new arrivals rejected an offer of drinks.

"Before you begin," said Knox, "I thought you might like to hear an interesting theory Mrs. Blake presented to me a few moments ago." He lowered his voice. "She believes that we may have a little volcano right in the middle of Central Park."

Janet McCoy said, "That's what we wanted to talk to you about. We believe that, too—except it might not be so little."

Arlene Blake had been watching her. "Why," she said, "you're Janet McCoy—the girl who's going to the Moon."

Robinson said, "Miss McCoy is also an expert on volcanoes, as are Mr. Weisman and Mr. Black."

The Mayor said, "But we're sitting on a mountain of granite. There's never been any volcanic activity along the East Coast."

"Not within the past 350 million years, at least," said Dave Black. "Our working theory, and that's all it is, concerns an eruption elsewhere—perhaps hundreds of miles out at sea—which is somehow being diverted so that it vents itself to the surface here."

"In the form of two puffs of steam," the Mayor said. "That doesn't seem so catastrophic."

"They killed one man," Janet said. "But, more than that, we're afraid those steam escapes may be just the first quiet warning of something much worse."

"You mean, it might blow a big hole in the Park?"

Janet, grimly, said, "I mean it might cover the whole city, Long Island, and the Jersey shoreline with six feet of ashes. Mr. Mayor, when Krakatoa erupted in 1883, it released as much energy as a two-hundred-megaton hydrogen bomb."

Knox, who had studied his physics, said, "In other words, we could be sitting on two hundred million tons of TNT?"

"Or on nothing more ominous than an underground bubble of hot water," said Robinson.

The Mayor asked hopefully, "Can't we make sure, one way or the other?"

Janet shook her head. "We haven't come that far in predicting eruptions, even with known volcanoes. And this one, if it exists at all, is a maverick. It may not even be there, or if it is, it may be, as Mr. Robinson said, just a bubble of hot water."

"Or," put in Dave Black, "it might be another Krakatoa. Though I tend to doubt that. If we do have a volcanic vent on our hands here, I suspect it's what we call an Icelandic type."

"I'm making everybody a drink," said the Mayor. "When I get scared, I have to do something with my hands. Jesus, how many types *are* there?"

Dave Black looked to Janet, who nodded. "Several," she said.

Looking at each person in turn and pointing at various bottles, the Mayor was getting drinks together without words and with remarkable efficiency. "Used to be a bartender in college," he explained. "Okay, let's say our baby's an Icelandic type. Just what does that mean?"

"Instead of a mountain blowing up," Janet said, "the lava flows from fissures and spreads out, creating plateaus which can cover hundreds—even thousands—of square miles."

"Jesus H. Christ," said the Mayor.

"Such magnitude is unusual," Janet reassured him. "Although the Columbia River Plateau, which covers parts of Washington State, Oregon, and Idaho, was formed by an Icelandic-type eruption. On the other hand, in Iceland itself, where I've just spent some time studying their use of geothermal energy, they've been both fortunate and successful in controlling the extent of lava damage. During the last major eruption, they actually saved a harbor by pumping cold water against the lava flow, slowing it and finally stopping it from reaching the harbor."

"So it *can* be controlled," said Knox.

"Sometimes," said Mort Weisman. "But, while I think we all tend toward an Icelandic type, if we have a volcano at all, it's wise to remember that there are other types, too."

Passing out the drinks, the Mayor said, "Lay it on me. My hands are busy. Of course, you may get a drink in your lap."

"The one most people think of has been classified by a bunch of geologists, mostly French and Italian, as the 'Vulcanian' type. Lava builds up in the crater like a plug in the sink, and when the pressure gets high enough, the whole thing blows sky-high. Vesuvius was of this type, and so was Krakatoa."

"Then there's the Pelean type," said Dave Black. "Named after Mount Pelée, on the island of Martinique in the West Indies. Instead of blowing the plug, which may be too heavy or too compacted, into the crater wall, the Pelean is the one that frankly scares the hell out of me. You can outrun lava, but with a Pelean eruption, the result is the *nuée ardente*."

"Pardon my French," said the Mayor, "but I don't have any."

"It means 'glowing cloud,' and that's what killed around thirty thousand people in 1902. Highly heated gases, filled with tiny particles of ash burning like the filament in a light bulb, spread out from the eruption at incredibe speed. When it passed through St. Pierre, every living thing in the city was killed except for one prisoner in a dungeon and a drunk who was passed out under a pile of his buddies."

"Finally," said Janet, "we have two relatively benign types. The Strombolian, which is usually so weak that its lava and rocks fall back inside the crater. And our own Hawaiian, where the gases don't normally explode, but leak out gradually. Lava may spew over the crater lip, but the Air Force has actually broken the lava flow by bombing. The lava can be diverted by piles of rubble, or earthworks."

"We've obviously got a crisis on our hands. What do you intend to do about it?" Arlene Blake asked.

Perry Knox tossed down his brandy.

"First," he said, "I've got a certain dinner guest to get rid of. Then we're going to get everybody I can trust together and see if we can come up with a solution other than evacuating the city."

"Look at the bright side," said Janet.

"*Show* me a bright side. Anywhere," he shot back.

"Well, if we've *got* to have a volcano, isn't it nice that it's an Icelandic one?"

22

By midnight, Linus McCoy was mean drunk. He walked straight, his voice was not slurred, and he seemed to make clear sense when he spoke.

But he had turned mean. This happened only rarely to him. Usually he reached a happy high and passed out. Tonight, however, being rejected by Janet and Paula within an hour of each other had planted an invisible seed of destruction within him.

The bar at Charley O's was crowded, as it always is between the end of work and the last safe train to Westchester. The booze flowed generously; the cheese and crackers were in heavy supply; the ambient noise level of the room was such that a minor earthquake would not have been heard. But Linus's voice had passed ten on the Richter scale.

"Cunts!" he announced, loudly enough that even those standing by the kitchen door could hear. "All women are cunts."

One of the bartenders, the normally smiling one with the totally bald head, said, "Buddy, watch your mouth."

"Tend to your ice cubes, Moon Head," said Linus.

The bartender made a growling sound in his throat. He moved toward Linus. Then a hand reached out from the crowd and yanked Linus to safety.

"You're snockered," said Rembert Brown. Mr. Brown was

a genuine certified client from National Petroleum. "No matter. I know where we can get you cleaned out."

"Rembert!" said Linus with delight, all the meanness gone as suddenly as a summer thunderstorm. "Whatever possessed you to kick the Texas cow shit off your boots?"

"Follow me," said Rembert Brown, who resembled nobody so much as Chill Wills, the superb Western character actor. Even his voice had the whiny twang of Wills. And his boots were genuine high-heeled dress, with inlaid silver dollars.

"I owe a tab," protested Linus.

"It's taken care of," said Brown. "Let's go, before you barf on the floor."

Too drunk to be insulted, Linus followed, out into a waiting blue Rolls.

"Ah," he said, recognizing the vehicle from other episodes. "The bar car."

"You were supposed to be at the Downbeat," said Rembert Brown. "I wasted a lot of time looking for you down there."

"Stood up by my own wife," complained Linus. "Famous lady. Going to the Moon. President said so himself."

"You got any idea where she is now?" asked Brown.

"Department of Energy. Energizing herself for Lunar mission, I suppose."

"No," said Brown. He told the driver, "Let's hit the Park, drive around."

The driver said, "Park's blocked off, remember?"

"Shit. Okay, just cruise around. Let's take First Avenue. It ought to be fairly empty by now. I've got to get this guy sobered up."

"He messes the floor, you clean it up," said the driver.

"Drive, peasant," said Brown.

Linus McCoy began to sing a dirty song about two virgins and a cannibal.

Rembert Brown took a seltzer bottle and sprayed it on the adman's face.

"The next one goes up your asshole," he promised.

"Alexander Cage?" the Mayor said incredulously. "What the hell does *he* want?"

"An appointment," said his secretary, fatigue pulling at her eyelids.

"Stall him. Maybe Friday."

"He suggests sometime within the next hour," said the secretary, bracing herself for the blast.

"We ought to see him," said Janet McCoy. "He's pretty well clued in on me. Why wait to find out what he's got up his sleeve?"

"Whenever he can make it," said the Mayor to his secretary. "And then you go to bed, you hear me?"

"I can last," she said.

"So can I," he replied. "But put one of the other girls on. I may need you later when things get really tough."

"Thanks," she said. "I'll use the upstairs maid's room, and I'll be on call."

"It's long past my siesta, too," Arlene Blake said.

"Take a break yourself," said the Mayor. "We're hacking out nothing but details." He looked around at the men and women in the room, who had now reached a total of seventeen. "Details about how to do nothing, I might add, except kill a good chunk of our population trying to evacuate them."

William Claflin, head of Civil Defense, said, "That's not fair, P.K. You know our Evac plan is predicated on two hours' attack notice. Give me two days, and we'll clear your town without losing more than four, five hundred people."

"Is that *all?*" Janet said. "I thought we were geared up to protect *everybody* from the Russians if they decided to send over a couple of their H-bombs. How come we'll lose five hundred people during a controlled evacuation with no panic?"

Claflin said, "How can you guarantee no panic? Miss

McCoy, I hate to admit it, but we already have signs of panic in the city at this very moment, thanks to irresponsible press reporting and rumors. Add to that the thousands of invalids, hospital patients, and folks who just won't get the word, and there's potential for casualties in excess of what I predicted. Unless we have enough time!"

Janet met his eyes. "I'm sorry, Mr. Claflin. You're right. I guess I was assuming the best of all possible conditions. I ought to know better than to expect that."

Arlene Blake said, "I can't help wondering—instead of enduring this possible crisis, is there any way we can avert it?"

Leslie Robinson spoke. "Strictly speaking, this matter should never have come through the Department of Energy. But since some of our personnel became involved in it, and since they happen to be highly qualified in this area, we seem to have inherited a good deal of the responsibility. As part of that, we are presently searching for ways to head off any possible volcanic eruption. You all know Miss McCoy's qualifications. I can speak as highly for those of Misters Weisman and Black. We are already in touch with top volcanic research centers around the world. And the principal Arlington government computer, normally devoted to matters of national defense, has been interfaced with all geothermal terminals, and is conducting a Random Access Memory search regarding both the possibility of a volcano beneath the city, and, if it should exist, methods of neutralizing it."

Janet McCoy said, "Even if we find that there's a ninety-five-percent chance of neutralization, do we dare risk all those lives? Remember the Three Mile Island nuke disaster?"

Bill Claflin spread his hands. "That's the big question. If we wait and nothing happens, or find a way to neutralize and succeed, we're home free. If we evacuate, and this whole thing turns out to be a false alarm, we know for certain that we will kill several hundred people, not to mention the millions of dollars of damage we will inflict on the city.

With all insurance canceled automatically the moment we declare an emergency."

The Mayor said, "I took a crash course in volcanoes earlier this evening. What if all we've got out there is a baby, who'll make a little mess that we can clean up and flush?"

Leslie Robinson said, "Who decides to take that chance?"

Bill Claflin said, "Who decides to order evacuation, knowing it'll surely cost lives? That's why Three Mile Island didn't."

The Mayor turned to Janet McCoy. "How much time do we have to make a decision?"

She shrugged. "An hour. A year. There's no way to tell."

"Those are extremes," said Claflin. "We probably don't have a year, but I think we've certainly got far more than an hour. My suggestion is to put all the brainpower we've got on the problem, check in twice a day, have contingency plans ready to go with instantly if things turn sour, and hold off on irreversible decisions unless we're forced into them."

The Mayor looked around the room. "Janet?"

"That's sensible." Mort Weisman and David Black nodded with her.

"Mr. Robinson?"

"I agree."

A new voice spoke: "I don't."

The Mayor looked around. "I beg your pardon?"

A slim man, hair stylishly gray, stepped forward. "I am Alexander Cage, of the National Petroleum Institute. I'm afraid I disagree violently with your rather cautious positions, ladies and gentlemen. Furthermore, I am in a position to offer to do something about it. Will you grant me fifteen minutes?"

Janet McCoy said, "Right to the second, good buddy. Then I have a few pertinent things to say to you."

"You," he said, "must be Janet McCoy."

"The one and only," she replied. "Is it a deal?"

"Consider it an ironclad contract," Cage said.

"Okay," she said. "What have you come up with that we

haven't? And how did you know about this mess in the first place?"

"Let us assume that I am omnipotent," he said, "and I will solve your problem. Fair?"

"What makes you think you know how to handle volcanoes?" asked Dave Black.

"Personally? I don't. But in combination with my associates in the oil industry, I believe we have more experience with matters beneath the Earth's surface than any other group in the world."

Grudgingly, Janet said, "We'll grant you that."

"I've got teams converging on the city from all over the country," said Cage. "Maybe they won't be needed—you may turn down my proposal. Or the problem may simply go away."

"Or," said Mort Weisman, "the problem may simply see to it that *we* go away."

"Exactly," Cage said. "Have you heard of Jack Ward?"

"The Demolition King?" Janet McCoy said. "Who hasn't? Paul Newman even played him in a movie a couple of years ago."

"He'll be here by dawn. What I propose is that while your teams are proceeding down their various avenues, we, of the oil industry, examine the situation and—based on our experience with drilling and underground exploration—see if we can offer any alternative options."

"You won't take any action without our approval?" said the Mayor. It was more of an order than a question.

"None, except to report our findings to you, and make our recommendations . . . if we have any."

Dave Black said, "I don't see what we can lose. We certainly won't be doing anything but studying the situation ourselves. Just so we don't get in each other's way." He looked to Janet for confirmation.

"It's worth a try," she said. During the conversation, the men and women in the room had split up into small groups, each earnestly discussing their areas of responsibility. The conversation level was approaching that of a din.

"Hold it down," said the Mayor. "Let's break up until morning. If you want to hang around, every room on this floor is available for your use. So are the phones. Two of the staff will be on duty to keep you fueled up with coffee. Or you can go back to your own offices. My personal recommendation is to take five or ten minutes to set up specific assignments, and then everybody go home and get three or four hours' sleep. Any of you who live too far out, use the rooms we keep at the Waldorf."

He was referring to the suites which were rented, on a yearly basis, to accommodate unexpected VIPs.

"What about our families?" asked one of the younger men. "I don't mind taking a chance while we try to figure this thing out, but I think my mind'd be a hell of a lot more on my work if I weren't worrying about my wife and baby."

Bill Claflin said, "Hold on. The surest way to start a panic is for the public to find out that those of us in the know are sneaking our families out of danger—"

"I wasn't suggesting 'sneaking'!" flared the younger man. "But unless I'm suddenly living in Moscow, I think I've got the right to send my family *anywhere* I want to *any* time I want to."

Mort Weisman spoke up: "Listen, I don't even believe we've got a volcano out there—but I sent my family out of town this evening. Bud, if you want your wife and family to take a trip, that's your privilege." He glared at the Mayor, expecting an argument. Instead, Perry Knox gave a gentle nod of his head.

"It's a matter of individual conscience," he said. "If any of you wants to evacuate his or her family, feel free to do so. But try to avoid gossip. We'll have enough of that without asking for it. As a matter of fact, although I neglected to say so, any of you yourselves who would rather not accept this unknown risk are free to go. The government of the City of

New York certainly didn't require you to sign an oath to go down with the ship."

Claflin said, "You don't need one. Not from me. And *my* family is staying. The rest of you can do what you want."

With an edge to his voice, Knox said, "Why don't you go on home, Bill? I want to see everyone right here for a working breakfast at eight-thirty."

"With any luck, Mr. Mayor," said Alexander Cage, who had kept himself to the side during the argument, "our oil team will have a report by then, and perhaps a recommendation for you to consider."

"Thank you, Mr. Cage," said the Mayor. "Can you answer one question, for my curiosity only?"

"Certainly."

"I know you're a good citizen and want to do your duty, and that goes for the oil companies, too. But just between us politicians, what's in it for you?"

"It would be nice to be one of the good guys again," said Cage.

Janet asked, "Are you speaking for the oil business, or for yourself personally?"

Cage considered the question. "Half and half," he said.

The Mayor went for the jugular. "Have you asked permission from your various companies?"

Cage laughed. "They have even more layers of committees than you do. It'd take them six months to agree to the fact that there might be an emergency at all. No, this is on my own."

Janet put out her hand. "Welcome to the good guys. We'll fit you for your white hat in the morning."

Knox waved for silence. "We've got six cars outside. They'll drop you wherever you're going. As far as getting back here in the morning, you're on your own."

Quietly, Cage said, "My limo makes seven." To Janet: "I'm going your way."

Amused, she asked, "How do you know?"

"Because I intend to find out which way it is and fabricate a destination of my own in the same neighborhood."

They spoke so low that no one else could hear them.

She said, "Isn't this pretty sudden, Mr. Cage?"

"Yes."

She considered. The scent of pink talcum seemed to flood her senses.

"All right," she said.

Janet had used pink talcum once herself. It was all she could buy at Anchorage when she and Linus spent their honeymoon at Alaska's Valley of Ten Thousand Smokes.

Her visit had been scheduled long before she met him in Mexico, and when she suggested—hesitantly—that she cancel it, Linus was firm in insisting that she honor her commitment.

So, one July morning the newly-wed Janet and Linus McCoy, and their guide, looked down into the most volcanic-damaged valley of North America.

She said, "Even today, almost nobody comes here. And I don't think anyone's lived in the Valley for at least fifty years."

Linus asked, "When did the big blast happen?"

"June sixth, 1912."

Only a few plumes of steam could be seen rising from the valley floor. At one time, there had been thousands. The sound made when Mount Katmai exploded would, if it had occurred in Chicago, have been clearly heard in Boston, and the corrosive acids released into the air would have eaten washerwomen's laundry off their lines in Brooklyn.

In 1918 the mountains and the valley were declared a National Monument by President Woodrow Wilson. Mount Katmai's peak, which had fallen into the earth over half a century ago, was now a cold blue lake. Twice the size of Delaware, and located at the base of the Aleutian Island chain, the Monument was visited by fewer than five hundred people a year.

Linus quipped, "Well, if you want to get away from it all, this looks like the place to do it."

"We've got good weather," Janet said. "The williwaws can be fierce here."

"What's a williwaw?"

"Like a Texas 'Norther.' Winds up to a hundred miles an hour."

He hugged her. "That's something we can do without."

She felt proud, as she continued her running history of the Valley. This was her field; her specialty. And Linus seemed proud of her, too.

The Valley was not as impressive as she'd hoped. A few years after the eruption, Dr. Robert F. Griggs, who led several *National Geographic* expeditions to the site, had written: "The whole valley, as far as the eye could reach, was full of hundreds, no thousands—literally tens of thousands—of smokes curling up from its fissured floor. Some were sending up columns of steam which rose a thousand feet before dissolving."

In some places, the verdant Valley floor, formerly filled with pines and other conifers, was covered with 700 feet of ash and pumice.

Linus said, in awe, "Sounds like it would have taken a hydrogen bomb to do as much damage."

"More like half a dozen of them," Janet said. "I've seen photos taken by the earlier expeditions. Most of the fumaroles have closed up since then. Still, I think it was worth the trip."

"Sure," said Linus. "It gives you something big to remember."

She glanced at him. They had not spoken much of her career but, at least to her, it seemed assumed that she would continue in it.

He mistook her glance and, with a pinch of her thigh, said, "Where are we bedding down tonight?"

"Baked Mountain. We can tie the plane down there in

case a williwaw comes up. I don't think it'd be too much fun to have to walk out of here."

Before the eruption, the Valley had been heavily wooded, populated with caribou, wolverines, wolves, and bears. Now . . . utter desolation.

"It's like standing on the surface of the Moon," said Linus. Janet said, "Thank God there wasn't a city here."

23

"You're not at all like I expected," said Alexander Cage.

Janet McCoy, alone with him in the back of the spacious limousine, now that the other riders had been dropped off, said, "Oh? What vision did you have in mind?"

He chuckled. "The usual stereotype, I suppose. Big, muscular, deep-voiced. Wearing hiking boots."

"Repressed spinster or bull dyke?"

He considered. "Neither. Perhaps an amoral Earth Mother. One who takes pleasure and casts aside the husks afterward, without thought of love or anything else—except that the appetite has been satisfied, and now it is time to get back to work."

"You've been reading some funny tea leaves," she said. "I would have thought you, or at least your staff, would have done better research on me. For instance, they might have turned up a certain husband."

"Ah, but they did," Cage said. "Did Linus never tell you that he is assigned to the National Petroleum account?" When she stiffened, but did not answer, he continued: "No, I suppose not. Well, you can't really blame him, can you? There he is, timid house-husband, his wife overshadowing him in ability, always away tending to her career. Why risk losing what little he has left by waving the red flag of crass commercialism at her? Far better to accept the meager rewards of his toil and spend them in secret."

Janet leaned forward. "Mr. Cage, I didn't like you before

on principle. Now you're making it personal. What the hell are you and your gang up to with Linus?"

"Very little," he confessed. "Naturally, we try to keep a keen eye on our competition. There'll be a large market for oil for some centuries yet, despite all the doom-sayers. Until recently, our strategy has been to minimize production while maximizing profits. I happen to believe in this system, or I would not lend my skills or my name to it. Supply and demand. It doesn't matter if gasoline goes to a dollar and a half or even two dollars a gallon at the pump—so long as the consumer is willing and able to pay the price, however reluctantly. The day he isn't is the day we've gone too far and must pull back. So, in answer to your original question, your husband has served us in the role of listening post. Through him, we received a more personal assessment of your success in the geothermal area than we could get through our more normal sources."

"You son of a bitch," Janet said.

"In fairness to Linus," Cage hurried to say, "he was an unknowing participant. But the young man does tend to overindulge and, while in his cups, has virtually no inhibitions. Besides—and I am sure this will come as a surprise to you, my dear—the poor soul is actually *proud* of you. He denies it, of course, even to himself."

"Let's see if I can get a few things in order," Janet said. "You've been monitoring alternate energy sources. Why? To block them so your own profits will stay up?"

"Not true," said Cage. "Our interest is merely in knowing what effect they will have on the total market, so we can take proper countermeasures to protect our stockholders—who, in case you wonder who really benefits, number at least twenty percent of the nation's adult population."

Janet sighed. "I took a course in writing way back in college. One of the visiting novelists told us, and used everyone from Iago to Hitler to prove it, that no villain ever *knows* he's a villain. I thought that was pretty silly at the time. I don't now. Cage, you really believe what you're doing is right, don't you?"

"Certainly."

"I won't emphasize the low-handed way you used my husband to spy on me. But what about the old people in Maine, literally freezing to death because you've run the price of oil so high that they can't afford to heat their homes properly? What about the near-doubling of the price of almost every commodity people must have to merely survive—either by increasing the cost of the petrochemicals from which they're made, or the energy it takes to produce them? How do you justify the quantity of human misery you and your associates have conspired to create?"

He replied calmly, "More people live better, longer, and happier today than at any time in history. The price they pay is only mere dollars, or rubles, or yen, and much of this is on luxuries. Where is it written that in each man's garage there should crouch three vehicles? Does the Bible promise us color television sets? Where in the Koran are ski weekends at Aspen offered? Act your age, Janet. I say again: if and when our profits really become too high, the market will react, and the public will pay the proper price. Not a penny more."

"And not a penny less," she said. "Pull this hearse over, Mr. Cage. I feel a sudden urge to stroll down the gutter and feel some good clean honest dog litter under my hiking boots."

"Indulge me," he said. "We're almost there."

"There where?"

"There is where a lady friend of mine is entertaining your husband. Or, if my information is correct, more likely trying to sober him up."

She struck his cheek furiously with her fist. It was no "how dare you" lady slap, but a genuine roundhouse that blazed stars before his eyes and made his ears ring.

But his reactions were still fast. He grasped both her wrists and twisted them until she cried out.

"You've had your sucker punch," he slurred, his jaw still numb from the blow. "Now settle down and pay attention. I didn't practically kidnap you from our illustrious Mayor because I'm interested in your fair white body. If what you and your egghead friends suspect is true, we've got a volcano getting ready to give Fun City a royal hotfoot. I have as much faith in government agencies being able to head off such a catastrophe as I do in the ability of jackasses to recite Shakespeare. I sense you share this view. So, like it or not, we're partners in saving this city. Now, can I let you go without getting sandbagged again?"

"You can let me go. We'll have to talk further about this partner thing."

He released her. "You pack a mean left," he said.

"When you've been camped at the twelve-thousand-foot level for two weeks with a couple of macho graduate students, it comes in handy."

"From my own experience, I assume that fair virtue emerged intact."

Janet laughed. In spite of herself, she felt a strange liking for this unashamed robber baron. "Just barely," she admitted.

Alexander Cage laughed, and—to her surprise—she joined with him.

Then, as the limousine purred through the shadowed city streets, she allowed herself to relax, and almost dozed.

Distantly, she heard Alexander Cage tell the driver, "Tie a tin can on this thing, will you, Tim? We're running late."

24

Linus McCoy groaned.

Janet McCoy brushed a cool kiss across his forehead. "I hope you don't die," she said. "I want to watch you suffer."

Eve Newhart told Janet, "He'll live. Or else I'll lose my faith in Maxwell House Special Blend."

Alexander Cage said, "Eve, dear, can you set us up with some more of that miracle brew? I'm afraid the night's hardly begun."

Linus stared at Janet. "What the hell are you doing here?"

"Good question. You answer it first. Somehow you never mentioned your connections with National Petroleum, although you were a fount of information about Armstrong Cork. How come, my dear friend?"

Rembert Brown, coming in from the kitchen, said, "Mrs. McCoy, I assume."

"Meet Rem Brown," mumbled Linus. "My client. No big damned secret. Just knew how much you hated the oil guys, and it didn't seem to be worth all the hassle."

"All right, Cage," Janet said. "You've set up this third-act confrontation. You must have your reasons."

"I do. Rem, thanks for locating the strayed lamb. Why don't you go home and get some shuteye? I'll call you around nine."

"Shit," said Rem Brown. "Us lackeys never get to hear the inside dirt."

"No," said Cage, "but they do get to keep their jobs."

"Duly noted," said Brown. "Good night, Mrs. McCoy. Believe it or not, underneath that sheen of alcoholic perspiration, you've got a pretty good man there. Don't be too rough on him."

Janet almost snapped an angry reply, but didn't. This man was obviously someone who cared about Linus, if only on a business-friendship level. So all she said was, "Good night, Mr. Brown."

Eve had served coffee by now. She let Rembert Brown out and, still standing at the door, gave Cage an inquiring look. He made a slight move of his head, and she nodded.

"I'll be in the study," she said. "There's a good 'Late Show' on tonight."

"Thank you, Eve," he said.

When she left, Eve closed the door.

"What is going on around here?" Linus McCoy demanded.

Alexander Cage said, "Your wife and I are going to try and save the Eastern Corridor from certain destruction—either immediate, through volcanic eruption, or prolonged, through energy starvation. Let us assume that you and your associates are correct: that there's a volcano under Central Park getting ready to explode. I have experts flying in. Maybe we can contain it."

"That's like trying to contain the Pacific Ocean," Janet said. "The forces within an active volcano are too powerful to be measured."

"Yet," Cage said, "the Pacific Ocean, no matter how powerful it is, has yet to erode a single inch of the Grand Canyon. That took the Colorado River to accomplish."

"Meaning?"

"That the Pacific has never been able to send so much as a single wave over the Rockies. It may well be that we can set up our own mountain barrier between the city and whatever it is seething down in those rocks."

"Genesis Rocks are their own barrier. They're the original primal crust of the planet, buried beneath miles of eroded debris. They restrain the molten core of this spinning planet. When they're breached, you can't just plug the hole with a cork."

"No, but perhaps you can divert the flow."

"To where?"

Alexander Cage smiled. "That is simple part number two. I have high hopes that Jack Ward can figure out a way to contain our problem. But if he can't, what would you think of maximizing the situation to our advantage instead of allowing it to cause nothing but profitless destruction?"

Janet stared. "You're in the oil business," she said.

He spread his hands. "I'm in the *energy* business. Look, if push comes to shove and Manhattan—and maybe even some of New Jersey, the Bronx, and Queens—has to be written off, why not take advantage of that unfortunate but unavoidable fact?"

"You're suggesting that we abandon the city and burn its carcass for energy?"

"You state it rather bluntly," he agreed, "but why not? If we have no real choice, isn't it best to take good from the bad?"

Janet said, "Aren't you the one who told the whole country, on *Today*, that my geothermal nonsense would never boil an egg?"

"That was this morning. This is now."

"Listen to the man," said Linus. "He's right."

Savagely happy to have someone to turn her frustration upon, Janet said, "What the hell do you know about it, buster? The only energy you're familiar with comes in 86 proof."

Quietly, he said, "Used to be, it was five-four tall and red-haired."

"Listen," Janet said, whirling on Alexander Cage. "Maybe what you're suggesting is making the best of a bad situation. But why did you have to get Linus involved?"

"Because I wanted to put pressure on you," he said. "I am a man who leaves nothing to chance. I'm well aware of the marital problems you two are having. But I rely on an instinct that tells me that something exists between you, despite your infidelities—on both sides—and your seeming incompatibility. You both still seek to *prove* something to the other. That is an advantage to me, since each of you can provide a service that will advance my own efforts. You, Janet—particularly since your nomination for the space program—can not only help me with the technical applications, but you'll make a super spokesperson to the public. As for Linus, he's invaluable as a link between us and the media."

Janet could barely speak. "Everything has happened only since the middle of the day. How were you able to get yourself so wrapped up in it so fast?"

"How does a centipede walk? Janet, I don't know how I keep all those legs moving in synchronization, but I do, and they always get me where I want to go. What's so wrong with that, by the way? If the city is to be lost to a natural disaster, isn't it sensible to try to salvage something from the wreckage?"

"Yes, it is. But I sense that you'd rather have the salvage part rather than getting a medal for saving the town."

"Your senses play you false," he said. And she believed him.

"All right," she said. "In theory, your energy scenario is practical. After all, that's why I just spent ten months in Iceland."

"Ten months, two weeks, four days," mumbled Linus. She tried to glare at him, but the tousled, little-boy look of his rumpled clothing, wild hair, and sleepy eyes, turned her suddenly weak and compassionate.

"Oh, hush up," she said.

"Take Lardarello, Italy," said Alexander Cage. "The steam bore holes there provide more than a thirtieth of the entire country's electrical power. And at a cost, I might add, of less than one fifth of conventional power plants."

"You've done your homework," Janet said. "You know of The Geysers, obviously."

"Situated in California," he agreed. "Producing absolutely clean, pollution-free energy at a cost well under that of conventional plants—and lots of it, too. My last reports were that The Geysers had broken through six hundred megawatts. That's enough to supply San Francisco and the whole Bay Area. Janet, we could both go on and on. The experimental plant you worked at in Utah. The tremendous success of North Island in New Zealand. And all of these plants are natural. Others can be man-made, or man-assisted, as I suggest here. Let's not overlook being able to tickle potential energy fields by shattering your primal—"

"Genesis," she supplied.

"Whatever. Genesis Rock, with controlled underground nuclear blasts, heating the surrounding rock mass and then using the old stonemason's fireplace principle of circulating cold water down the shaft to drive hot water up—which would power the electric turbines to create useful energy."

Janet finished her coffee, which had gone cold. "Mr. Cage," she said, "I feel like saying 'Gol-leee!' Why aren't you down in Washington, working with the Department of Energy?"

"Because, believe it or not, I honestly believe that I get more good done by indulging in my individual private enterprise—for which you may substitute greed—than I would under some federal bureaucrat's thumb."

Suddenly, surprising them, Linus emitted a magnificent snore.

"Why don't you both stay here?" asked Cage. "You'll never squeeze him into a cab, and my car's gone."

"What about you?"

"Surely you could tell that Eve and I are more than employer/employee. There's a Castro in the den. We'll pull it out for you and Linus. There's little enough left of the night as it is."

"My father taught me never to sleep on important decisions," Janet said. "So here's my position: I disapprove completely of you personally, of your goals, and the way in which you achieve them. But logic tells me that we're on the same side this one time, and we're both going to need all the help we can get. So why don't you let your girlfriend out of there and I'll make up the bed for my erring spouse while you sneak whatever phone calls you're dying to make. We'll talk again before we see the Mayor, and maybe by that time my subconscious will have come up with some sensible way to convince him and my sometimes bright, sometimes flatheaded, boss that we're seriously considering dislocating the lives of ten million people for the greater good of the other two hundred and forty million."

He tipped her chin up with his fingers and, gently, kissed her on the lips.

"Janet McCoy," he said, "you are one hell of a terrific woman."

25

Jack Ward never had any intention of picking up the airline ticket offered by Alexander Cage. Instead, he made two phone calls. By the time he had driven across town to the small municipal airport that had been a bomber training base during World War II, his two passengers were waiting.

Lincoln Fence's father had either a mean sense of humor, or was drunk—or, more likely, both—when he named his first son Lincoln. By the age of five, the boy was Link Fence, and had given up fighting over it. Tall, heavy-set, his custom-made ten-gallon hat cost more than most men's suits. But his well-worn jeans and frayed flannel shirt cost less than most men's hats, so all in all, Link felt that he had evened things out. To look at the 48-year-old Texan, no one would have guessed that he owned a ranch that was measured in square miles, not acres; drove a spotless Rolls Silver Ghost; paid taxes on some three-quarters of a million dollars a year —and avoided taxes on at least twice that—and would follow Jack Ward into an oil-rig fire in a bathing suit . . . stark naked, for that matter . . . if Ward asked. It had been said (and often by his competitors) that Link Fence was the best demolitions man in the world. Modestly, he admitted to the honor.

Ross Weems, his young assistant, might have just left a classroom at the Harvard School of Business. In a day when complex units were discounting for $12.95, his Texas Instruments calculator had been custom assembled and, even using standard components and integrated circuits, had cost more than $3,000. It was as much a part of Weems as his fingers.

With Jack Ward ramrodding the organization, picking up the jobs, handling the clients, and providing personal color for the publicity that brought even more business (it never hurts to have Paul Newman play you in a movie!), and Ross Weems calculating every predictable—sometimes the unpredictable, too—aspect of a job, and finally with Link Fence's incredible ability to place just the right charge in exactly the right place, the Fire Devils, as they called themselves, had saved hundreds of millions of dollars for the big oil boys by capping runaway wells, and rejuicing fields that were apparently running dry, but which actually only needed the magic touch of the Fire Devil formula of steam, explosives, and the knowledge of how and where to apply them. In the process, they earned several millions for themselves. Many had tried to follow in the steps of these three; none had succeeded, and several had died. Even for the Fire Devils, their work was always dangerous; for those misguided adventurers who thought that, having worked a season or two with the Devils, they could go out and start their own business, it was often fatal.

Jack Ward glanced at the Rolex Oyster he wore only when on a job. Normally, he liked a Timex. But when you're holding up a client for the kind of fees the Fire Devils charged, it helped to impress them once in a while. Like Link, with his five-dollar shirts and eight-hundred-dollar hat.

"Two minutes late," he said. "Sorry, boys. Something came over the news just as I was leaving. Tell you about it up there."

Ten minutes later, they were "up there"—the specially built Lear Jet, fully loaded with all the special gear (including explosives of several types that were not covered by permit, and were therefore more than slightly illegal)—climbing through 20,000 feet. Normally, Jack would have been at the controls himself, but tonight he'd hired on Bill Leonard, one of the best jet jockeys the Air Force had ever been foolish enough to let retire. They'd be going into Teterboro, over in Jersey, and he wanted a man he could trust to stay with the plane.

"Alex Cage called me," said Jack. "Had a real hair up his ass. Offered five grand for me to come up for a consultation." He chuckled. "Man ought to know better. Five bills around here is just shit paper. But I figured he must have something pretty big. Now, he don't work outright for any of the companies anymore. So if it was an offshore rig on fire, or any of the usual stuff, we'd of heard from them direct. Me and that damned cat, we'll never learn. I let my curiosity get the best of me, and I figured you boys'd want in, too, if it looked interesting, so what was the point of this consultation crap? I figured we'd go up ready to work, if we feel like it, and if we don't, we'll take Mr. Cage's five G's and throw a barbecue for the kids over at the state boys' farm. Getting to be that time of year, anyhow."

"What the hell are you making a speech for?" asked Link. "I knew what was on your pointed head before you said three words. I got here, didn't I? You don't need to explain nothing."

"The same goes for me," said Ross Weems. "I owe myself a trip to New York anyway." He brushed at the sleeve of his Harris tweed jacket.

Link groaned. "Boy," he said, "it breaks my butt to see you throwing your money away on them old-fashioned clothes. I don't think you own a suit that's been in style since 1943."

Their disparity in clothing created constant friendly bickering between them. It was true that—originally to distract from his youth—Weems sought out the old double-breasted pinstripes, the heavy tweeds, the flared trousers of the rock era, and wore them with élan and utter disregard for the stares of others, particularly workmen on an oil site when he arrived as one of the Fire Devils. He had learned to get in the first punch, and although slim, his reflexes and strength were sufficient enough to guarantee there would probably not be a second one. His only mistake had been made during an Alaskan pipeline spill, when he had had enough ribbing from a husky worker. Just as he swung, Weems realized that the worker was a woman—not uncommon on the Line—and he pulled his punch. Still, he sent her reeling. As he stood, open-handed and stammering apologies, she got up and proceeded to punch the steaming piss out of him. He took the punishment, as he had to. And, later that night in Fairbanks, having driven sixty miles in forty-below weather, she showed up at his hotel room with three fifths of Black Velvet.

"Reason I'm talking," said Jack Ward, "is that news item on TV. I think I may have a notion why Cage wants us up there so bad. There was some kind of accident in Central Park. Some jerk was blasting, and he set off steam eruptions."

"Shit," said Link, "he maybe vaporized a couple of underground pools."

"If I remember my geology," Ward said, "that whole city's planted on solid rock. At least, that's what everybody's thought up to now. But what if they tapped into something else? You'n' me, we've hit our share of rock faults. What if those shitheads have pried one open, clear down to God knows where? Boy, I guarantee you, capping that mother would be one sumbitch of a job."

Weems had already attacked his calculator. As a whim, he'd had each entry button emit a different tone, so one could never be sure if he were actually working or merely playing the melody of "By the Time I Get to Phoenix." "Very unlikely," he said. "The molten core beneath the Eastern seaboard is hundreds of miles down."

"And you'd try to tell me, Mistah Clothesrack, that we ain't never hit no flue, or fissure, or running sill that went that distance? And even more? Add it up, fellers. Cage is running out in front on his own. He as much as said there weren't no way in the world I'd turn down this job. Much as told me I was one of the good guys. You can shit in my hat if Central Park ain't what it is!"

Link Fence let out a whoop.

"You've got it right on, baby!" he bellowed. "We're on our way to cap us a rip-raring volcano!"

Ben Keller had pulled all the strings he could find, called up every IOU, prevailed on every friendship—and his energetic measures had paid off.

Most important was permission from the Fire Department to hook into their hydrants. Ben could have pumped water from the Receiving Reservoir, but that would have taken equipment trucked in from elsewhere at a cost of hours. As it was, the NYFD provided him with a pumper and all the hoses, and hooked it up to the Recreation House of North Meadow within an hour after the Chief had okayed Keller's request.

Conferring with Al Taylor, his demolitions chief, Keller had come up with the idea that the two fissures must be connected underground somewhere. Whatever—and wherever—the heat that had produced their deadly steam, most of it was gone now. Flushing through one fissure to the other would leach off any remaining heat, and even if there had originally been water chambers down there, keeping the water circulating would siphon off any future blast-related rise in temperature. With luck, the Trench could be back on schedule—or at least, working toward it—in a few days.

Ben and his small group of workers had examined the accident site carefully for hours. Their joint opinion was that they'd been the victims of a freak blast effect that couldn't happen again as long as the rocks remained below boiling temperature.

But, with the sprawling breakdown in communications that always accompanies events overseen by conflicting authorities, and even while the Mayor of New York and dozens of high officials agonized over which option to exercise, the only message received by Ben Keller had been to expect an inspection team in the very early morning and to do everything to assist them in their investigation of the accident.

This, Keller was prepared—even anxious—to do. Because he was determined that by the time the team arrived, "shortly after dawn," as his instructions had indicated, he intended to make damned sure that the investigation was of a *former* accident site, now well under control and back in full operation again.

Normally, he never drank on the job. But this was that timeless hour between midnight and the first dull glow of dawn, so he sweetened his coffee with some ginger brandy and passed the bottle around.

Telephones worked overtime that night.

The Gracie Mansion switchboard resembled the Christmas-tree display at Rockefeller Plaza. The Mayors of Jersey City, Hoboken, and the smaller upriver towns had been alerted to stand by for a "possible civil alert, highly confidential and not to be made public at this time." Some, tracked down at their late dinner parties, or in more dubious surroundings, had to bite their tongues to keep from telling the Mayor of New York where he could stuff his "possible civil alerts." Still, the man would probably be the next Governor of New York, so even hostile politeness was better than flying off the handle. As for President Foster, he was accustomed to Sky Is Falling crises, particularly from that locale.

So the President merely instructed Mayor Perry Knox to keep him posted, and not to make panic waves in the media. The Governors of New Jersey and Connecticut were more reasonable, but somewhat miffed that the Mayor apparently did not trust the security of their aides to spell out the real danger rather than warn vaguely that one might materialize.

Perhaps, thought Knox, this is only an effort in futility. These characters aren't going to be ready to act even if I *do* blow the whistle tomorrow, or the next day, or next month. He smiled grimly as he finished his last call and leaned back to doze in his chair, nearly unaware that Ann had covered him with a light blanket. Well, he'd done his best: spread the blame and covered his ass.

Bill Claflin, at Civil Defense Headquarters, got no sleep at all. The worst part of the night was the fact that he had thought through it a dozen times before.

The truths were immutable. You simply cannot take several million people and spill them out into the surrounding communities and countryside, even if the necessary time and transportation were to be had. Where would they sleep? Who would feed them? How would the authorities control the mindless anger of those who had been invaded and the fearful hostility of those who had forcibly been torn from their homes? For starters, who would establish a circle of safety? Must Fort Lee, New Jersey, be evacuated, while neighboring Saddle River stayed put—unaffected except for the sudden influx of thousands of frightened, hungry, resentful refugees?

Planning such scenarios was part of Claflin's job, and he had done his homework carefully and often.

The answer always came back the same:

In case of any emergency which did not provide several days' warning, it was absolutely impossible to evacuate Metropolitan New York City. Period.

Alexander Cage's telephone calls were conducted with more finesse than the Mayor's. For one thing, Cage was talking, however once removed, to his bosses.

The message he gave them was the same: An opportunity had arisen for the Oil Industry to come to the aid of a major

American city—indeed, perhaps to save it from destruction. The costs would go into the millions. The immediate returns might be nil. Or, and here the carrot supplemented the stick of public opinion, it was entirely possible that a new source of revenue had been discovered which would dwarf the latest seven percent "inflation" boost in crude-oil prices. No, details were impossible. Cage must be taken on past performance, must operate independently and swiftly, and be assured of a war chest of sufficient money to get the job done. If things went wrong, if the project subsequently soured, he stood ready to assume responsibility. What did the Seven Sisters have to lose?

Mere money . . . which now flowed with more volume and from more wells than any "black gold" had ever gushed in the past.

Some—indeed, a majority—of the chief executives of the major oil companies were crap rollers who often went on a hunch and a tiny scrap of blue sky. They were well known to Cage, and he called them first. Then, when he reached more timid souls, he had big names already on his "Go" list to reinforce his recommendation.

Eve Newhart had long since fallen asleep when he finished his calls.

Too bad. If there was one thing action like this did for Alexander Cage, it was to make him horny.

Chief Charles Nelson Neal turned into the Boy's Gate at West 100th Street and Central Park West. He had been off shift for hours, but couldn't sleep, and so renewed his love affair with the city where he had been born, grown up—become one of its "finest," and first been called "pig"—by driving around the empty streets. From the corners of his eyes he saw many things that, had he followed all laws and statutes, would have pulled him over. Pushers stalking their victims in Needle Park on Broadway. Blond and "black is beautiful" hookers displaying all the thigh nature had provided, with a tuft of pubic hair slipped under the vinyl shorts as a bonus. Soon it would be too cold for the short shorts, and then Neal and his regular old-timers would have to find some other scenery to admire. A teen-aged Puerto Rican walking too fast with a portable television set. Good, otherwise honest citizens, letting their dogs crap on the sidewalk in violation of the "scoop" law. Uncovered garbage cans, some alive with stray cats and in those bad streets where cats did not venture because of cruel boys, rats squirming amidst the litter. Every storefront barricaded with steel bars like one long street after the next of prison cells. And, from rooftops, the occasional brick or beer bottle aimed at Neal himself; missiles from above hurled by frustrated hands belonging to disenfranchised persons whose only goal seemed to be to "get even."

Neal saw lights in the MTA Trench work-area. That probably meant coffee. He could use some.

Anything to take the now-sour taste of what had once been the sweet wine of city life from his mouth.

Mort Weisman and David Black had gone to Mort's apartment. To Mort's dismay and David's amusement, Mort's wife had left a note that, while cordial, would have frozen ice cream. She did not particularly like being ordered out of town on unexpected visits, and Mort should remember that she still had a key to the apartment and that once the children were safely grandparented, there was every possibility that anybody trying any funny business around home might be interrupted in full swing by the Outraged but Still-Loving Wife.

Mort found some beer. David Black spread papers, including a map of the metropolitan area, out on the kitchen table.

"My wife's like that," he said. "Call her."

"Now? It's after midnight! She'll scream like a wounded banshee."

"But with love," said Black, unpacking his drafting tools. He began to make marks on the map.

Mort Weisman hesitated, then dialed a number. It must have rung only once, because the mechanism had barely stopped clicking when he said, "Hello? Sharon? Yeah, it's me." Pause. "Well, who did you think it was, Robert Redford? Yeah, I'm home." Pause. "Okay, I guess. Look, I'm sorry. I just read your note. I know I didn't . . ." Pause. "Oh. Oh. Oh. Okay, hon. Kiss the kids." He looked around, lowered his voice. "I love you too." He slipped the receiver back into its cradle.

"She said she almost came all the way back to tear up the note. Women! It's right before her monthly, and she gets moody."

"Better moody than dead," said Black. He had completed some rough drawings on the map. "Take a look at this. What do you see?"

"Circles," said Mort. "I see circles."

"You see Icelandic circles. And you see circles of destruction, depending on what kind of malignancy we may have down in the basement."

"Icelandic ain't bad," said Mort, tracing pencil marks that only occasionally lapsed outside the boundaries of Central Park.

"No, but what if we get another Vesuvius? Say good-bye to Long Island, and maybe Metuchen, New Jersey, depending on which way the wind's blowing."

Weisman considered. "I think Janet's right. Everything points to Icelandic, if we've got a volcano at all. The only thing I don't understand, Dave, is how evenly the lava flow is contained within the Park, according to your sketch. What's going to hold it in there?"

Grimly, David Black said, "The buildings that surround the Park, stupid."

26

"Hold on, Cowboy," said Ben Keller. "I heard all about you guys, and I'm pleased to meet you, but this is my construction project, and I make the decisions."

"Man," said Jack Ward, "you're plumb out of your gourd. You already lost one man out here already."

"I've got a schedule to meet," said Keller. "If you're worried, why don't you just head on down to your hotel and leave the work to me and my crew. You ain't got no business here anyway."

The three Texans had driven directly from Teterboro Airport to the construction site. They had not even taken time to check in with Alexander Cage. And, when they introduced themselves to Keller, his reception had been cordial—at first. They were, after all, top professionals together. But that changed when Keller described his plan to flush the fissures with cold water.

Link Fence frowned at that. "Sounds mighty risky," he said. "Maybe those two holes ain't even connected. What if they both go down deep and connect up with another heat source? It could be worse than before."

Matters weren't helped any that Chief Neal was standing nearby, drinking coffee. True, it wasn't Neal's job to enforce lack of permits. Keller wasn't even sure if there *was* a permit to cover what he intended to do. He chose to interpret his plan as coming under the general umbrella of complicated permissions that the construction firm had obtained for the Trench. Still, Neal could make trouble. Under the guise of letting the three Texans inspect the now-cold fissures, he led them away from the construction shed.

"Why don't you wait a couple of hours?" suggested Ward. "I've got some instruments I'd like to drop down those holes. They'll give us a better picture of what's going on."

Keller gave a violent shake of his head. "Rush hour's coming up, and we've got hoses all over the lousy road. You want to come in here and run things, give my boss a call. He's in the office by nine."

"You wouldn't have his home number, I suppose?" asked Ross Weems.

"Not with me. And it ain't listed."

"We're wasting our time here," Weems said bluntly. "The man is lying—he isn't going to pay any attention to what we say. We need bigger guns. Let's go."

Keller had never been spoken to in such a manner. He braced himself for a rush at the dapperly dressed young man.

"Don't try it," said Jack Ward. "This ain't fair-fight time. All three of us will cold-cock you. Just take my advice, mister. Stay the hell away from those fissures with your fire hoses."

Chief Neal, who had been attracted by the altercation, said, "What's going on, Ben?"

"These wise guys are interfering with the job," said Keller. "I ain't got time to argue with them."

"Do you men have business here?" asked the Chief.

Jack Ward recognized the hardness underneath the polite question.

"Not officially," he said, "so I guess we'll be moving on."

"I'll follow you out," said Neal. "You really shouldn't have brought that jeep in here if you aren't part of the construction gang, but at this hour I'll overlook it."

"Thanks," said Ward. "See you around."

Once in the jeep, he jabbed a thumb at the mobile phone and told Weems, "Cage gave me three numbers. Try them all." He handed Weems a slip of paper. "Meanwhile, let's get the holy hell away from this excavation. That crazy bastard might just blow us all to Kingdom Come."

They were driving south on Central Park West, just passing the Museum of Natural History, when Weems located Alexander Cage at Eve Newhart's apartment.

Briefly, Ward explained the situation.

"What if we can stop him from flooding those fissures?" asked Cage. "Can you cap them off?"

"No way to tell. But they didn't look too bad. At least, not up here on the surface. Who knows what may be happening a thousand feet down!"

He heard voices, but could not make them out.

"Hey, Cage," he said, "I'm talking to you."

"Sorry. I was getting some advice. Get on down here." He gave the Chelsea address. "By then, I should know what we're doing."

"That'll be the day!" said Jack Ward.

When Cage hung up, he turned to Janet McCoy. Still half-asleep, she was trembling.

"Get the Mayor," she said. "Nobody knows what will happen if that idiot tickles those fissures with cold water. He's got to be stopped."

Cage, already dialing, said, "You said you've heard of Jack Ward?"

"Who hasn't?"

"If *he's* worried, *I'm* worried."

"We shouldn't have waited," Janet said. "My God, we could be killing people because we wanted to be completely sure before we warned them. It's Three Mile Island all over again!"

"Shhh," he said. "Mayor Knox. This is Alexander Cage, and it's urgent." Pause. "Yes, I know he's asleep. Wake him at once!"

"Sure," said Janet. "Take it out on some poor secretary."

"That poor secretary," said Cage, managing a smile, "sounded like around two hundred pounds of Irish cop."

Janet had not undressed to doze on the Castro beside the snoring Linus, but she now became aware of how disheveled she must appear. "I'm going to get cleaned up," she said. "Yell if you need any questions answered."

Into the phone, Cage said, "Mayor, I'm sorry to disturb you, but your construction foreman is preparing to flush out those fissures with water. No, I don't know why. But Miss McCoy says it could be disastrous. And my own experts, who have just left the scene, confirm that opinion. He must be stopped, and instantly. Yes, yes, Miss McCoy and I will join you as soon as we can. But get someone on the radio and shut off that water!"

While conversing with Cage, the Mayor had been waving at his assistants, and the emergency radio frequency was already available by the time he hung up the phone.

Without preamble he said, in a voice that automatically cut into every precinct station, every firehouse, every squad car and portable walkie talkie carried by any city employee:

"This is Mayor Knox. Top Priority. All units in the proximity of West 97th Street and Central Park West, converge on the MTA construction site." He had already nodded at an aide, who was frantically searching for the telephone number of the construction shack. "Under no circumstances are the workers to be allowed to pour water down into the construction site. Repeat, no water under any conditions."

He clicked off the microphone. "Somebody'll be there in two minutes," he said.

The aide said, "The phone's ringing, sir."

Knox grabbed it. "Hello, this is the Mayor. Of New York, damn it! Where's the construction foreman?" His voice tightened. "Then get him! No, wait. Tell him this is an order! He is not to pour any water down those holes. Do you hear me? He . . ." His voice trailed off, as he listened. Then he shouted, "Well get it shut off! *Shut off right goddamned now!*"

He slammed down the receiver.

To those who had gathered in the room, most not having the faintest idea what he was talking about, he mumbled, "They've already started pumping."

Being arrested saved Jack Springfield's life.

He had just darted across West Drive near the Winterdale Arch when Chief Charles Nelson Neal put the spotlight on him and gave a brief honk of the horn that said "Halt!" more clearly than words.

The old man had been on his way to the Delacorte Theatre, where he hoped to find an open door for the night. But, with his duffel bag, and at this late hour—early, actually, with dawn only an hour or so away—he appeared suspicious.

The questioning was brief. No, he hadn't any address, or identification, either. The stuff in the bag was his, but it was obviously the gear of a vagabond.

"Why don't you come down to the station house with me, old-timer?" the Chief suggested. Actually, it was an act of kindness. The night was chill, and the old man would be more comfortable in a warm cell, unbooked. He could be referred to the proper social-welfare departments in the morning.

"I was just passing through," protested the old man. "I ain't done nothing wrong. I ain't stole nothing, honest to God."

"Get in," said the Chief. He thought of the days when the vagrancy laws allowed officers to pick up any suspect who appeared indigent. Civil-rights activists had taken care of that. Now any bum who wanted to could wipe a greasy rag

across your windshield and stick out a grimy hand for his "pay."

Jack Springfield was terrified of what might await him at a police station. Some mind-reading computer that would instantly display on its screen: WANTED FOR MURDER IN TENNESSEE.

But he was more terrified of the massive .357 Magnum revolver on the policeman's hip.

"Yes, sir," he mumbled. Neal opened the rear door, and the old man tossed his bag inside, then followed it. When the door was slammed, there was no way for it to be opened from the inside. And Neal was protected by bulletproof mesh between the front and rear seats.

"I'm not busting you," he told the old man, to let him off the hook. "But you could get hurt out here. This place is full of scumbags who like to beat up on people, just for the hell of it. You spend the night at the Precinct House, and we'll find you someplace else to go tomorrow. I'm not even going to book you, in case you're worried about acquiring a criminal record." Inwardly, the Chief chuckled. The old fart probably already had a half dozen raps for minor offenses—drunk and disorderly, petty theft, breaking and entering some side-street saloon. Well, so what? He felt sorry for the tattered relic, and that was one of the privileges of being Chief: you could do pretty much what you damned well wanted to.

Jack Springfield was saying, "I sure do thank you kindly for that, Mr. Policeman . . ." when the world suddenly seemed to come to an end.

Part Three

The fiery discharges from volcanoes are believed to come from the fires of hell in the interior of the earth, from the shrieks and groans of the departed spirits suffering the tortures of the damned.

——Dante, *The Divine Comedy*

27

At exactly 5:11 Ben Keller gave the signal for the New York Fire Department pumper to begin spewing water into the two fissures. Hoses ran from the standpipes to the pumper, where the water pressure was increased. As it rushed through the heavy canvas hoses, the water stiffened them and made them throb against the ground.

The first results seemed satisfactory. The water made a gurgling noise, and because of its excessive pressure, much of it spilled out of the fissures and ran down the rock faces.

Ben Keller watched, arms crossed. Al Taylor had assured him that there was no possibility that any future blasts could vaporize underground pools. That had probably been the result of the double charge, a mistake Taylor vowed never to repeat.

The water continued to flow, at more than five hundred gallons a minute. Except for the minor overflow, the fissure seemed able to absorb it all.

"That must be one deep motherfucker," said Ben Keller.

Those were his last words, never to be inscribed on his tombstone.

With an incredible belch, the solid rock heaved and began to reject the liquid diet Keller had been feeding it.

Steam burst from a dozen new fissures.

Keller was dead before he even knew anything was wrong. He had been taking a deep breath, inhaled boiling steam, and his life slipped from his body instantly.

Al Taylor was not so lucky. He heard the underground rumbling, and tried to escape.

The steam caught him from behind and threw him, a tumbling doll, into a sheer rock face. By then his skin had been boiled lobster-red, and although his body twitched and his lungs screamed for some seconds, the man himself was dead from the instant his skull met the unyielding rocks.

The NYFD officer in charge of the pumper shouted, "Shut her down!" just two seconds before the blast wave of consuming steam enveloped him and overturned the vehicle. Its unintelligent motors, relieved of human command, continued to pump water down the greedy fissure.

Unseen by any human eye, the fissure branched three times, each diversion widening, and connecting with a sill that penetrated the bedrock at the incredible depth of 5,942 feet below the Park surface. Pumping magma like an artery filled with healthy blood, the sill emerged from the Atlantic Ocean, and until the assault by Al Taylor's explosives, had been isolated from the surface by the clogged vertical dikes.

It had been through one of those dikes that the Genesis Rock was ejected, hurled like a spitball from far under the earth by the pressure of a petulant steam flow which only wanted to be left alone.

Had the two original fissures been allowed to cool naturally, the chances would have been good that they would have solidified again, and that the present eruption would never have occurred.

But happening it was.

The original casualties were in the MTA Trench. But that was only the beginning.

Its fury unleashed, the sill and its tentacled dikes cracked the solid rock which had clogged them for millennia and, as the Fire God decreed, sought release to the surface.

The most dramatic of these releases was in the center of the huge Receiving Reservoir. As a holding tank for much of the city's potable water, the Reservoir, with its gigantic gatehouses and its cluster of ten-foot pipes had been completed in 1862. It spanned more than a hundred acres and was connected by huge conduits to more than a dozen watersheds and upstate lakes.

One gatehouse was located near East Drive and the Metropolitan Museum of Art. It was safe from the sudden unleashing of raw natural energy.

But the other gatehouse, just behind the Tennis House off the 97th Street Transverse, was Siamese-twinned to a tilted sill, which was fed from one of the dikes that had been unleashed by Ben Keller's assault on the earth's bowels. Just as a champagne cork, driven by mounting internal pressure, will eventually be ejected, a huge chunk of solid rock was forced through the sill and emerged, explosively, into the Reservoir itself.

It was followed by superheated steam. The effect was both instant and devastating.

The eruption blasted up through the city's drinking water, hurling suddenly boiling liquid over a half mile of Park and city.

No lake has a clean, sandy bottom; smoking debris was thrown into the air at the same time.

Since the rim of the Lake was higher than the surrounding park, the mud flow began immediately.

It rushed down the East Drive, spilling through the Memorial Engineer's Gate and cascaded eastward along 90th Street, sweeping trashcans, automobiles, and unfortunate pedestrians before it as it sought the lower level of the East River. But to find that homing place, it had to sweep clean the corners of Fifth Avenue, Madison, Park, Lexington, Third, Second, First, and York.

At York, the deadly mixture of scalding water, sand and mud, boulders, rusted beer cans, and various gases spilled over the pitiful walls of Carl Schurz Park and enveloped Gracie Mansion.

There was no warning. The Mayor was still on the telephone, sending emergency fire units toward the MTA Trench site, when the very walls began to smoke as windows shattered, and the foul effluvia burst within. All on the ground floor died instantly.

Those upstairs perished slowly enough to experience fear. Arlene Blake awoke with the stench of sulfur choking her. For a fleeting moment, she had a sensation of intense terror. Then the coverlet over her burst into flames and she threw herself to the floor where, for an agonizing moment, she flailed for life while her mind, still cool and logical, analyzed what was happening to her. Then its impulses were short-circuited by death. Ann Knox, who had been awakened by the telephone conversation and had started down to the study, was trapped on the stairway and screamed in horror as the viscous mass surged up to envelop her.

The house itself began to burn quickly. Smoke and fire alarms went off, but the firehouses had already been overloaded by the many alarms triggered by the fiery flow toward the river. In any event, nothing could have been done to save either the Mansion or its occupants.

The elapsed time since Ben Keller had said, "That must be one deep motherfucker," and the total destruction of Gracie Mansion, was less than 45 seconds.

To those struck by the mud flow, time had no meaning. One moment all was well; the next, the world had collapsed, and every ear was filled with screams and cries for help.

But to those a few blocks away, the sensation was only that of an odd increase in air pressure and a slight rise in heat. Since the Reservoir's destruction had not been an actual eruption, but rather an expulsion of its contents by the pressure of superheated steam, there was no flash of light, or even much noise to give warning. Inured to the constant clash of 6:00 A.M. garbage cans, the sound of East 90th Street dying was merely a minor irritation—just enough to make people roll over in bed and mumble, "The Sanitation guys are out early. They must be bucking for a raise."

28

Thirty blocks south, where Central Park West becomes Eighth Avenue, Jack Ward and his companions felt the dull, almost soundless movement of air.

"Jesus H. Christ!" said Jack, grabbing for the mobile phone. "That crazy bastard's pulled the plug."

He slammed on the brakes and skidded the jeep around to face north. Against the sky, forever illuminated by the city's lights, he saw a plume of boiling steam twisting up above the trees.

"No fire," commented Link. "Just steam."

"That stuff's a lot closer to us than the Trench," said Weems. "I think he blew a hole in the bottom of the Reservoir."

On the third ring, Eve Newhart answered her phone.

"Put Cage on," said Jack Ward.

"He's just leaving—"

"Stop him! Move, woman!"

In a moment, Cage's voice said, "Who the hell is this?"

"Ward."

"Jack, I'm on my way to the Mayor. We put out an order—"

"Your order came too late," Ward cut in. "Your Mr. Keller has just vaporized a big hole in the Reservoir. You 'n' me better get together fast."

Cage hesitated. "Go to Civil Defense headquarters. You

want to see a guy named Bill Claflin. Tell him Janet McCoy and I are on our way over. I'll call the Mayor."

"On our way," said Jack Ward.

Only after he'd hung up the phone did it occur to him that, as many times as he had visited New York, he didn't have the faintest idea where Civil Defense headquarters was located.

"Gracie Mansion's not answering," said Eve, who had been dialing while Cage and Janet huddled over one of the maps of Central Park she'd gotten from Mort Weisman.

Janet gave her two numbers. "Try to get Mort Weisman or Dave Black at these numbers." Then, to Cage: "All bets are off on the geothermal idea. If there's enough heat so close to the surface as to blow through the Reservoir, this whole city could be a cinder cone within twenty-four hours."

Linus, who had risen, Lazarus-like, from the Castro convertible bed, appeared in the door. "What's going on?" he asked. Amazingly, the short amount of sleep seemed to have cleared his brain of its alcoholic fumes.

"Honey, we're in the middle of trying to find out whether or not we have a volcano in Central Park," Janet said, absently, still studying the map. "Sit down somewhere and—"

"Sit, hell!" Linus turned on the television set. "Got any radios around?"

"There's one in the stereo," said Eve, dialing the telephone. He found it and began scanning the frequencies.

The TV screen, which, soundlessly, had been displaying a 19th rerun of an old *Rockford Files* show, suddenly went red and dark letters appeared: SPECIAL NEWS BULLETIN.

Janet pushed the map away as Linus turned up the sound.

"Here we go," she said softly.

A voice, at first over the lettering, then the face of an obviously-hastily-commandeered announcer appeared, still clipping on his lavalier microphone, said, "An enormous explosion has rocked Central Park, the second of the day. Unconfirmed reports are that the giant Receiving Reservoir has been breached, and that a scalding mudslide swept eastward in the Nineties blocks, with heavy casualties being described."

He paused as a hand reached into the picture and gave him a sheet of paper.

"Oh-oh!" Linus said, recognizing the sudden tension of panic which gripped the announcer.

"Official . . ." began the announcer. His voice broke, and he turned his head away from the camera and coughed. When he began again, his voice was unsteady. "Official fire department sources have informed the press that the mudslide has torn a path of destruction several blocks wide, with East 90th Street as its center. The flow is still in progress, carrying debris and boiling water as high as second-story windows." He choked. "At the foot of 90th, just before plunging into the East River, it is reported that it enveloped Gracie Mansion, the Mayor's residence, and that the building is completely aflame with few survivors." His hand shook as he put the paper down. "Naturally, we'll bring you updated reports as soon as we get them." He looked down at the paper again. "There's nothing here about the Mayor or Mrs. Knox."

Another announcer stepped into the frame. "Things are pretty hectic here just now, folks," he said. "We've got camera teams and reporters on their way to the scene, and we ought to be bringing you some live minicam pictures soon." He gave the first man's shoulder a squeeze. "I don't mind telling you, we're shook up. But we'll tell it to you straight, as soon as we get it."

"My God," said Alexander Cage. "The Mayor's dead."

"We don't know that for sure," Janet said.

Before he could answer, Eve handed her the phone. "I've got Mr. Weisman."

Janet said, "Mort? Is Dave with you?"

"Yes."

"Have you heard?"

"No," said the geologist. "But something tells me what you're going to say isn't good."

"The construction foreman pumped water down the fissures."

"Kee-rist! Anybody hurt?"

"There must have been a labyrinth of dikes and sills down there. The whole shaboom went up. It took out half of the Reservoir and created your classic mudslide."

"East or west?"

"East. All the way to the river, two stories high." She hesitated. "Gracie Mansion's gone. We think the Mayor's dead, along with everybody else who stayed behind."

"Then there's no doubt," said Mort. "We've got an Icelandic situation on our hands."

"We're gathering at Civil Defense headquarters. Can you and Dave get right down there? Number Seven Centre Street, basement. Use the West Side. Everything east from the Park to the river is ten feet deep in pyroclastic flow deposits."

"Got you. We'll bring all our material." Mort paused. "Funny, what you think of. That young guy at the Mansion. I hope he got his family out of town."

"Whether or not," Janet said, "he was probably at the Mansion." Her voice broke. "Get moving, buddy. We've got work to do."

Linus, freshly washed, took the phone from her and placed it back in its cradle. "Fat chance of getting a cab at this hour," he said, speaking from long experience in returning home just at the crack of dawn. "Is there anybody we can wake up to borrow a car?"

Cage said, "I can have mine here in ten minutes. I was just going to call for it when—"

"Too long," said Linus. "See you guys downstairs in two minutes. Hon," he asked Eve, "you got a sharp knife?"

She went into the kitchen without a word and returned with a butcher knife.

"Linus!" said Janet. "What are you doing?"

Grimly, he said, "I'm going to pick the easiest parked car to bust into and hot-wire it. See you as fast as you can make it."

He left, leaving the door open behind him.

Janet had been gathering her notes and maps.

Alexander Cage said, "Life is full of surprises, isn't it?"

"I'm ready," she said. "Let's go."

Eve Newhart said, her voice trembling, "Alex, what should I do?"

"You're safe here," he said. "I hate to leave you alone, but I'll probably have calls coming in and the office isn't open. If they call here, you can refer them to Civil Defense." He brushed a kiss against her cheek. "Also, you'd better call the Waldorf—tell them where we're going."

"Be careful," she said.

"You too." To Janet: "Let's go—before your husband gets busted for car theft."

"If I know Linus," she said, trying to smile, "he's already got us the sharpest car on the block."

Linus was waiting with a ten-year-old Marathon, the civilian version of the Checker taxicab.

With a sheepish grin, he said, "I decided to choose roominess over style."

The moment Janet and Cage had left the quiet of the building, the screaming awakening of the stricken city became noticeable. Sirens wailed in every direction. Lights were going on in apartments as far as they could see. Normal traffic was light, but the heavy roar of fire engines raced up Eighth and Tenth Avenues.

Cage pushed Janet in beside Linus, and climbed into the back seat. "Let's break some speed limits," he said.

"With pleasure," said Linus.

Janet McCoy felt a strange sense of pleasure as her husband reached over and squeezed her knee. Her mind was completely occupied with the disaster around them, but her body reacted as it always had.

As he drove, reaching forty miles an hour by the first corner, Linus blinked the headlights with his left foot and kept the horn blaring *beep-beep . . . beep-beep!*

"Get your ID ready," he told Cage. "I hope a cop picks us up—then we'll get an escort."

But there's never one when you want one. The Marathon arrived at Civil Defense headquarters, at Police Plaza, behind the Municipal Building, without once having been challenged by one of New York's Finest.

29

Slowly, the mud flow from the Central Park Reservoir lessened. It had choked half a dozen crosstown streets all the way to the Franklin D. Roosevelt Drive and had leaked vanguards up and down the intersecting avenues and streets.

Capriciously, it spared some who were directly in its path, dividing into two streams which swept by harmlessly. Others, unaware until the final moment, were struck down by a furious stream of scalding water, mud, and rocks.

Hardest hit were those buildings which faced onto East 90th Street. With their lobbies and elevator shafts blocked, and hundreds either dead or terribly injured on the first two floors, the remainder of the building's tenants were trapped, unable to do anything except climb to higher floors in an attempt to escape the rising heat and steam. Burrowing under the streets at every manhole and crevice, the mudslide had shorted out electrical and telephone cables within the first half minute.

With the street lights gone, the view from the higher windows was that of a darkened canyon which contained a slithering, sometimes glistening mass that moved steadily toward the East River.

Cautiously, with floodlights beamed downward, helicopters approached the path of the mudslide and its source, the Receiving Reservoir. Geysers of steam rose thousands of feet into the air.

One newsman, who normally reported on traffic conditions for the "drive time" radio audience, went on the air.

". . . it's like looking down into a big kettle of boiling water," he said. Janet, who had been scanning the radio dial of the speeding Marathon, found his signal and turned up the volume.

"Something seems to have exploded in the Reservoir," reported the helicopter newsman. "A large portion of the east wall has been torn away, and what looks like mud or lava has choked three or four of the East Side crosstown streets all the way to the river. Power seems to be out in a square covering the entire East Side from 86th to 94th Streets. I can see several fire engines converging on the area, but other than that, traffic has been halted—whether by the blackout or by individual policemen cannot be seen from this height."

"Classic Icelandic pattern," said Janet. "Alex, we've got to get this whole damned city evacuated. The mud's only the beginning. If this eruption follows the usual sequence, molten lava comes next."

Calmly, Cage said, "Why not wait and see what the experts have to say, my dear?"

"Don't 'my dear' me!" she flared. "I *am* one of the experts!"

The newcaster's voice, which had been droning on, became excited. "We're making a pass over the Reservoir itself. The turbulence is something else. There's steam all around us. It's like being caught in a whirlpool. Our floodlights are ineffective . . . they reflect back from the steam and blind us. Wait a minute. Wait a minute. Something's happening. My God! It's awful! I can't describe . . . Let me try . . ."

Silence.

"He must have crashed," said Cage.

"No," Janet said. "I can hear his carrier wave. His radio's still on the air."

From the radio speaker came a rasping cough, a desperate attempt at drawing breath.

The newscaster's voice was barely audible: ". . . some kind of gas. Pilot's unconscious. We're spinning in." He coughed again, and when his voice returned, it was weaker. ". . . can see all the way down to the bottom now. The water's literally boiling away. I can see . . ." He hesitated. "Laura, I love you!"

Tersely, Janet whispered, "What? What do you see?"

"I always have," mumbled the newscaster. "What the hell *is* that down there?" More rasping coughing. "Fire. My God, the bottom of the Reservoir is on fire! Mary, mother of God, forgive me, I never . . ."

The drone of the Radio Frequency carrier wave ceased.

"*Now* he's crashed," Janet McCoy said numbly.

Linus screeched the car into a bus stop.

"Civil Defense," he said. "And it looks like they're open for business."

The building was flooded with light. Cars were parked haphazardly, some in the middle of the street.

Janet had caught Alexander Cage's arm. "Do you realize what that newscaster said? The eruption's broken through the bedrock. That fire he mentioned—it has to be magma . . . molten rock. What you call lava."

"What will it do?"

"Who knows? If the pattern continues, it will flow up through the crater and spread out over the city. Unless it's obstructed—in which case it might explode like Vesuvius."

Grimly, as they got out of the car, Cage said, "Then I guess our first priority, if we can't contain it, is to see that it isn't obstructed."

Linus McCoy said, "Am I included in this clambake, or am I off duty now?"

Janet flared, "Of course you're included. What is it?"

"The hairs on the back of my neck are signaling that TV cameras approach. If you don't want to be interviewed, we'd better get inside."

"No interviews!" snapped Cage.

"Wait a minute—" Janet began.

He cut her off. "Let's see where we are before we scare hell out of the city."

"*Mister* Cage," she said, letting him lead her into the Civil Defense building, "This city is already on the edge of sheer panic. We're not the only ones who heard that broadcast."

"More to the point," said Linus, "assuming the Mayor's dead, and everybody else is running around like a chicken with its head cut off, who's boss now?"

Janet hesitated, looked at Cage.

Her voice was flat. "God help me, I suppose I am."

Chief Charles Nelson Neal slammed on his brakes and leaped out of the police cruiser.

Staring at the turbulent steam boiling up from the middle of Central Park, he whispered, "Holy shit!"

His command radio had errupted with a dozen overlapping calls. He grabbed for the microphone and said, "This is Chief Neal. Clear the frequency. Come in, Centre Street."

"Centre Street. What's happening, Chief?"

"It looks like somebody dropped an atomic bomb in the Reservoir," said Neal.

"Negative," said Centre Street. "There's been another accident at that subway trench. Our report is that they poured water down those steam fissures and instead of cooling them off, there was an even bigger explosion. The Commissioner requests that the area be cordoned off until we find out what's going on."

"Roger," said Neal. "22nd Precinct, did you copy?"

Sergeant Linda Zekauskas's voice blasted through the speaker. "Five by five, Chief. The troops are already moving out. What's your twenty?"

"Two minutes. Suggest you evacuate the precinct house at once. Set up temporary command post at the Metropolitan Museum of Art. You're too damned close to that Reservoir."

"My sentiments exactly," she said. "We're already advancing to the rear. How do we get into the Museum if we can't find the guards?"

"Break in," said Neal.

She tried to laugh. "That'll set off the intrusion alarms."

"And you'll be responding to them. Move your ass, Sergeant!"

"I didn't know you cared," she said. "22nd out."

Neal opened the rear door.

Jack Springfield looked up at him, bewildered. "What's going on, Officer?"

"Some kind of accident," said the Chief. He fumbled in his pocket, came up with a twenty-dollar bill. "Here. Take this and get your tail the hell out of this Park. Head west. Find yourself an all-night movie, or coffee shop, or better still, take a bus to California."

Hesitantly, the old man said, "That's mighty kind of you, Mister Policeman. But I got a little money of my own."

Neal stuffed the bill into Jack Springfield's breast pocket. "Get moving," he said gruffly, "or I'll really have to run you in."

The old man crawled out of the car and gave a thank-you nod of his head.

To Chief Charles Nelson Neal, he said, with honest feeling, "You take good care of yourself, you hear?"

30

It wasn't the War Room, but the conference room wrangled by Alexander Cage had almost as much equipment. There were closed circuit television monitors hooked up via Ma Bell to command posts around the entire five boroughs, a twenty-channel hot line connected with Washington's most important offices, including the White House, and at this hour of the morning, most importantly, gallons of black coffee, despite the latest plantation freeze in Brazil.

Mort Weisman and David Black were pinning their maps and calculations to convenient walls and easels. Somehow, the *News* photographer, Tom Chastain, had managed to insinuate himself into the group, and his motorized Nikon was whizzing away at three frames a second.

Janet McCoy was huddled with Alexander Cage and Leslie Robinson. It was obvious that they were having a heated argument.

Jack Ward and his associates were studying a map of the Park which Mort Weisman had given them.

William Claflin was talking into three telephones at once. It was apparent that he was rapidly approaching the end of his short fuse.

Half the men—for most of those in the room were male—were in uniforms of one kind or another. The rest were in casual civilian clothes. There seemed to be an informal pecking order; certain men stopped talking and listened when other men spoke.

During a lull in the general noise, Claflin's voice was heard yelling into a telephone, "I don't give a damn *who* runs it—Amtrak or New York Central or the goddamned Atchison, Topeka and the Sante Fe. I want every railroad car within three hundred miles rotating in and out of Grand Central and Penn Station as fast as they can turn around. We may have to move five million people, you shithead!"

In their corner, Alexander Cage said, "Wait. Let Jack Ward give us his recommendation."

Leslie Robinson said, "This is something for higher authority to decide, Janet. We take our signals from Washington."

"Really?" she asked. "*Who* in Washington? They're there and I'm here. Are you trying to tell me that if President Foster himself got on that phone and ordered us not to evacuate this city that we should listen to him?"

"Yes, we should," said Robinson. "Jan, maybe you're too close to this thing—"

"I *know* volcanoes," she said. "Do you?" She whirled on Cage. "Do *you?* My God, haven't either of you read history? In every major volcanic catastrophe, there's always been sufficient warning—which was always ignored! And you're perpetuating the stupidity that always gets people killed!"

"Janet," Robinson said gently, "we're only suggesting a little restraint. You've been warned as well as we have. Setting off a panic will result in thousands of casualties."

"What you refuse to understand," she said, "is the panic is already breeding. You don't have a deaf-and-dumb populace out there, waiting to hear your soothing words of wisdom. They heard that poor chopper reporter crash into the Reservoir. They can hear the sirens in the streets. They can see the steam rising from the Park. What they need is to be told *what to do!*"

"They will be," Robinson said. "Believe me."

"You still have time," she accused. "And you're frittering it away with protocol and polite meetings. Well, I won't go that route. Unless one of you comes up with something sensible, I'm going public with what I know, and then you'll by God have your panic, like it or not."

"Give us one hour," said Cage. "It may be possible to contain the eruption. Jack and his boys are working on that right now."

This seemed to calm her. "Ward's the best," she agreed. "Okay, boys. One hour. But let's spend it figuring out how to get as many people out of the danger area as possible."

"Agreed," said Robinson.

A uniformed policeman tapped his shoulder and pointed to one of the telephones.

"Thank you," said Robinson. "Hello? Waldo? Yes, I did. No, things are going as well as you could expect. Hmmm? Oh, all right, I'll put her on."

He handed the telephone to Janet. "It's Waldo Wynn from NASA."

She gave a tight smile. "Not missing any bets, are you?" Then, into the phone: "This is Janet McCoy." She listened for a moment. "My advice, Mr. Wynn, is to bail every living soul out of this city and to hell with the consequences. Yes, I know we'll lose lives that way. But if we don't move them, we could lose a few million more." A pause. "I'm sorry that you have to take that line, but it's your privilege. All right. Talk with the President. You can cancel my NASA appointment—be my guest. No, I can't make any promises. What I do depends on what happens in the next hour." She gave the phone back to Robinson. "He wants to talk to you again."

Not wanting to hear just one side of the conversation, she went over and confronted Jack Ward. They had met briefly a few moments before.

"How are things going, Mr. Ward?"

Ward waved a hand. "Make that Jack, ma'am. Somebody says Mr. Ward, I always look around to see if my daddy's standing behind me."

Janet managed a weak smile and a nod as reaction to the old backwoods shit-kicking.

Ross Weems, his calculator seemingly attached permanently to his left hand, said, "It really depends on whether or not we have what you call an Icelandic lava flow rather than an out-and-out blowup eruption."

"Latest chopper reports indicate that the lava is rising slowly. Everything points toward Icelandic."

"How much of that stuff do you figure is down there?" asked Ward.

"Impossible to estimate. Perhaps enough to cover the whole island of Manhattan six feet deep."

Link Fence spoke for the first time. "Then we got to contain that lava. I was talking with those two other geothermal guys. They seem to think that the buildings surrounding the Park will act as a natural barrier and slow your lava down. But a lot of it'd still leak down the side streets, and from what I've heard about lava, once it starts moving, it doesn't like to stop. I don't think the present protection of the buildings is going to be enough."

Janet had spoken with Mort and David about the possible containment of the lava. Now she nodded. "I agree. They'll help some, but not completely. What can we do?"

Link said slowly, "I've already put in some calls. If the situation calls for it, and I guess we'll know that pretty soon, we may have to distress some property owners."

"Distress them how?"

"By blowing down the corner buildings to block every street through which that lava can escape from the Park."

Janet gasped. Already prepared for destruction by natural forces, it had not occurred to her that it might be achieved by man-made havoc.

Jack Ward said, "We've already got bulldozers standing by to shove up earth walls across the 79th Street Transverse to the south, and across 97th Street in the north. We can put up levees there high enough to contain the lava if we get moving right now. But, ma'am, unless we start blowing those buildings pretty soon, and if that stuff keeps climbing up out of that Reservoir, it's just going to run out over the sides the same way that mudslide did, and burn its way down to both the Hudson and the East rivers."

To Link, Janet said, "You mentioned some calls."

"Yes, ma'am. Me and Mr. Cage have got around fifty of the best nitro boys in the world on the way here. We're stealing explosives from every oil-supply warehouse in the Northeast. If we get the word, we're ready to go."

"I see," she said. "But it seems that there's nobody to give the word."

"That's the way it looks," said Jack Ward.

Janet's jaw tightened. "Okay, buddy. Let's go see what we can do about that."

Ward grinned. "I'm right behind you, little lady." His hand cupped, and he nearly patted her pert behind, but some instinct warned him against the friendly gesture.

Still, Janet had caught the motion from the corner of her eye.

"Go ahead, tiger," she said. "Everybody else around here is giving me a pain in the ass. Why should you be an exception?"

Ward laughed.

"If you don't mind," he said, "I think I'll pass this time."

President Howard Foster slammed down the telephone receiver. Without using the intercom, he shouted, "Where the hell is that lousy Waldo Wynn?"

His personal secretary said, "The East Gate just reported that he's signed in."

To Vice-President Arthur Rand, Foster said, "John F. Kennedy was right: never trust the experts. Do you know what we've got? A goddamned girl telling us to evacuate the entire New York metropolitan area, just hours after I practically canonized her on national TV. An oil lobbyist suggesting we abandon the city and turn it into a source of electric energy."

"That might be the best move," said Rand. "Your own

man—Robinson—agrees that if the city can't be saved, we might as well get some good out of it."

"Good? Out of New York? That place has been nothing but a rotting albatross around the country's neck since they inaugurated George Washington on Wall Street."

"The old town's had its good moments," said Rand.

"Arthur, get the hell off your cheerful kick and start suffering with the rest of us poor bastards. What the hell are we going to do? Every expert I talk to has a different answer."

"You've put the machinery into action," said Rand. "The armed forces are moving in with everything on wheels. They'll get those people out. What makes you think you personally have to be at the wheel of a two-ton truck?"

"I have to admit one thing," said Foster. "It's one hell of a temptation to let New York go. Maybe we should have let Shawcross and his Afro American Army of Liberation have the place. Then he'd be stuck with the problem."

He was referring to the Labor Day weekend of two years before when an ex-Marine major general named Stanley Shawcross had headed up a black army which struck the city, isolated it, and for some 72 hours, held the United States Government at bay.

"Wrong," said Rand. "First, Shawcross is dead, killed by your own zap team of loyal blacks. Secondly, they didn't want Manhattan. They wanted New Jersey as a separate nation. Finally, blacks and whites are now closer than ever before. Who's crazy enough to want to go back to the way things were before the insurrection?"

"Simmer down, Art," said the President. "You know I'm just shooting off my mouth."

"I know," said Rand. "And if it helps you, go right ahead."

There was a discreet buzz. His secretary's voice said, "Mr. Wynn is here."

"Send him in."

The NASA Director wasted no time on polite greetings. "I hear we're in a peck of trouble," he said.

"You're in just as deep as the rest of us," said Foster. "Your protégé, Janet McCoy, is inches away from going on television and informing the population of New York that they've got a volcano under their city and that they'd better get the hell out."

"Isn't that precisely what's happening?" asked Wynn.

"Yes and no. Things may not be as bad as they seem." The President chewed on his pipe stem. "Civil Defense and the military are already on the move. But if people start running too soon, they'll clog all the roads and make our efforts useless."

"Mr. President," said Wynn, "I've heard rebroadcasts of a reporter who crashed into the volcano. It isn't exactly a secret. If you want to prevent panic, you're going to have to get the word out pretty soon. The Governor of Pennsylvania did when it looked like the Three Mile Island nuke plant might melt down."

"Getting it out in the right way at the right time is what counts," said Foster. "And that's where you come in. Get to the McCoy girl. Shut her up."

"Why don't you call her yourself, sir? I'm sure she'd obey your instructions."

"Well, I'm not," said Foster. "She sure as hell didn't listen to me, or her father either, when she was ten. You're the one with the big carrot—the Mars mission. Wave it in front of her. We're having a staff meeting an hour from now. Then I'll go on the air. We can't have her taking the zip out of that."

"Mr. Vice-President," said Waldo Wynn, "do you mind if I speak with the President alone?"

"Arthur can listen to anything I say," said Foster.

"Perhaps. But not to what *I* want to say. Please?"

Rand gave a questioning look. Foster shrugged. Rand left the room.

"Okay, Waldo," said Foster. "What's the big deal?"

"First, and reluctantly, Mr. President, I quit."

"You what? Knock off the horseshit, Waldo."

"No, Howard, *you* knock it off. I've known you since when. Yes, I supported you for President. I thought you were a good man, and I still do. But from the first day you entered this office—actually, even before—you've treated the Presidency like a monarchy. You pulled a grandstand play to keep Congress from canceling Air Force One and damned near pushed us into World War Three. When we lost our crewmen on Apollo 19, you covered it up—in fact, you're still covering it up, just like you're still covering up the Jesus Factor atomic project. And when General Shawcross backed you into a corner, you handled the uprising like MacArthur driving the bonus squatters out of Hooverville. Now one of our major cities is in mortal danger, and you refuse to listen to the one person on the scene who is qualified to help save as much as possible. No, sir, Mr. President. I will not telephone Janet McCoy and instruct her to call off the dogs. If anything, I intend to urge her to unleash them. So—that's it. I suppose you can have me thrown in the can for treason or whatever, but that's where I stand!"

There was a long and very quiet pause in the Oval Office.

When the President spoke, it was in a voice that could barely be heard.

"Well, I'll be a cockeyed son of a bitch."

"I'm sorry, sir," said Wynn. "I didn't intend to be insulting. But I meant every word."

"I know you did, Waldo," said Foster. "And I appreciate it more than I can say. All right. Let's erase the past three minutes. You've just come through that door. What do you recommend that I do?"

"Get in touch with Janet McCoy at once. Listen to her assessment of the situation. Listen to her recommendations. Then give her authority to put them into action."

"You'll help me?"

"To the limit."

"Good."

The President pressed a button. "Martha," he said, "please connect the conference line to Civil Defense headquarters in New York City."

31

Cameras, whose lenses alone had cost nearly $100,000, aimed themselves at the upper East Coast of the United States. Special filters, image enhancers, and zoom mechanisms went into operation.

From Boston to Wilmington, Delaware—from Middletown, New York to the icy depths of the mid-Atlantic—every inch of the spinning Earth was faithfully recorded and transmitted down to the hungry computers of NASA, the Department of Defense, and even the headquarters of one of America's largest oil companies, which had been using rented satellite time to chart the course of the Gulf Stream with infrared photography, to guide its huge tankers into its flow and thereby save precious fuel.

David Black had convinced Janet that the mysterious lines on his earlier photographs should be investigated more thoroughly.

"If there's a sill coming in from the Baltimore Trench, that could explain everything," he said. "It'd be like a big pipe, funneling magma from the plate fault lines. If we could block that sill, or divert it, we'd shut off the flow."

Leslie Robinson, who had just been given new orders by the President, unable to locate Janet McCoy, held scant hope for such a venture. "Do you know how long it takes to arrange for satellite time?" he asked. "I've been trying to get a survey of the western Andes for two years."

Black said, "We're talking about saving a city, Les, not chasing down something for the history books."

Alexander Cage said, "One of my clients has satellite use with infrared capability. I think Exxon's been using it to vector their tankers. Let me get on the horn."

The destruction of Gracie Mansion and the death of the Mayor were confirmed.

"So who's running the city?" asked Mort Weisman.

"Deputy Mayor Hughes," said Bill Claflin, still handling half a dozen telephones. "But we can't find him."

Janet McCoy arrived, after having spent five minutes with Mort Weisman. She said, "I promised everybody an hour. It's almost up. The street out there is jammed with TV cameras. Unless we come to some sort of workable decision damned soon, I'm going to advise the people of this city to evacuate it—on foot, if necessary."

Claflin said, "Young woman, that would be the height of irresponsibility. You'd be directly responsible for the death and injury of hundreds."

"Mr. Claflin," she said, "don't you know I realize that? But what about the millions we'll lose if we sit tight, waiting for something to bail us out, and that thing in the Park blows?"

"How likely is it to 'blow?'" asked the Civil Defense man. "My ears aren't plugged with glue. You speak constantly of an 'Icelandic' effect. Isn't that a slow disgorgement of lava, one that could actually be fled from on foot, if necessary?"

"Yes," she admitted. "Lava isn't like that earlier mudslide. It moves relatively slowly."

Claflin said, "You're right about one thing. Somebody's got to address the public, because by now the whole city has been alerted by the media. My men are working on two fronts. The first is immediate—to rescue as many as possible from the mudslide area. That's already under way with every man and piece of equipment we've been able to muster. The second front is already being prepared. All available means of transportation are being mobilized and are converging on the city. But it'll be some hours before they're ready to operate effectively."

"What are you asking of me?"

"Only that, if you do decide to speak to the press, you try to get across some important points."

"Which points?"

He handed her a Xeroxed sheet of paper. "I've got a list of nine evacuation staging areas here. People should prepare to get to them. But only *prepare*. It'd be madness if they headed there right now. We've got a 10:00 A.M. start date for evacuation." He glanced at a clock on the wall. "That's a little over four hours from now. I'll be making my own announcements with the details. But it's obvious that you'll capture the major attention of the immediate audience, and the overall plan would probably be better coming from you."

Dryly, she said, "Why?"

"Because the President has endorsed you, for one."

"He's what?"

He nodded toward the bank of TV sets against one wall. "They're playing reruns of his speech."

"Excuse me," she said.

She went over and chose a set which displayed a close-up of President Howard Foster. He was in mid-paragraph of an obviously prepared speech.

". . . so that, at this moment, no one is precisely sure how real the danger to New York City really is. But to avoid confusion, especially when many key officials are missing or out of communication, I repeat that this Administration has decided to place on-the-spot command decisions in the hands of Miss Janet McCoy, one of our most respected experts on volcanoes. Other city, state and federal agencies will continue their assigned duties. But if eventual decisions must be made instantly, with no time for consultation with higher authority, including the White House, Miss McCoy will make them. This message will be repeated several times on videotape, while we in Government are actually holding necessary meetings and continuing our response to this dangerous natural disaster."

The screen went dark and a voice said, "One moment, please. Stay tuned for a message from the President of the United States." Then the same broadcast began again.

"My men can be ready to start laying charges by 9:00 A.M.," said Link Fence. "That gives somebody else three, four hours to get those buildings evacuated."

"Think what you're doing, Janet," said Robinson. "You're ordering the destruction of hundreds of millions of dollars in private property. The legal results alone could bankrupt the city."

"Somebody's got to start things moving," she said. "Okay, Link, you get your men moving. Just leave the wires disconnected so that if the lava doesn't come after us, we won't have accidental explosions."

"I'll do my best," Link promised. "With this many guys laying that much stuff, we're bound to have accidents. But we won't pull the Big Plug until we hear from you."

To Bill Claflin, Janet said, "Here's a map of the area which we plan to blast. Obviously those people must be gotten out of there well in advance of your ten o'clock deadline."

"Already working on it," he said. "We're going through each building floor by floor. A lot of sleepy people are mad as hell, but they're the ones who slept through the mudslide and don't know what's happening. On the West Side, we're going to split them between the Coliseum and Columbia University. On the East Side, because the mudslide's got most of the Nineties blocked off, we're using the U.N. grounds and buildings to the south, and the Abraham Lincoln Housing Project to the north. Just as halfway stations. They'll be ferried to departure zones from there."

"Move them fast," she urged. "We're working against an artificial deadline you set up yourself. The volcano may not give us that much time." She turned to Jack Ward. "How about the heavy equipment?"

"Churning away," he said. "Give me three hours, we'll have a pair of levees stretching all the way across the Park high enough to hold in a couple of million cubic feet of lava."

Wearily, Janet reached for one of the ever-present polystyrene cups of coffee.

"Okay," she said. "I guess that leaves me with only one more little chore."

Linus said, "Let me do it, babe."

She squeezed his hand. "Wish you could." She looked around, found one of the Civil Defense assistants. "Tell the press we're making an announcement in the main auditorium in ten minutes."

Leslie Robinson and Alexander Cage drew her off to one side. "Be careful," said Robinson. "The President's been forced to place you in charge because you were the only right person in the right place at the right time. But don't forget that we're only forty minutes from the White House by jet chopper."

"Les," she said wearily, "if Howard Foster showed up and lifted this load from my shoulders, I'd gladly promise him the votes of everybody in Litchfield, Kentucky in the next election. But let's not count on it."

Cage said, "I just received word that Exxon's satellite output is being fed into the Omaha SAC computers. They're scanning for heat with infrared."

"Coordinate that with Dave Black, will you?" she asked. Then she turned in a half-circle, as if looking for something she might have forgotten. Her eye fell on Linus. She said, "We may be here for days. We'll both need clothes and stuff. Can you hot-wire another car and get up to the apartment?"

Bill Claflin said, "He can use a CD car."

"On my way," said Linus.

Janet brushed a kiss against his cheek.

"Hold it," said Tom Chastain of the *News*, and immor-talized the moment on film.

32

The police helicopter, orbiting the Receiving Reservoir, radioed, "The light beneath the water is definitely getting brighter. And we can see that the water level is going down steadily. Either it's boiling away, or it's leaking into the ground."

"Keep your distance," warned the dispatcher at Centre Street.

"No sweat about that," said the police pilot. He had heard the newsman's last words as that unlucky chopper spun in.

"We have a question from Civil Defense," said the dispatcher.

"Go ahead, Civil Defense," said the police pilot.

To his surprise, a woman's voice asked, "Has there been any radical change in the surface of the remaining water? Any debris being thrown up, for instance?"

"No," said the pilot. "Like that other guy said, it's just like looking down into a boiling kettle."

"Thank you," she replied. "Be careful. If it does blow, you don't want to be right over it."

"Many thanks," he said, clicking off his microphone.

Silly broad, he thought. If that thing goes, anything anywhere in the sky over Manhattan is going to get knocked down like a fly hit with a spritz of bug spray.

Chief Charles Nelson Neal found his way blocked by an advancing line of heavy bulldozers, throwing up huge

mounds of earth along the south side of the 79th Street
Transverse. He backed up, found a way up a side entrance
to Belvedere Castle and spun dirt, chasing the lead bulldozer.

Its operator, a big black man wearing a yellow hard-hat,
yelled down, "Better get out of the way, man. Got us a
mountain to build!"

"I'm from the 22nd Precinct," Neal shouted. "What's
going on here?"

"Big earthmoving project," said the operator. "Orders
from Civil Defense. Got to ask you to move, Mistah Law.
Don't want to get your shiny new car dusty."

Anger swept over the Chief. "You're destroying Park
property," he said. "Who's your boss?"

The black man smiled. "According to the orders we got
an hour ago, he's the President of the United States."

Unaware that the mudslide had claimed the life of Arlene
Blake, Professor Jess Hawley dialed her number every five
minutes.

Finally, frustrated and angered that he could find no useful action to perform, he got dressed and, brandishing a
briar walking stick, set off into the night.

Paula Armstrong, awakened in her East 67th Street apartment by the wail of sirens, peered out her windows. The
streets were oddly empty, even for this predawn moment.

She switched on her television set and almost choked.

"Holy shit!" she said. "That's Linus's old lady!"

Joan Weldon, sitting in her window seat, had a crow's-eye
view of the confusion below. Obviously something serious
was occurring to the north of the Dakota. She could see the
whirling plumes of white steam and the parade of shrieking
police cars and fire engines continuing up Central Park West.

The night was slowly turning to day outside. Soon it

would be light enough to see without the glare of street lights and flashing blue lights.

She touched the remote-control unit attached to the windowsill, and the Sony 19-inch set lit up on Channel Two.

President Howard Foster's face was just fading to black.

An announcer, standing outside a floodlit building, appeared.

"In just a moment," he said, "we're going inside for a briefing by Miss Janet McCoy about the Central Park disaster. As you may know, Miss McCoy has been named by NASA as one of the scientists to study volcanic conditions on the Moon. In an unprecedented move, President Foster, saying that she was the best-qualified person available on the scene, has placed her in charge of the response to the possible volcanic eruption in Central Park."

"Ye gods," said Joan Weldon. "Eruption?"

"I can't see a monitor," said the announcer, "but I'm told by CBS control that they're running some footage of the sudden mudslide that took hundreds of lives, including that of Mayor Perry Knox. This is Carl Benson, standing by outside Civil Defense headquarters in Manhattan."

Garishly lit by aerial floodlights, Joan watched the slimy flow of mud, moving faster than a man could run, cascading down East 90th Street.

A voice-over announcer said, "This footage was taken some minutes after the original slide swept away lives, cars, and even Gracie Mansion, with the Mayor, his wife Ann, and numerous aides and guests. Three streets—East 89th, 90th, and 91st have been completely blocked by the slide, all the way from Fifth Avenue to the East River. In addition, side excursions of the mud—a mass consisting of scalding water, bits of silt, rock, and assorted debris, have penetrated north-south streets, in some cases as far as several blocks from the original path. Residents of apartment buildings on the three principal crosstown streets are trapped. Some are making their way over roofs to buildings outside the limits of the slides."

The footage picked up, with its zoom lenses, a group of such refugees, carefully working their way downtown over TV-antennaed rooftops.

"Fire Department and Civil Defense units are on the scene," the announcer went on. "There is no way of predicting the total loss of life at this time, but official estimates place it in the hundreds, and perhaps thousands."

The picture flickered, and was replaced by Carl Benson, outside Civil Defense headquarters.

"I understand that the press conference within is about to begin," he said. "As I said, the spokesperson for the Disaster Team is a young woman, named only yesterday as our first woman geologist to be sent to the Moon, Miss Janet McCoy."

He waited, and eventually the station cut to the cameras inside the building.

The viewers and listeners on radio numbered in the tens of millions by now. Phones had been ringing, doors knocked upon, neighbors awakened. Their reactions were varied, but principally subdued. Unlike the Orson Welles "Martian Invasion," few ran outside peering into the heavens for signs of impending destruction. Accustomed to the calm presentation of violence—war and accident and natural disaster—on television, the American viewers seemed able to retain their cool under almost any threat.

A wide shot of the auditorium stage appeared first. Several people were milling around the podium. Two men were setting up a large map of Manhattan Island.

"We're on the air," called one of the cameramen. He had just been informed of that fact by the talk-back earplug.

A husky man stepped forward and held up both arms. "Can we have quiet, please? Hold it down."

Anxious for their stories, the reporters and media people complied.

"I'm Bill Claflin, in charge of Civil Defense," said the man. "In a few minutes, I'm going to talk directly to the people in the affected areas. But first, and I might add, by order of the President of the United States, I want to introduce one of the world's foremost experts on volcanic activity. Miss Janet McCoy."

The cameras came in close on Janet as she approached the cluster of microphones.

"Thank you," she said. "Time may be short, so I won't try to fill you in on details you may already know, or which wouldn't help you anyway. Then I'll take questions from the press, before stepping aside for Mr. Claflin, who will inform you of the Civil Defense plans already underway."

She looked down at the brief notes she had made. "Early yesterday, steam began venting from fissures in Central Park, just north of the Reservoir. At that time, we began investigating the possibility that there might be volcanic activity beneath the Park, although all geologic information until now indicated that this was highly unlikely. However, this piece of stone, which is referred to in the scientific community as a Genesis Rock, was found in Central Park, indicating that there might be possible unanticipated changes occurring beneath the layers of bedrock under the city."

The zoom lenses filled the screen with the small stone.

"Then, just hours ago, a volcanic eruption occurred under the Reservoir itself, apparently caused by attempts to cool down the steam fissures. A giant mudslide escaped and caused considerable damage and many casualties in the East 90's. I'm sorry to report that Mayor Perry Knox was one of those who died."

She looked at the sheet of paper Claflin had given her. "I have been informed that evacuation procedures and staging locations have already been established. Mr. Claflin will describe them to you. Meanwhile, I urge that every person be prepared to leave the city on literally ten minutes' notice. Stay tuned to your TV or radio station—both, if you can. Don't panic. Even if the worst occurs, we will not have a Mount Vesuvius, where everything blows sky-high. More likely, if the eruption does occur, it will be in the form of relatively slow-moving lava spilling out of the Reservoir and flowing over the Park. If this happens, we hope to contain

he lava by creating artificial levees and blocking the streets
n the danger area so that most of the damage will be con-
ained within the Park itself."

She cleared her throat. She felt thirsty, and hot, and very
ired. "Are there any questions?"

NBC asked, "How do you plan to contain the lava within
he Park?"

"Teams of heavy-equipment operators are presently con-
tructing levees that stretch completely across the Park,
rom Central Park West to Fifth Avenue. The lower boundary is roughly 79th Street, although, if there's time, an exten-
sion will curve uptown around the Metropolitan Museum of
Art to attempt to save it. I understand crews are already
removing the most valuable paintings." She paused. "Up-
own, the boundary is just north of the 97th Street Transverse."

CBS asked, "But what about Fifth Avenue and Central
Park West? You surely can't bulldoze levees there."

"No, we can't. We rely on the bulk of the buildings themselves to absorb the impact of the lava. As for the side
streets, demolition teams are already planting charges. If it
appears likely that the lava flow will escape from the Park,
we shall have to sacrifice certain buildings to create a barrier."

New York magazine said, "Those certain buildings would
nclude the Guggenheim and perhaps the Museum of Natural History, not to mention the Metropolitan, wouldn't
hey?"

Janet nodded. "I'm afraid they would have to go—to keep
he flow from covering the entire uptown part of Manhat-
an."

Local station WOR said, "Exactly who decides which
buildings will be destroyed and which will be spared?"

Janet said, "Geography. In order to block the streets,
corner buildings will have to come down."

ABC said, "And what if all this is only a false alarm? Half
he city is already in panic."

Janet looked at the famous woman reporter and, her voice trembling, said, "If I'd had my way, this would have been announced twelve hours ago, and by now half of the city's people would be safe. Have you forgotten the Three Mile Island nuclear accident in Pennsylvania? 600,000 people were lied to until, if it had become necessary, there wouldn't have been time for them to get out. As it is, I'm praying this is a false alarm. If that happens, I'll fall on my knees every night and thank God." The ABC reporter started to answer, but was shouted down by CBS.

"We're wasting valuable time right now," said the gray-haired reporter. "I agree with you, Miss McCoy. Let's get the hard information out to the people as fast as possible and the hell with second-guessing who should have done what, when."

Gratefully, Janet said, "Thank you, Walter. Let's get Mr. Claflin up here. He's got the detailed plan."

He took up his notes. "Now, first, and I know we keep saying it, but there is no cause for panic. We're going to take the city in sections, starting closest to the possible danger and working outward. Please, you viewers and listeners, get pencil and paper, and take notes. Send your children or other persons in the room to every apartment in your building—make sure that they are listening. If you know of invalids or other shut-ins and do not feel you can assist them yourself, telephone 911 immediately so the authorities can send help."

He paused emphatically. "Most important, do not leave your homes or present location! Do not try to get your car and drive out of the city. If our streets and exits become blocked, the fear of a few thousand can cause millions to be trapped. Orders have been issued to the police department that any unofficial vehicles seen moving will be stopped—by force, if necessary."

Claflin stepped up to the map of central Manhattan. "The chief danger seems to lie here, beneath the hundred-acre Receiving Reservoir. Therefore, our first priority is the evacuation of those living along Fifth and Madison Avenues from 79th to 97th Streets on the East Side, and from those same streets bordering Central Park West and Columbus Avenue on the West Side. This evacuation is taking place as I speak."

He drew a circle around the area mentioned. "For those of you outside the immediate danger zone, prepare one small suitcase with your most important valuables, drugs and medicines if you are under a doctor's care, any irreplaceable documents, and the like. One small suitcase per family unit is all that will be allowed should a general evacuation take place."

He gave a hand signal.

Outside, hundreds of air-raid sirens sounded their mournful wail.

"Should power fail, and evacuation must be ordered, you will hear those sirens. They will go off in a sequence of five, a pause of thirty seconds, and then a repeat sequence of five, and so on. That will be your signal to report immediately to staging areas which I will now announce."

He looked down at the cameras. "I hope you media people will run constant repeat tapes of these instructions."

"You got it," said CBS.

"Good. Now, for those living in the area from East 79th Street to East 59th, your staging area is . . ."

As Claflin droned on, Leslie Robinson gave Janet a brief hug. "You did good," he said. "My God, isn't it like the blitz in London all over again?"

Her eyes blinking, she said, "The Londoners didn't panic, did they, Les?"

"No," he said. "Hitler kicked them in the gut every night, and every morning they crawled up from the Underground and started piling bricks back on top of bricks."

"So will the New Yorkers," she said, and then, with a puzzled expression, fainted into his arms.

33

Waldo Wynn was drinking some of President Howard Foster's best scotch when the private buzzer sounded and Foster's secretary said, "The Governor of New York is on the line, sir."

"Terrific," said Foster. "Plug him in."

He punched the amplifier button. "You might as well listen in, Waldo. You may find yourself running for public office sometime."

"Mr. President?" asked a deep male voice.

"I'm here, Steve," said Foster.

"I've just been informed of the situation in New York City," said Governor Stephen Bennis. "It appears that you've moved in and Federalized my city."

"Sorry about that," said Foster. "But you were unavailable."

"Well, I'm available now. Is it my fault I was on retreat and nobody bothered to alert me to the situation?"

"Crap!" said the President. "You were retreating somewhere upstate with that hunting-and-poker club—miles from a phone, as usual. Meanwhile, things have been happening fast and somebody had to take the reins—particularly since, as you may not know, Mayor Knox was killed."

Bennis made a choking sound. "No, I didn't know that. Okay, Howard. What can I do?"

"Nothing. We've already got all our options in operation."

"But I can't just lay back and let the cavalry ride to the rescue. I'd never be elected again."

"No, you wouldn't. And that might be a good thing for New York State."

"Mr. President—"

"I'm only joking, Steve. Look, get yourself a sharp stick and stir the hell out of your bureaucrats. If we have to evacuate the metropolitan area, we don't need a bunch of up-state farmers chasing the refugees off with pitchforks. Send out your state troopers, start getting every basketball court, every skating rink, every conceivable shelter that can hold a family—or even a single person—ready to accept them if worst comes to worst. Can I count on you for that?"

"All the way," New York's Governor said gratefully.

"Fine. I've got calls in to New Jersey and Connecticut already. I'll refer them to you now, and you can coordinate everything. That way, it'll look like you've been busier than a beaver covering trout shit."

"I'll be in my office within twenty minutes," said Bennis.

"There!" cried Dave Black, pointing at a facsimile satellite photo which had been transmitted from the Exxon headquarters. "See that hot spot! That's where the sill burst through."

Comparing the photo against a larger-scale map, Mort Weisman said, "Could be. See? You can see the heat flow going up to Iceland and all the way down to the Caribbean." He looked at Black. "You know, Dave, there's only one way—one chance in hell—of shutting that flow off."

Black nodded. "A massive disruption of the ocean floor. At least a ten-megaton hydrogen bomb, and it had damned well better be placed in exactly the right place—or we'll be worse off than we are now."

"Are you all right now?" Robinson asked.

"I've been all right all along," protested Janet.

"Sure, that's why you keeled over. Luckily you were out

of sight of those reporters. Sit down and take it easy. I recommend a good slug of brandy. You stay put. I'll go find some."

Still feeling dizzy, Janet nodded. Robinson left.

Mort Weisman and David Black found her and, without preamble, jabbed excited fingers at the satellite photo. Janet listened carefully.

"What it comes down to," she said, "is that we're pretty sure our magma flow is coming from an offshore source. If we block the sill, what's already under the city will cool down and solidify."

"Right," said Black. "But if we miss the target, we might enlarge the flow pathway and dump twice as heavy a load on us."

"Won't the shock wave force whatever's already in the sill up into the Park?"

Mort Weisman nodded. "Janet, no matter what we do, the Park has had it. The question is: can we shut off the flow so that only a limited amount of magma escapes, and maybe, that way, keep the damage contained. Otherwise, I'm scared shitless that the whole city might get a dose of lava if our levees don't hold."

"Let's go," she said, getting up. The sudden motion made her light-headed.

"Where to?" asked Black.

"We're going to make a conference call to the President."

Linus McCoy was glad the electricity was still on. It saved him from having to climb the nine flights of stairs.

Inside the apartment, he went to the closet and flipped through the clothing hanging there. Janet had only a few dresses anyway, and he finally chose a blue one that he had always liked on her.

He decided he'd need a suitcase, and went to his own closet for it. When he opened the door, the first thing he saw on the shelf above the clothes rack was the unopened bottle of Chivas.

Linus hesitated, then reached for the bottle.

What the hell. One quick drink won't hurt.

The old man passed the 107th Regiment Monument on his way to the Tavern on the Green. Some mornings—not too often, because he didn't want to wear out his welcome—Jack Springfield said good morning to a genial Italian chef who could always be counted on to come up with some delicious leftovers from the previous evening's dinners.

A voice startled him.

"Morning," said a tall, elderly man who carried a briar walking stick.

"Same to you," said Jack. He nodded over his shoulder toward the clouds of steam rising from the Reservoir. "I wouldn't go up that way if I were you."

The other man chuckled. "I was about to suggest the same to you. I've seen you often in the Park. You live here, don't you?"

Jack felt a trust for the stranger.

"For a spell," he admitted. "But it looks to me like it's time to move on. Too bad. I sort of got used to the place."

The man nodded. "So did I." He put out his hand. "Jess Hawley's the name."

Jack shook it. "Springfield," he said. "Jack Springfield, from down Tennessee way."

As he spoke, he realized that he had not given his name to a living person for more than six years.

"Let me buy you a cup of coffee," said Hawley.

"I got a better idea. One of the chefs at Tavern on the

Green is kind of a buddy of mine. He'll spring for both of us."

"Fine," said Hawley. "Lead the way." It would be nice to have someone to talk with on this oddly frightening morning.

Jack stumbled. Hawley caught his arm and kept him from falling.

"Slipped on a rock," said Jack. He bent over and picked it up, made ready to throw it off into the bushes. But it was a funny-looking little cuss. Kind of milky-white.

Impulsively, he put it in his pocket. He hadn't had a good pocket piece since he had to spend that 1879 Morgan silver dollar he'd carried for years.

34

The Joint Chiefs of Staff had hastily assembled key staff members in the War Room beneath the White House. It had been chosen because direct television linkage with New York's Civil Defense was already operating.

President Foster gave a brief résumé of the information he had received from Janet McCoy moments before. She and Leslie Robinson were waiting, seen on the War Room's monitor.

"Questions?" asked the President.

Air Force asked, "Miss McCoy, how much time do we have?"

Janet said, "Every minute counts. No more than three or four hours. General evacuation of the city is set to start at 10:00 A.M."

Army said, "We're already helping in that part. But frankly, we don't have any weapons system capable of doing the job."

Navy said, "We do. The nuclear sub *Rickover* happens to be within a few hours of the position you've given us."

The President asked, "*Rickover* carries Trident missiles, doesn't it?"

Navy said, "Yes, sir. But we also have antisub underwater drones that can be guided to a five-foot target from a hundred miles away."

"Our estimate is that an explosion in the ten-megaton

range will be needed to excise the necessary amount of sea bottom," said Janet.

"No problem," said Navy. One of his aides leaned over and whispered into his ear. "Wait a minute. I've just been told that our antisub drones are of a much lower yield. Maybe we could shoot a flight of them—four or five, and—"

Foster shook his head. He turned to Air Force. "You've got the hardware. Can you deliver it?"

Air Force said, "We can deliver to the surface of the water, Mr. President. But even using radio detonation, I don't think we could guarantee that the device would settle to the bottom in precisely the right spot. I understand the depth we're facing is almost twelve hundred feet."

The President frowned. To Navy, he said, "Have your sub steam toward the target location at flank speed."

Navy made a motion, and one of his aides leaped up and hurried out to the communications room.

"With your permission, sir," Navy said, "I'd like to present the problem to *Rickover*'s skipper, Captain Scott. He might come up with something."

"Do it," said Foster. Another Navy aide hurried from the room.

To Air Force, he said, "Could we lower a device on a cable from a helicopter?"

Before Air Force could answer, Navy said, "Mr. President, I believe the currents in that area are so strong that any chance at the kind of accuracy Miss McCoy says we need can only be provided by a powered, controlled device. A bomb on a cable could be swept hundreds of yards off course."

"We'll give it a try if you want, sir," said Air Force.

The President gave a nod of thanks, but said, "A try isn't going to be good enough. Whatever we do has to work right the first time."

The first Navy aide returned. His hands trembled as he handed Navy a sheet of paper.

Navy read it and his face went visibly white. "My God!" he said.

"What do you have?" asked Foster.

Almost inaudibly, Navy said, "Captain Scott has come up with a solution. But it's . . ." His voice trailed off. He handed the sheet of paper to the President.

Foster read it. His lips tightened. "Can *Rickover* be on target in time?"

"Yes, sir. ETA, two hours and eleven minutes."

"Then, unless you have an alternative plan, we'll accept Captain Scott's suggestion."

"Sir!" Navy protested.

The President said, "You needn't say it. I know exactly how you feel. But we're talking about saving a city containing some nine million Americans."

The aide spoke for the first time. "Sir," he said, "Captain Scott told me that there are several other vessels in the target area. They'll have to be told to clear out. Maybe *Rickover* could surface and—"

He stopped. Navy had gripped his wrist so hard that the young officer winced.

"That part is understood," said the President.

Navy said, in a choked voice, "All right, Mr. President. I will obey your order. There seems to be no alternative. Will you excuse me? Time is short."

"You're excused," said Foster. "Try to remember, you are acting under direct orders. This was not your decision, and you are in no way responsible for it."

"I'm responsible for anything that happens to the lowest rank on the smallest vessel in the fleet," said Navy. He and his staff left.

Foster rubbed his eyes wearily. "That poor son of a bitch," he said. "I don't envy him."

Janet McCoy said, "Mr. President, I'm confused. Are we going to be able to destroy the underwater sill or not?"

Foster said, "The answer is yes, Janet. An atomic device

will be placed precisely on target and detonated before
10:00 A.M. this morning."

"Thank you," she said. "My associates and I are sure
enough of the results of that action that we can now recommend only a minimal evacuation of the city. That will save
quite a few lives."

To himself, unaware that the sensitive microphones
picked up every word, President Howard Foster said softly,
"Yes . . . but not all of them."

Alexander Cage had held private talks with the team from
Texas. To Jack Ward, who was coordinating the logistics of
the demolitions men, he said, "Remember, Jack, we want to
save the rest of the city, certainly. But leave the possibility
open that we can reenter the Park when things cool down
and perhaps tap into all that geothermal energy."

"Mr. Cage," Jack said quietly, "do you mind if I say one
little thing?"

"Say anything you want," Cage answered.

"I been listening to you working on that little girl, and everybody else you can get to listen, and if you'll take my honest opinion, you're as full of shit as a Thanksgiving turkey. If
we can contain that lava, it's going to cool down, and you
won't have no geothermal or any other kind of energy. And
if we don't contain it, this whole city's going to be one big
chunk of steaming lava."

Cage almost stammered. "I thought you agreed with my
plan."

"At first, maybe. But I seen and heard too much since.
Now, if you'll step aside, me and my boys have got us some
blasting to do."

Numbly, Cage did just that. He stepped aside.

Linus McCoy was on his fifth drink when the door
opened. He turned one bleary eye toward it and saw the sil-
houette of a woman.

"Janet?" His voice was slurred. "I meant to come right back, but—"

"Wrong," said Paula Armstrong, putting a large straw bag down near the door. Her contemptuous look could have melted the glass in his hand. "I was scared, so I came looking for your help." She gave a bitter laugh. "Fat chance. Okay, friend. I'm not the motherly type—you're on your own. Good luck. As for me, I'm getting out of town. If you can walk, I advise that you do the same."

He stumbled toward her, splashing the straight scotch over the glass's rim. "Listen, Paula, I—"

"Bye-bye," she said, slamming his own door in his face.

Linus stumbled over the forgotten straw bag and lurched against the wall.

Joan Weldon packed one small suitcase with three contracts for upcoming motion pictures, nearly five thousand dollars in hundred-dollar bills, and one publicity photograph of her with Humphrey Bogart taken when she met him at the Brown Derby.

Her telephone rang. She rushed to pick it up.

Then she heard the voice and the heavy breathing on the other end of the line and, with a hysterical laugh, she pulled the phone jack from its wall receptable. In the middle of New York's catastrophic turmoil, she had just received an obscene phone call.

Chief Charles Nelson Neal found Sergeant Linda Zekauskas operating a mobile radio unit in the main lobby of the Metropolitan Museum of Art.

Cheerfully, she said, "Found the door wide open. They're carting away all the paintings."

The Chief said, "I've been talking with Civil Defense. We may have to get the hell out of here, too."

"The bulldozers are cutting us off from the Reservoir," she said. "Why don't we stay put for a while? My feet hurt from all this running around."

The Chief looked down at her fondly. He still remembered how loudly he had protested when she was assigned to him. . . . My God, that was nearly ten years ago.

Gruffly, he said, "Okay."

She handed him a sheaf of messages.

"Thanks," Neal said. Then he added, "You do good work, for a Polack."

Tom Chastain collared Link Fence. "Okay if I follow you around?"

"Won't bother me," said the Texan. "Of course, you might get your fool head blown off."

"Which side are you going to work?"

"Fifth Avenue," said Link. "The other teams are already wiring things up along Central Park West. I hate to say it, but I don't think there's any way we're going to be able to save the Museum of Natural History, or the Planetarium."

The *News* photographer said, "Just save the people, buddy. They're the only ones who count."

Link gave a mean chuckle. "You're just on their side because they buy your newspaper."

Chastain liked the big man. "You are absolutely right," he said.

"Well," said Link, "let's get the lead out. Hope you got plenty of film."

35

The evacuation of the area in immediate danger went relatively smoothly.

Police helicopters circled at rooftop level, calling down instructions with their loud-hailers at full volume. Crews of firemen, trained to evacuate burning buildings, found the job much easier without the threat of flame and smoke.

In those buildings which still had electricity, they took elevators to the top floor and systematically worked their way down to ground level, literally herding the evacuees before them. Each team was accompanied by pairs of armed policemen or military troops, who were beginning to arrive from nearby bases. Once out of their apartments, none of the refugees was allowed to return, no matter how plaintive their pleas or what important valuables had been left behind.

Invalids and the elderly were transported in their own wheelchairs, in improvised ones made from kitchen chairs, or on firemen's backs.

Once on the street, they were boarded onto a motley armada of vehicles that ranged from regular buses to grocery trucks and, with each street moving in only one direction—toward the nearest staging area—left their city lives behind . . . perhaps, most thought, forever.

It was full daylight now, although the sun was obscured by the pall of steam and microscopic particles rising from the Receiving Reservoir. It looked like a big, perfectly round orange ball in the sky, rising above the East River.

As each building was emptied, its doors were splashed with paint and, where possible, locked or barricaded.

"It won't keep them out a hundred percent," said one street-wise police lieutenant. "You'll have looters running around in there before we're out of sight."

Angrily, one of the refugees said, "I hope the hell the volcano gets them."

Speed. Terrible risks. The hell with neatness—all that's needed are piles of rubble blocking the streets. Stick the wires on with masking tape. Shove the nitro in any crack, under any windowsill, in any shaft. The whole building doesn't have to come down—just enough so the bulldozers can shove together a levee of stone and metal high enough to withstand the lava flow.

Teams of police, aided by hastily recruited young men and women, many who had served prison time for precisely what they were now doing, raided parked cars—hot-wiring them and then driving them, bumper to bumper and door to door into the intersections along the endangered parts of Fifth Avenue and Central Park West. Their mass would serve as partial protection if the lava flow began before the buildings could be dropped.

One tall black boy, smashing a new Caddy into an already-parked Dodge van, laughed. "I ain't had so much fun since I got busted for doing ninety on the Triboro Bridge!" he shouted.

The worker nearest him, a uniformed policeman, yelled, "Cut the bragging and steal more cars, Turkey!"

Near the mudslide, the work was more grim. Terribly burned casualties were still being brought out. Some of the buildings on East 90th Street itself were inaccessible, and rescue teams were going in, lowered to the roofs by helicopter. Those found alive were brought out the same way—over the roofs to buildings with open exits when possible, or lifted, trembling, by hoist and flown to the nearest open area.

The dead were simply left behind. There was no time. Not to comfort the wailing pleas of mothers whose children lay, suffocated, in their nurseries. Not for wives whose husbands had gone somewhere else in the building to help, and had not returned. Not even for the priests who had to be physically dragged away from their performance of the last rites.

One young priest decked two policemen who were trying to get him out of a room that was already chokingly dense with gases from the mud flow. A third policeman returned the favor with his nightstick, and the priest was carried to safety.

Some, and who knows what dark fears clouded their minds, hid from their rescuers. Perhaps they were protecting their possessions. Some might have seen the hurrying, shouting men as more dangerous than remaining in what had been their safe, secure refuge against the noise and violence of the city outside.

Others, resourceful, helped. They pointed out apartments where there might be someone ill, or deaf, or too old to flee alone. They guided the blind, comforted the crying children, lent their own flagging strength to those who weakened.

"Wherever these people go," Chief Charles Nelson Neal broadcast, "they're going to have to eat. Break into the stores. Fill the floors of those buses and trucks with canned goods, bread, anything that doesn't have to be cooked."

Within minutes, to the delight of the younger members of the teams, groups of men and women who in other circumstances would have been called looters, were smashing the windows of the Safeways, the A&Ps, the Gristedes—even the small mom-and-pop grocery stores. In those few occasions where the owners were present—one was a delicatessen proprietor—they were astounded to be told by the nearest policemen that their property was being "requisitioned" for the emergency.

Violence was scarce. A few fights occurred. Some of the food procurers were cut by broken glass as they wheeled shopping carts, piled mountainously high with hastily collected food. But, considering the haste and the confusion, most of the supplies were delivered intact to the shuttle buses and trucks.

The narrow streets echoed with the roar of engines. It was like being inside a giant indoor Indy 500.

Gradually, and well before the 10:00 A.M. deadline, the area which Janet McCoy and Bill Claflin had decided was in the most immediate danger had been cleared of all but a few renegades and frightened souls still hidden in the closets of their own apartments.

In one way, this was Manhattan's darkest hour.

In another, it was her finest.

36

In every Maria Montez–Jon Hall movie, it was always the spectacular lava flow that posed the most danger to frightened natives. In the original film, *One Million B.C.*, which starred Carole Landis and Victor Mature, a racing wall of lava overtook and enveloped the fleeing cave-people.

But, in actuality, lava is perhaps the least dangerous of a volcano's weapons. Lava moves slowly—people can usually stroll out of its path.

Nor is lava particularly dramatic in appearance—at least, not to the naked eye. Once cooled, lava—or magma, as the experts prefer to call it—looks like a burnt-out clinker from a coal furnace.

It is only under a microscope that lava takes on its magnificent structure of interlocked crystals of feldspar and brightly hued olivine and pyroxene, intermingled with iron oxide. Since any crystalline object is, like a snowflake, a model of orderly patterns, so lava, when highly magnified, keeps its various minerals in their proper and easily identifiable places.

Lava is Nature's prime example of natural order and beauty.

But try telling that to the pilot of a police helicopter who has just watched the last of the Reservoir's water forced over the huge Gate House pipes, replaced by a seething mass of hotly glowing melted rock.

"The lava's busting out!" he radioed. "On the south Gate

House. The whole Reservoir is nearly filled up with the stuff."

His words were heard in the Civil Defense command center under Police Plaza.

Leslie Robinson looked at Janet McCoy.

"You're my boss," she said.

"Not in this. The President put you in charge."

Janet gave a mirthless laugh. "Women's Lib, look what you've done to me!" She turned to a communications technician. "Will you patch me through to President Foster?"

Awed, he answered, "Yes, ma'am."

The evacuation continued.

On West 89th Street, just a few buildings in from Central Park West, the black iron-grated door to a basement entrance opened and a tall, red-haired woman emerged, a huge black Labrador retriever straining at his leash.

A passing fireman yelled, "Lady, get the hell out of here! They've just put out a signal that the Reservoir's getting ready to overflow."

"I'm on my way," said the woman, in a mid-Pennsylvania accent. She hooked the dog's leash to the door and hurried back inside, calling, "Stay there, Spookie! I forgot something!"

Frustrated, the fireman threw up his hands. "Shit!" he bellowed. "People don't *want* to be helped!"

Inside the handsome brownstone, the tall woman looked around for what she knew would be the last time. She noted how tall the potted birch tree had gotten, in its two-story-high corner of the dining room. A home economist, the tools of her trade were all around. But none could be taken. The microwave ovens, the handsome copper pots and pans, the carefully sharpened knives . . .

Within her small suitcase were the legal papers she would need later, and the few photographs she had been able to gather in the short time available. But she still had a free hand.

It reached for a moody watercolor painting of sailboats in the fog, signed by Warren Rogers . . . hesitated. Then she turned to a sideboard and, instead, took up a silver chafing dish. Its value in money was relatively small, but she had used it for many years, and it was almost a part of her.

She hurried down the narrow hallway and let out a small cry when she found the fireman unhooking the big black dog.

"Lady, I was just letting him loose so he could get away. Who the hell knew whether you were coming back again?"

Her anger subsided. The man was right.

"Thank you," she said. "We're going now. Spookie, thank the man."

The dog leaped up and presented the startled fireman with a wet kiss.

The leash looped around her arm, the small suitcase in one hand and the silver chafing dish in the other, the tall woman strode west, toward Columbus Avenue.

Behind her, she began to hear the sound of explosions, but she did not look back.

"Mr. President," said Janet McCoy, "the lava is overflowing. I've ordered the blasting to begin."

Foster hesitated. "Is there any way to know whether or not the flow will be contained?"

"No, sir."

"What's your own opinion?"

Janet looked at the color television monitors, showing pictures transmitted by the hovering police and media helicopters.

"If the rate of flow continues as it is presently, I'd have to say no. There are bound to be breaches in our barricades. And once the lava finds them, if its momentum continues, it will cover most or all of the island."

"Can we relieve some of the danger by sacrificing streets as lanes for it to flow down to the river?"

"Some. But our plan has been based on the assumption

that we'd block the sill out in the Atlantic. Many people would be trapped because they haven't been evacuated. We had planned to start general evacuation around an hour and a half from now, but the lava didn't wait for us. Now there isn't time."

Softly, the President said, "We *are* prepared to destroy that part of ocean floor, Janet. But there is only one way to do it, and it is an unpleasant one. I alone will give the order. However, my decision must be based on the best information I can get."

"I understand that," she said.

"Not completely," he answered. "Use the scrambler phone."

She picked up the red instrument. The sound from the closed-circuit monitors ceased, and now she heard his voice, sounding vaguely like Donald Duck.

Calmly, President Foster told her what the price the destruction of the underwater sill would be.

For a moment, Janet could not speak. Then she said, "Give me five minutes to check with our people in the field. You'll have my firm answer then."

"I'll be waiting," said Foster.

"Hook me into the Command frequency," Janet told the communications man who had been assigned to her.

Three minutes later, she was reconnected with the War Room beneath the White House.

"Giving us every break in the book," she said, "we still can't make it."

"Estimated casualties if we don't block the flow?"

"We'll lose the city all the way down to 42nd Street, and maybe beyond. River to river. And up to at least 125th Street. Half a million people at the very least."

"Thank you," he said. "Nothing can make my job easier, but at least those numbers may comfort me later."

Without a good-bye, he broke the connection.

37

The giant buildings collapsed like huge mounds of children's blocks. Guided by Link Fence's radioed instructions, his demolitions men sent rubble cascading into the side streets in a desperate attempt to isolate the middle of Central Park.

Like Thor hurling thunderbolts, a procession of explosions crashed up Fifth Avenue and Central Park West.

On Fifth, at East 79th, the Ukrainian Culture Center, formerly a chateau for Peter Stuyvesant's descendant, Augustus Van Horne Stuyvesant, shuddered under the explosive assault and, in a cloud of red dust, fell down into the street. The same fate befell One East 75th Street, the Edward S. Harkness House, built in 1907–09 of white Tennessee marble. Now occupied by the Commonwealth Fund, it was surrounded by an intricate black wrought-iron fence which had to be smashed down by the demolitions men.

Its sacrifice was demanded by the assumption that the hastily-thrown-up levee around the Metropolitan Museum of Art would fail and the lava would cascade down Fifth Avenue.

The dust and small bits of debris were still settling when bulldozers moved in and began turning the rubble into twenty-foot-high barricades.

Nor was the original home of the Woolworths on 80th Street spared. At one time, the Five-and-Ten magnate planned to establish an entire square-block kingdom, cometing with that one already located blocks away by the Vanderbilts. Early death ended that dream, although he did construct four more houses, one of which sheltered the parents of the well-known Barbara Hutton.

On the West Side, the north wing of the American Museum of Natural History, with its 58 halls and 13 acres of floor space, fell under the demolition-men's charges. One workman turned away, with tears in his eyes, when the Theodore Roosevelt Memorial at the Central Park West façade crumbled.

The Hayden Planetarium, with its famous "theater of the stars" fell, too. Its huge dome, shattered by a carefully placed charge, crumbled inward like a crushed egg.

To those who had been evacuated, the sound behind them was only a reminder of all that they had lost. It was like thunder in the distant mountains. Although smoke and dust and the acrid odor of explosives filled the air, few noticed these irritants. Their thoughts were filled only with already-fading visions of their homes and their possessions and their very living pasts which had been left behind.

In the underground Emergency Operating Center at 7 Centre Street, beneath Police Plaza, Janet McCoy sat numbly. She had replaced the scrambler telephone in its cradle, but her hand seemed to burn from its touch.

Alexander Cage had sent out runners to raid nearby liquor stores. He handed Janet a stiff brandy. She sipped it as if it were pure water.

"Forgive me," he said. "I'm a greedy son of a bitch. All I kept seeing were the dollars, not the lives."

She choked on the drink. "I'm not one bit better than you," she said. "All I saw was the glory."

Professor Jess Hawley, disobeying the very advice he had given Jack Springfield, was walking carelessly up Central Park West. He paid no attention to the shouted warnings or the sound of distant thunder. His mind was a blur.

Above him, weakened by the nearby explosions, a cornice trembled itself free from its moorings and fell.

Life, dreams, and—mercifully—sadness, vanished for the elderly Professor.

A nearby demolitions man, who had called out a warning, fell to his knees and was violently sick.

Joan Weldon descended the stairs from her apartment in the Dakota because the elevator's power had gone off.

The guard at the courtyard gate was still at his post.

"Good morning, Miss Weldon," he said. "Would you like a taxi?"

She stared at him. "Would I . . . are you kidding, Matthew?"

He stepped out onto West 72nd Street and blew his whistle.

Immediately, a Yellow Cab—a huge Checker, no less— pulled up.

Matthew opened the door. "Have a good day," he said.

"How the hell did you do that?" Joan demanded. Matthew smiled and shrugged.

"Luck of the Irish," he said.

She pressed a hundred-dollar bill on him. He tried to wave it away.

"Wait until Christmas, ma'am," he said.

"Today *is* Christmas," she said.

He took the money. He looked around, at the dark clouds of smoke and the fiery glow from the northeast.

"Be careful," he said.

"You too," she said.

"Where to?" asked the driver. "That phony. He slipped me twenty bucks to stand by for five minutes. I was just getting ready to haul ass, pardon my French."

She leaned forward to read the name tag on the dashboard. "Mr. Hepburn," she said, "do you have a family here in the city?"

"Not no more," he said. "The old lady moved down to

Florida two years back. Today I've been thinking I should have gone with her."

"The best way to Florida," she said, "is via New Jersey."

Hepburn shrugged. "All right with me," he said. "If we can get through the tunnel."

"Leave that to me," she said.

He started to say that he had liked her movies very much, but decided against it. Instead, he drove with all his skill at the very top speed that the bottomless potholes in the corroded streets would allow.

"Wait a minute," she said, pointing up ahead. "Stop by that man."

Jack Springfield gave a start when the cab suddenly screeched its brakes alongside him.

A beautiful woman leaned out and said, "We're on our to Florida, old timer. Would you like a lift?"

Looking back at the smoldering rubble surrounding Central Park, the old man said, "Don't mind if I do."

38

"Captain Scott?"

"Yes, Mr. President."

"Are you in position?"

"Right on the button."

"What about your crew?"

"We surfaced and offloaded everyone but the three men we absolutely had to retain to operate the sub."

"Plus yourself."

"Yes, sir. *Rickover*'s my ship."

"I'm afraid the news is bad, Scott. If we don't block that lava flow, we'll lose half a million people—maybe more."

"I anticipated that, sir."

"Are you prepared to detonate?"

"The button's uncaged and activated. Shall I do it now?"

"No . . . not until I . . . Captain, how the hell can I say what can't be put into words?"

"Mr. President, nineteen years ago, a boot recruit fell on a live grenade that got loose during practice. He saved my life. One for one. Don't blame yourself. Four of us for half a million isn't such a bad trade."

"About your family . . . Don't—"

"You don't have to say it, sir. Aren't we wasting time?"

"Shall I—"

"I wrote some quick letters. They're with the offloaded crew. Don't trouble yourself. *Just let me get on with it!*"

"I understand, Captain. Good-bye, and God bless you."

"Thank you, sir. *Rickover* signing off and lowering her flag."

There was a pause, a low hum of carrier wave. Then total silence.

One of the War-Room officers, monitoring satellite transmissions, cried, "Holy Christ!"

The President looked up.

A huge white glow had spread over part of the North Atlantic.

39

The buildings crumbled, barely ahead of the lava flow.

The Italianate mansion at 1100 Fifth—91st Street. Next, the often criticized, but never ignored Guggenheim Museum at Fifth and East 89th Street. Designed by Frank Lloyd Wright, it had often been called a "brick clothes-washer." Within its spiral halls, one filmmaker sneaked in and, using a slow motion camera, a battery-operated light attached to his camera, and a pair of Schwinn roller skates, glided from top to bottom to produce an Academy Award short subject titled *Whiz*. The old Payne Whitney house at 972 Fifth, now used by the French Cultural Service. The Marymount School, once a row of private houses. At East 86th, the massive, controversial "French Classic Eclectic" house, once occupied by Mrs. Cornelius Vanderbilt, and now owned by the Yivo Institute for Jewish Research.

Helicopters reported the continuation of the destruction.

Their pilots, with reckless abandon, hurled their craft into violent turbulence created by the rising superheated air.

But still the lava gained.

Daredevil youths, careening through the clogged streets in hot-wired cars, tried to stem the flow of the ever-encroaching lava. Like a demolition derby, they crashed the cars into each other to make as tight a mass as possible.

Some of the daredevils did not walk away from the collisions.

Below Police Plaza, Mort Weisman sought out Janet McCoy.

"They've blown the Atlantic sill," he said.

"I know."

"I think it's helping. The flow traces on the infrared transmissions from the satellite are starting to dim."

Thinking of the men who had sacrificed themselves aboard the *Rickover*, Janet said bitterly, "Maybe it would have been better to bail everybody out of here last night and let the goddamned volcano have the city."

Mort stared at her. "You don't mean that. Listen, we're holding our own. The levees are working. If that sill's really blocked, it'll start cooling down pretty fast. So we'll *have* a solid-rock park instead of crabgrass. Who cares? At least the city's still here. And you did it."

"Yeah," she said, "I did it. I guess I've come a long way, huh, baby?"

President Howard Foster maintained a stern expression as he took the elevator up from the War Room to the main foyer. Instead of going into the Oval Office, he let himself quietly into the small room to one side, which he and other Presidents had often used for privacy.

He poured a stiff slug of Jack Daniels and gulped it down.

Then he sat at a battered desk, cradled his face in his trembling hands, and wept.

Tom Chastain persuaded a police car to rush him downtown to the *News* office, promising the officer glossy blow-ups of the shots he took with the crumbling Fifth Avenue behind the cruiser.

There, he locked himself in the darkroom and devoted himself to his only love.

Eve Newhart waited by her telephone.

Alexander Cage never called.

Jack Ward gathered his team together.

"Who we going to bill for this bastard?" he asked.

Ross Weems cleared his throat.

"You got something to say, Ross?" asked Ward.

"I'll say it for him," said Link Fence. "Jack, you try to make one goddamned dime off this mess, and I will personally tromp you into a pile of chili beans."

Jack Ward grinned.

"That's fine with me," he said. "I just didn't want you boys to think you was getting the dirty end of the stick."

Chief Charles Nelson Neal switched off the walkie-talkie. He grabbed Linda Zekauskas by both shoulders and rammed her healthy breasts against his not inconsiderable belly.

"It's cooling down!" he bellowed. "We held it!"

Linda had been waiting for this opportunity for several years. She ground her pelvis against his and said, "They got some funny-looking beds back there in the Egyptian exhibit. Let's go take a look at them."

Waldo Wynn tapped on the door of the President's private retreat.

"Go away," said Foster.

"Like hell," said Wynn. "I smell booze."

He went in and, taking the bottle from the President's limp hand, swigged directly from its neck.

"*Rickover* pulled it off! They were right on the dime with their location. The lava flow's down to a trickle. It's already starting to harden up in the Park. We didn't lose more than a few side streets."

"Tell that to Mrs. Scott," said the President.

"Howard," said the NASA Director, "you did what you had to do. I hope if I'd been sitting in your chair I would have had the same guts you did."

Trying to smile, Foster said, "Don't kid yourself, Waldo. I didn't do it myself. I made that poor goddamned girl push the button. You take care of her, you hear? If you don't, you've got me to answer to."

Tossing down another slug of sour-mash bourbon, Waldo Wynn said, "Mr. President, that's one thing you don't ever have to worry about. I haven't been able to put Janet McCoy out of my mind since the first moment I met her."

Linus McCoy had just struggled up from befuddled sleep when the door of the apartment opened again.

"Paula?" he called.

"I'm afraid she's gone," said Janet McCoy, pushing aside the battered straw handbag. A black lace bra spilled out. Janet glanced at it casually and felt nothing. No surprise. No jealousy.

"Jesus!" Linus said. "Babe, I'm sorry. I meant to come right back. But then I took that first damned drink. How the hell can you forgive me?"

"Easily," said Janet. She sat down beside him on the sofa. Her lips caressed his cheek. "Forgiving's easy. Forgetting's what's hard."

"My God!" he said. "The evacuation—"

"Under control," she said. "The Navy blew a hole in the lava stream. Now we've got a park made of solid rock. But pretty much of everything else is safe."

Linus looked down at the bottle of Chivas, almost empty. Silently, Janet handed it to him.

"Go ahead," she said. "It can't hurt anything now."

He sipped gratefully. "Jan, I need you."

"I know you do."

"I'll try to be better."

"No, you won't. Nobody changes, not really. Not you, not me. Whatever we are, we remain. I'm sorry, Linus. You *do* need me. But I don't need you. There's still half of my productive life ahead, if I'm lucky. I can't handle that and carry you, too. Try to understand. I can't be your mother."

Bitterly, he said, "Just as I couldn't be *your* father!"

"I deserve that," she admitted. "And I'm sorry." She kissed him softly. "Funny. You're the drunk, you're the one who couldn't pass up anyone even slightly available. And yet, it's I who feel the need to be forgiven. Forgive me, Linus. And forget me. You can get by. You can function. Have your fun and the hell with everything else. That's what you were meant to do. It isn't your fault."

"Then you're leaving?"

"Today. You can get the divorce. No alimony, no property settlement."

His voice husky, Linus said, "No regrets?"

Her eyes misted. "Lots of regrets," she said. "But then, nobody's perfect."

The police sergeant in charge of the guard detail at the Lincoln Tunnel under the Hudson River almost saluted when the beautiful tawny-haired woman leaned out of the Yellow Cab and said, "Officer, you probably don't know who I am, but . . ."

He gulped. "I've seen all your pictures, Miss Weldon."

"Well, MGM's filming this slight disaster right now, and I was told there'd be a studio car waiting for me at this end of the tunnel. Have you seen it?"

"No, ma'am. But they aren't allowing any traffic through the tunnel."

"I understand. Golly. They need me for some close-ups with the City in the background." She hesitated. "Perhaps we can walk through?"

The policeman looked around. What the hell did it matter?

"Cabbie," he told Hepburn, "you drive Miss Weldon. The tollbooths are closed, so don't you try sticking her for an extra buck and a half, you hear?"

The cabdriver, numb at the exhibition of near hypnotism he had just seen, said, "Count on me, Sergeant. In fact, I'm shutting down my flag." He threw the switch, disconnecting the meter. "I didn't know I had a real movie star in my hack!"

"Let them through," called the Sergeant.

As the Checker cab began to move, Joan Weldon threw him a kiss.

Deep under the river, Jack Springfield shook his head and said, "I'll be a ring-tailed monkey!"

Joan laughed. "Boys, I don't think any of us really want to see much of Fun City for a while. Why don't we really go to Florida? I've got enough cash to cover gas and motels."

"Fine with me," said the cabdriver. "This wreck is mine, free and clear. I can drive it anywhere I want to."

She looked at the old man. "And you?"

"It'd be nice to be warm," he said. "But I pay my own way, or it's no deal."

Joan understood pride. She said softly, "Of course you will. Tell you what. Give me all your money. I'll keep track of the bills. When we hit Miami, I'll give you back what's left."

"That sounds fair enough to me," said Jack Springfield.

He fumbled in his pockets and came up with some crumpled bills and tarnished coins. He ladled them into Joan Weldon's outstretched hands.

"What's this?" she asked, as the Checker emerged from the west end of the tunnel and found itself flooded with bright sunlight.

Jack Springfield took back the small object she held out.

It was the milky-white stone he had found in Central Park.

"It ain't much," he said. "Just a lucky rock."

ABOARD *Rickover II:*
PARKING ORBIT 130 MILES UP

Two more orbits and the slingshot effect would hurl them out of Earth's gravitational field, and the nine-week trip to Mars would begin.

Janet McCoy had the acceleration couch in the rear. The pilots were up front. But she could see, and control, the color-television scanner, and make videotapes on the refined Sony Betamax with tiny 1/8-inch metal tape crawling at 3/16 inches per second. At that speed, *Gone With the Wind* would be only slightly larger than an aspirin.

The Eastern corridor of North America swam past the television's zoom lens.

The water surrounding the continent was incredibly blue. Seen from this great height, the Earth itself was a mottled hue of brown and green.

The two years since the Central Park eruption had gone swiftly. There had been the good times, when she found that she had been accepted completely by NASA's personnel, and the better times when she found love for Waldo Wynn, who, privately, was an amazingly shy and gentle man. There had been no mention of marriage, by mutual unspoken agreement, nor would there be until her return from the Mars mission.

And there were the bad times. Linus's suicide, if it could

be called that. Blind drunk one night, he had strolled casually in front of a Fifth Avenue bus.

The changes in the cities of America . . . the gradual decentralization, the continuing battle to destroy slums and all the misery that went with them . . . the award to her of the Presidential Medal of Freedom by President Foster . . . all were only a blur now, as she reached for the zoom control of the television camera.

In a little more than two hours, *Rickover II* would hurl itself into space. Destination: Mars.

But now, just for a moment, she would record a snip of videotape to view while working on the hostile surface of the Red Planet, one last close-up of home, the good, green Earth.

She zoomed in, and the eastern seaboard filled the screen. Manhattan Island came into view.

The lens was so powerful that she could see cars and buses moving in the midtown streets. There were people, too, but so small they were only specks on the TV monitor.

The camera found Central Park.

What once had been the Receiving Reservoir was now a glistening mass of hardened lava. She had walked across it often since that November day two years ago. But this was the first time she had viewed it from a height.

The shimmering lava, contained by shattered buildings, and earth levees, and the courage of four men aboard the nuclear submarine *Rickover,* had arranged itself into the shape of a perfect heart.